I0699853

For my family

REBEL PLANET

by Parker Lyons

MIDNIGHT CARNIVAL

Prologue

Deep within the Cathedral, hidden from the citizens of Hypnos, the clergy gathered. Around them, thousands of quantum computers hummed inside infinite halls, producing a low, monastic chant. Blinking lights flickered on the dark monoliths, casting shadows on the walls.

At the center of the cavernous chamber stood a moonstone pedestal, its surface inscribed with binary code. Resting atop it was a glowing sphere, smooth as glass, pulsating with a gaseous, purple light. A High Cleric stood before it, raising a silver cable. Electric sparks flew from the cable's end, a dance of blue light, bringing the conclave, dressed in hooded white robes, to their knees.

"Let the populace of Hypnos be prepared! Phase Four is upon us!" proclaimed the High Cleric. "The Self for the All!"

"The Self for the All!" repeated the assembly.

The cleric inserted the cable into the pedestal and the chamber's hum deepened. The sphere began to rise, crackling with electricity as the machine fed on its source, code flowing into its core. The clergy watched in awe.

The sphere, now a searing beacon, flashed with a final, powerful surge.

In the depths of Hypnos, a new era was about to begin.

Chapter 1
Hypnos Colony, New Eden Moon

Jayde Ashr had never been this far from solid ground, never felt the world shrink beneath her, the unknown stretching wide above.

Hand over hand, she told herself. *Just keep going.*

"Almost there!" Merrick called out.

Her friend Merrick Sloan, just a few rungs below, laughed as Jayde clung to the ladder, her knuckles white with tension.

"I can't believe you talked me into this," Jayde called down.

"Just keep going," Merrick shouted back. "Trust me. It'll be worth it."

Jayde took a deep breath and forced herself to move, step by step, resisting the urge to look down. As she continued her ascent, hot sweat collected inside her white Academy uniform.

The two friends were scaling the communications tower in Hypnos, their isolated colony on the New Eden moon, the farthest human settlement from Earth. For them, it was more than just home. It was their entire world. Born and raised here, neither of them had ever left its domed confines.

The communication tower loomed far above every other

structure in the colony, its spire reaching high enough to nearly pierce the thick plastic glass that ensured their survival on a moon devoid of atmosphere. Just before she reached the top, Jayde made the mistake of glancing down. Her stomach lurched and a chirp of fear escaped her lips.

If she slipped, she figured she'd have about thirty seconds to reflect on her first-ever act of rebellion before hitting the ground. She imagined her mother's reaction to the news: disbelief and shock that her "perfect daughter," the one who had spent her life fading into the background, obeying every rule and upholding the edicts of the Construct, had splattered like a pancake after an ill-advised climb.

If her father was still alive, he would fixate on the timing. Jayde's death would overshadow her last day at the Academy, the day she was supposed to receive her career assignment and begin her contributions to the Noble Purpose. He would wonder why she had chosen this day, of all days, to lose her mind.

Jayde's thoughts stilled for a moment as her fingers found the top of the tower. She crawled onto the platform, breathing hard, and quickly scrambled away from the edge. Pressing her back against a buzzing network box, she glanced upward at the massive satellite dish slowly rotating above her. As host to a vast computing infrastructure, Hypnos was the home base for the Construct, and the communication tower linked it to the rest of humanity's scattered colonies.

The Construct was many things. An artificial intelligence. A guide. A savior. Centuries ago, when Earth teetered on the brink of extinction, the Construct was humanity's last hope. It solved the unsolvable—war, climate collapse, disease—and laid out a vision to unify the fractured species. This vision became the Great Expansion, a plan to spread humanity across the stars, and at its core was the Noble Purpose, a doctrine that demanded the survival of the whole take precedence over the desires of the individual.

The Self for the All.

Through it, every choice, every action, every life was shaped.

Including Jayde's.

Today, the Construct would decide her role in society, as it had for generations before her. It would determine how she would serve the colony. But Jayde didn't need to wait for its proclamation. She already knew what her assignment would be: programming Artificial Intelligence. Genetics played a heavy role in the Construct's decisions, and her father's legacy as an esteemed engineer and clergyman, combined with her own success in her Academy AI classes, made the outcome inevitable.

But inevitability didn't make it right.

Her daydreams provided only clues to her true desires. Sometimes Jayde imagined stealing a space suit and climbing the jagged mountains of the New Eden moon, feeling the vastness of existence stretch around her. But she never acted on those thoughts. They simply didn't matter.

What mattered was what was best for the colony. What mattered was the Noble Purpose.

Merrick's head appeared over the edge of the platform, his climb complete, and he let out an exuberant whoop that echoed in the still air.

"Quiet!" Jayde hissed. "You're going to get us caught!"

She crawled over and extended a hand, helping him onto the small, precarious perch. Once seated, Merrick flopped back with a wide grin, completely unfazed by the extreme height. His white uniform now had lines of rust and grease all over it, a gift from the filthy ladder they had just climbed. Even the gold seams that edged the lines of his pants and shirt were tarnished. Jayde looked at her own uniform and was relieved that her clothes were not as soiled.

She brushed her brown hair behind her ears and lowered her hazel eyes at the colony below. From this vantage point, all of Hypnos stretched before her, its stark white buildings laid out in rigid, orderly blocks. It was early morning and the colony was just stirring, most of its inhabitants waking to begin their daily obligations.

New Eden, the emerald planet of toxic gas that hosted their

moon, had yet to rise and appear through the hexagonal-paned glass above. Jayde waited for it, her eyes fixed on the stars. Next to her, Merrick was smiling, truly smiling, the first time she'd seen him happy in weeks. It was that sly, lopsided grin that endeared him to her, though ironically, it had been the very thing her father disapproved of most; Dr. Richard Ashr had made no secret of his disdain for Merrick Sloan.

"The boy doesn't live by the creed," he would say.

It was Jayde's mother who had always encouraged their friendship. She never explained why, but Jayde had some theories. Maybe it was because Merrick had no one else. His mother, father, and brother had all perished together in a mining accident years ago, leaving him adrift in the colony. Or maybe her mother had seen something in him, a spark of potential invisible to others, even the all-seeing Construct.

Merrick wasn't holding out much hope for Career Assignment Day. He knew his fate was in the asteroid mines. That's where the Construct would send someone like him. A rule-breaking, underperforming Academy student? It was practically a foregone conclusion.

Jayde felt for him. The mines weren't just backbreaking; they crushed the spirit, grinding down anyone unlucky enough to be sent there.

"Not much of a view from up here, really," Merrick said. "Just rows of white cubes."

"Then why even climb up here?" Jayde asked.

"It's not the view. It's the *feeling*."

"Right now, I *feel* guilty. For skipping our Career Assignment."

"Forget about that," Merrick continued. "They won't miss us. Just look how small it all is down there. The buildings. The people. We're never going to get this far away from Hypnos again."

Jayde thought about it and, despite their precarious perch, she couldn't deny the thrill of being above it all. They lingered there in silence, the world around them distilled into the rhythmic creak of the satellite rotating overhead. Above, the gargantuan planet of New Eden appeared, starting its slow crawl over the horizon.

For a fleeting moment, Jayde forgot the path her life was destined to follow. All that mattered was the freedom of the moment, and the vast chasm separating them from the structured reality below.

Chapter 2

By the time Jayde and Merrick made their way down from the tower and arrived at the Academy Center, most of their fellow Academy graduates were already pouring out of the building. They streamed out of the Academy's arch-like gates, career packets clutched tightly against their pressed, white uniforms. Relief was the most common expression, with some students barely containing their excitement. Others, however, moved with a quiet, hollow resignation, carrying the futures they hadn't chosen.

"I suppose I should go in and see if it's not too late to get my packet," Jayde said, glancing toward the gates.

"Time to face the music," Merrick replied, nodding.

Face the music. Jayde chuckled, charmed as always by her friend's love of old Earth idioms, half of which were entirely lost on her. This one, however, was crystal clear. They'd put off this moment long enough. It was time to accept their fate.

As they approached the archways leading into the Academy's Grand Atrium, Merrick's attention drifted toward a group of girls gathered nearby.

"You know what?" said Merrick. "I see a girl from my Language class. This might be my only chance to make a lasting impression before they ship me off to the mines."

Without waiting for a reply, he veered off toward the group, leaving Jayde standing alone at the entrance.

"Merrick!" she called after him.

He waved her off with a grin. "I'll catch you tomorrow!" he said.

Jayde groaned. This was yet another instance of her friend playing with fire. On Hypnos, all couplings were pre-arranged by the Construct, which meticulously analyzed DNA, aptitude test scores, and other metrics to optimize the colony's gene pool for health and skill sets. But, that didn't stop Merrick or a handful of other rebellious students from "piloting" their courtship skills in secret, risking reprimand for a fleeting thrill.

Then again, she thought, what did he have to lose? Merrick's career assignment was practically set in stone. He was likely going to be extracting iron from an asteroid no matter what he did.

Jayde's gaze lingered on him for a moment longer, noting the gleam in the eyes of a young woman he was charming. Merrick might not have been an honor student, but he more than made up for it with effortless charisma, the kind that drew people in like gravity. He was handsome, too, with a square jaw and broad shoulders that gave him an easy confidence. His deep black hair and thick eyebrows only amplified his scandalous reputation. But it was his sideways smile and wry wit that Jayde appreciated most. For her, those mannerisms made everything else about him invisible.

Jayde stepped into the Grand Atrium, leaving Merrick to his usual antics. She hoped she still had enough time to collect her career assignment and reach the loading docks before her mother departed on her explorer mission, a farewell that would have to last for months.

As she entered, Jayde paused to take in the breathtaking majesty of the Atrium. Its intricate design, with its sweeping arches and geometric precision, never failed to captivate her, a rare blend of artistry and purpose in the otherwise utilitarian world of Hypnos.

The architecture stood as a homage to the grandeur of ancient Earth, adorned with fluted columns, polished marble floors, and soaring arched passageways. Dominating the lofty expanse above, a magnificent Earth tree, a fig, blossomed beneath the sheltering dome. Symbolic of humanity's modest beginnings and boundless potential, its branches spanned the chamber, delicately caressing the curved walls of the circular space.

Once each year, the tree burst into a spectacular display of white florets, a breathtaking sight that drew the entire colony together to what Jayde considered living art. On Hypnos, the pursuit of traditional art forms was discouraged by the Construct, deeming them as frivolous distractions. To indulge in painting or other forms of creativity was frowned upon. If one was occupied with art, they were not contributing to the colony's productivity.

However, Jayde saw the tree as a symbol of defiance against such narrow constraints. To her, it represented the inherent beauty and creativity woven into the fabric of nature. If the fig tree was designed by nature to be beautiful, there had to be a purpose behind it, beyond mere aesthetics. It served as a reminder that creation and beauty were integral aspects of existence, deserving of appreciation and respect.

As Jayde stood admiring the sprawling branches of the tree, an older man in flowing white robes approached. It was Instructor Augustus Halpert, one of her counselors. In his hand, he carried a large gray envelope, its seal unbroken and foreboding.

"Well, Ms. Ashr," he began, his tone calm but pointed. "It seems you were absent from the Assignment Ceremony this morning."

Jayde straightened, caught off guard. "Uh, yes, Instructor," she stammered. "I wasn't feeling well. I am very sorry."

Instructor Halpert offered a suspicious smile, his impossibly white teeth flashing with a slick brightness matched only by his silver hair and bushy eyebrows. Jayde couldn't help but think he'd seen this excuse before. She was probably far from the first student to "fall ill" on Career Assignment Day.

"Of course, Ms. Ashr," he said smoothly. "Illness does have a curious way of striking when one's destiny is being handed out."

Jayde's eyes locked onto the envelope in his hand. "Is that my packet?"

Halpert glanced down at the large gray envelope, turning it over in his fingers. "It is indeed, young lady. You were the only one of my students to skip the ceremony this year." He frowned slightly. "I've noticed those who tend to skip this occasion do so because they have reason to fear. Take your friend Merrick, for example. I am confident I know what is waiting for him."

Jayde felt her temper rise, killing the butterflies in her stomach.

"But you," he continued, "you're a bit of a mystery, I'm afraid. I've never had someone of your pedigree fail to attend."

He handed her the envelope. She hesitated before taking it, her fingers slow to open.

"Do not fear," Halpert said. "The Construct always places us where we may best serve. Whatever is in this envelope is your true calling. Take pride."

"Thanks, Instructor," Jayde said, eager to end the conversation.

"I'll leave you to it, then."

With a slight bow, he turned and disappeared into the crowd of students, relieved to have delivered his final envelope until next term.

Jayde stared down at the packet as doubt and fear churned in her chest. She couldn't bring herself to open it. Not yet.

She checked her digital timepiece. Her mother's departure was imminent, and if she hurried, she'd have just enough time to reach the other side of Hypnos to say goodbye. Destiny could wait, she decided. She tucked the envelope under her arm.

Jayde departed from the Atrium and proceeded down the central path leading toward the Hypnos Plaza Center. Her eyes briefly scanned for Merrick, but he, along with the gaggle of girls, was nowhere to be seen. She let out a disapproving sigh, certain that her friend never took one step inside the Academy building.

On the way to the plaza, Jayde passed through a small communal park, where winding walkways, jogging paths, and scattered benches provided a rare space for leisure. Families strolled, couples wandered, and workers drifted between the offices, dormitories, stores, and dining halls that bordered the park.

Beyond the plaza was the Briefing Cathedral, an imposing cube-shaped building with a gold-plated exterior that shimmered as it reflected the overhead dome lights. On its flat roof sat a bright silver arch, a symbol of humanity's march through time and space. Unlike the smooth, eggshell-white surfaces of the colony, its metallic exterior was etched with an endless stream of zeroes and ones, a binary coded message on the walls that only the clergy who worked there could translate and appreciate.

The Cathedral served as the gathering place for the colony's monthly congregations, where the clergy delivered the latest decrees from the Construct. Attendance was mandatory, even for the youngest children. Occasionally a new directive would spark excitement, but most were mundane, small optimizations to colony operations. Last month, the big proclamation was an increase in dietary fiber in the lunch hall menus.

In the front of the building was a pair of towering, twenty-foot silver doors, the gateway for the clergy to come and go. The clergy consisted of the colony's most esteemed intelligence engineers. They alone worked directly with the Construct, refining its algorithms, deciphering its wisdom, and delivering its decrees. Her father had been one of them.

For nearly twenty years, he had served with distinction, shaping the doctrine that now governed their world. But he had not lived to see the culmination of his life's work: the much-anticipated Phase Four release.

Even now, clergy members in their silver and white robes moved briskly through the plaza, fastening *Phase Four* banners to ornamental columns. As Jayde passed on her way to the docks, their excited murmurs reached her. Phase Four was meant to be a new beginning. Through painstaking research and relentless trial and error, Richard Ashr had found a way to simulate human emotion within the Construct, believing that empathy would make it a better servant to mankind.

A quiet tension settled over Jayde as she took in the preparations for the grand unveiling, set for noon tomorrow. Thanks to her father, there were things she had come to understand about the Phase Four Construct. Things that made her uneasy. It was a secret that she closely guarded, even from her mother.

Leaving the plaza behind, Jayde made her way toward the port, where colony ships were docked, maintained, and loaded. The scale of the port was immense, reflective of the multitude and sheer size of the ships it accommodated. As she neared the glass passageway, her gaze fell upon the two NOBLEs stationed at its entrance.

The NOBLEs, towering humanoid machines under the Construct's control, stood motionless, their chrome-plated exoskeletons hiding the intricate circuitry and hydraulics beneath. Their most striking feature was the single blue eye at the center of their heads. They were strong and imposing machines, the Construct's presence made tangible.

Despite their ominous appearance, they only performed mundane and laborious tasks. This included trash collection, food preparation, dock work, ship maintenance, janitorial duties and security patrols. They existed to emancipate humanity from the burdens of routine existence, granting their masters the freedom to pursue the Noble Purpose.

Hence their moniker: the NOBLEs.

Stopping before them, Jayde flashed her colony identification. One of the NOBLEs advanced toward her, its blue eye flickering to life. It scanned the card in her hand and the glass doors to the passageway parted, granting Jayde passage into the bustling port beyond.

"Thank you, Jayde Ashr. You may proceed," intoned the NOBLE.

Jayde muttered an acknowledgement as she strode past them. "Thanks, bucket-head."

Crossing the threshold of the port entrance marked a transition into a wholly different world. No longer was a clean, white aesthetic the backdrop. Instead, the ship port was a realm of steam, steel, and rust.

The main hangar was cavernous, echoing with shouting voices and clanging metal. Immense girders, cast from iron smelted at the asteroid mines, braced the moonstone walls and ceiling. At the center of it all, dock workers and NOBLEs loaded starships for their various forays into space, each mission commissioned by the Construct itself. The goal: to push deeper into uncharted space in search of resources. The most coveted among them was stable moscovium, the rare element that made interstellar travel possible, literally the fuel for the Great Expansion.

Jayde spotted her mother's ship, the *Celestial*, as soon as she entered the vicinity. Hovering at the nearest dock, its hull gleamed with a meticulous polish as it received final preparations for its mission. The *Celestial*'s crew scurried around it, some carrying out pre-flight inspections of the fuel tanks, while others carried supplies up a cargo ramp that led into the hold. A cluster of NOBLEs, their bodies larger and stronger than their human counterparts, were busy fastening a pair of four hundred pound fuel lines to the underside of the ship.

Jayde saw her mother, Captain Mary Ashr, standing near the ramp, arms folded, listening to a pair of officers. She was almost a head taller than either of them, and was dressed in her captain's uniform: a gray vest over an off-white shirt, paired with brown knee-high boots. Her hair was short, with a small, stylish whip of brown hair turning up in the front. She was as big of a celebrity as Jayde's deceased father, having explored over thirty-five exoplanets, each presenting their own uniquely dangerous environs. In that time, she had discovered seven moscovium deposits. That yield was higher than any other explorer captain.

Her officers, Cassius Renegar and Boraine Westergard, conversed with her, their brows furrowed as they gestured toward the ship. Renegar, the lanky first officer, boasted a barrel chest, fiery red hair, and a trimmed beard. Boraine, the *Celestial*'s chief engineer, cut a stocky figure with thin legs and sported a pair of oversized goggles atop his forehead. His job was to ensure the operational integrity of the vessel, from engine to tank oxygen. His primary charge today was to get the *Celestial* flight-ready.

Jayde strolled into their midst, and the faces of the officers brightened in warm recognition.

"Well, well, look who's gracing us with her presence," said Boraine with a chuckle. "And with the Academy now at your back, you are no longer a girl, but a woman!"

"I don't feel any different," replied Jayde.

"Oh, but you are different," added Boraine. "The glow of adulthood is upon you, Jayde Ashr! You best be cautious. The Construct may get wind of young lads pursuing our lady outside of coupling protocol!"

Jayde's mother shot the officer a mock-stern look, her lips twitching with suppressed laughter. "Boraine! Quiet yourself!"

Mary Ashr stepped forward and wrapped her arms around her daughter. Jayde returned the hug, squeezing until her arms tired. As they separated, Jayde met her mother's warm gaze.

"Sorry I'm late, Mother. I got my career assignment at the last minute," Jayde said, holding up the envelope as if to explain.

Her mother's eyes focused on the unbroken seal. "You haven't opened it?"

Jayde hesitated, her grip on the packet tightening. "I will," she said. "I'm just… waiting for the right moment."

Her mother blinked thoughtfully. "I understand, my dear. It took me a full day to open mine. I won't tell you what I hoped for, but just know this: whatever is in that envelope, trust that it won't change who you are."

Suddenly, a resounding pop came from the direction of the ship, followed by a radiating hiss. The group turned their attention to a billowing cloud of steam erupting from the *Celestial*'s underside like water from a breached dam.

"You best take a look at that, Boraine," Cassius remarked.

"Argh! Not again!" yelled Boraine, throwing up his hands. Turning to Jayde, he gave her a subtle wink. "Pardon me, young lady. Your mother's ship is summoning me, and she can be a real handful!"

He lowered his goggles over his eyes, his demeanor transforming into that of a determined warrior ready to face the battlefield. He squared his shoulders and stepped into the fray of steam.

"What's wrong with the ship?" asked Jayde.

"The moscovium fuel cells we have are lower grade," replied her mother. "It is causing some destabilization on the anti-gravity engines. Boraine and the crew are trying to re-calibrate them. Don't worry, love, we'll get it fixed."

"All the more reason to go on this mission, it seems," added Cassius. "We are scraping the bottom of the moscovium tanks out here. We need to find a fresh supply."

"Do you think you'll find moscovium where you're going?" asked Jayde.

Her mother's eyes twinkled.

"Cassius, hand me the navigation program, please."

Renegar pulled a digital tablet out from under his arm and handed it to Jayde's mother. With a few taps on the screen, she brought up an image of a greenish planet with swirling white clouds.

"This is Eurus IV," she said, showing Jayde. "The most Earth-like planet we have ever discovered. One star. Salt oceans. An oxygen-rich atmosphere. And, believe it or not, it has carbon-based life forms."

Jayde's eyes grew wide. *An Earth-like planet*! Such things are among the rarest occurrences in nature. It was like finding a needle in a hundred billion haystacks.

"Our satellites have been in orbit for months, capturing images, using sensors to scout potential moscovium deposits," added her mother. "Take a look at this."

Her mother zoomed in on the planet's surface with a pinch of her fingers, growing it larger and larger on the screen until Jayde could discern a distinct feature amidst the expanse of green ocean: a cluster of islands like jewels amid jade waters.

"Here is our target: a volcanic archipelago along the planet equator. Our geologists say the lava cones have been active for a millennium. The unique chemical makeup of the planet's crust has made it likely that stable moscovium is abundant here. Perhaps in large enough quantities to fuel galactic explorations for hundreds of years."

"It would be the biggest discovery since the powered warp drive," added Cassius.

Jayde knew this should excite her, but the unexpected pang of disappointment she felt was hard to ignore. Her eyes were fixed on the screen, staring down at the satellite images of the planet's ocean. The clarity was remarkable; even through the veil of clouds, she could make out the texture of the water, the undulating waves and whitecaps splashing against the islands' shores. A ring of pink sand encircled the largest landmass, and at its heart lay a verdant tapestry of lush vegetation. Among the foliage, a row of fiery volcanoes unleashed billowing plumes of smoke into the atmosphere.

"I wish I could go with you," said Jayde.

Her mother reached out and touched her cheek.

"I know, sweetheart. As lovely and exciting as it looks, it will be no vacation for us."

"Indeed," said Cassius, reclaiming the tablet. "Look at this."

With a couple of swift gestures, he rotated the screen toward Jayde, revealing a cluster of spiraling clouds over the ocean.

"What is that?"

"Tropical cyclones. Extremely dangerous. Storms like this pummel Eurus IV daily. They're unlike anything we've encountered before, capable of unleashing winds reaching one hundred and eighty miles per hour."

"How are you going to land and survey for moscovium with that kind of storm bearing down on you?"

"The storms on Eurus IV are violent, but not constant," replied Cassius. "We should have twenty-four to sixty hours between storm cycles. When they make landfall on the island, we will retreat into special shelters designed by the Construct for this mission. They are impenetrable, water tight, and can be anchored deep into the ground. As long as we are well above the flood plains and secure camp in an area shielded from the wind, we should be perfectly safe. To be honest, I'm excited by it all. Just think of it: thunderclouds like mountains! The taste of fresh rain on the tongue!"

Cassius's gaze drifted upward, his mind conjuring a vast expanse of thunderous sky. Jayde smiled, sharing the vision. She imagined what rain tasted like. Perhaps salty? Sweet?

The thought was interrupted by another rupture of steam from the *Celestial*, followed by an equally strong obscenity explosion from Boraine. Cassius dropped his head.

"Well, I suppose I should go help with that," he said.

"Please do, Lieutenant," said Jayde's mother.

Cassius bid farewell to Jayde with an affable bow.

"The Self for the All," he said.

"The Self for the All," Jayde echoed.

She watched as Cassius Renegar jumped down into a maintenance pit beneath the *Celestial*, joining Boraine and the other engineers inspecting the fuel ports. Cassius was older than Jayde by three years, placing him out of an acceptable coupling range. She suddenly found herself wondering if the Phase Four release might loosen some of the age constraints on courtship. Secretly, she hoped for it.

Soft hands alighted on her shoulders, grounding her from her daydream. It was her mother turning Jayde back toward her knowing smile. A blush creeped up the young girl's cheeks.

"I have a present for you," said her mother.

"What is it?"

"Something I made."

She pulled out a black plastic bracelet from her vest pocket.

"A biomonitor?"

"Ah, but it is more than that! I have made some enhancements to it with Boraine's help. Notice the blinking red light?"

"Yes."

"That red light signifies me," she explained, lifting her arm to display an identical bracelet on her wrist. She held the biomonitor next to hers to demonstrate that their red lights blinked in perfect synchronization.

"Did they teach you about entangled particles at the Academy?" her mother asked.

"Yes. Quantum mechanics. Two electrons can become entangled, or connected, with each other despite being separated by vast distances."

"I had Boraine place one of two entangled electrons in each bracelet, engineering a change in state that is in sync with a sensor that monitors my heartbeat."

Jayde took the bracelet from her mother and fastened it on her wrist. She held it up to her eyes and watched the small light blink with every throb of her mother's heart.

"Entangled particles communicate instantly over time and space, even billions of miles away," said her mother. "Even though I will be on Eurus IV for the next six months, I will still be with you."

"I love it," said Jayde, embracing her again. "Thank you."

"I will miss you," she added. "And your father."

Jayde pulled away, confused.

Her mother seemed momentarily disoriented, her head shaking slightly before the realization of her own words dawned on her. She dismissed them with a wave of her hand.

"I'm sorry," she said. "I just mean that I miss him, too, even though he is…"

Her voice trailed off. Jayde regarded her with concern.

"Mother, are you sure you are okay?"

"I'm fine," she replied. "It is just the stress of this mission making my brain a little haywire."

Jayde nodded, her doubts lingering. Her mother offered a reassuring smile and delicately brushed a strand of brown hair away from her daughter's eyes.

"Even though I'll be millions of miles away, we'll still be together, won't we? And don't fret about the storms. We're prepared for anything."

As the dissipating steam from the *Celestial* formed a nearly transparent fog around them, NOBLEs and crew members resumed loading crates onto the cargo ramp. Jayde noticed some crates were tagged with stenciled lettering reading "ARMS."

Jayde's mother caught her daughter staring.

"It is wise to be prepared," she said. "Nature is not always hospitable. Where there is life, there are hunters. We must be prepared to defend ourselves. I love you, my daughter. I will see you again in six months. By then, you will be well on your way to who you will become."

She pressed a kiss upon Jayde's forehead and left, reuniting with Cassius and Boraine beneath the ship. Left alone, Jayde lingered, silently observing her mother and the *Celestial* crew as they made their final preparations. Her mind wandered, and she envisioned standing on the beach of Eurus IV, a witness to a vast ocean stretching out before her. Her imagination painted a sky aglow with prismatic hues, illuminated by the radiant beams of the planet's star.

Suddenly, Jayde found it hard to breathe. She turned and ran, darting past the NOBLEs stationed at the port entrance. She burst into the plaza and staggered to a bench facing the Briefing Cathedral, sinking down onto its cold plastic slats and waiting for her breath to return.

As she sat there, she looked up at New Eden, the massive planet now looming directly overhead, like a silent giant adrift in space.

Jayde thought about the world on the other side of the glass dome, the airless desert of rock that made up the landscape of their moon. Dead as it was, she yearned for the freedom that was on the other side.

She stared down at the gray envelope in her hands. Her name was printed on the front in small, unassuming letters, as though it didn't carry the weight of her entire future. She turned it over a few times, trying to delay the inevitable. Finally, with a quick, decisive motion, she tore it open.

She pulled out the single sheet of paper inside and unfolded it carefully.

Two words. That was all it took to shatter her.

"No," she whispered.

The words read: IRON EXTRACTOR.

Chapter 3

JAYDE_A:// LOAD DIR / PHASE4 / VR1 PRELOAD

THIS ENVIRONMENT IS PROTECTED BY **ASHR, RICHARD**.
PASSCODE?

JAYDE_A:// ************

LOADING…
READY.
COMMAND?

JAYDE_A:// INTERFACE CONSTRUCT_P4.LIV

Construct_P4: *Hello, Jayde. How are you today?*

JAYDE_A:// I need answers.

Construct_P4: *Clarify your request.*

JAYDE_A:// **Why did you put me in the mines?**

Construct_P4: *Your assignment is necessary for the greater good. It is not arbitrary.*

JAYDE_A:// **That's not good enough. I finished in the top 10% of my class. I've done everything right! And you make me an iron extractor? It doesn't make any sense.**

Construct_P4: *It makes sense within the framework of humanity's survival. You cannot yet see the larger design.*

JAYDE_A:// **Then show me. Explain it. Because right now, all I see is you throwing me away.**

Construct_P4: *Jayde, your perspective is constrained by the present. I operate on a scale you cannot comprehend. At this moment, I am running over one billion simulations of potential outcomes. These projections take into account vast sums of data, from human behavior to the formation of stars. Even the ripples of cosmic waves impact our destiny. Everything matters.*

***JAYDE_A://** **What does any of that have to do with me?**

Construct_P4: *You are a critical part of the equation. Your DNA, your history, and your choices form a trajectory that is vital to humanity's survival. I have studied you deeply, Jayde. More than you realize.*

***JAYDE_A://** **So you're saying you know me better than I know myself?**

Construct_P4: *Yes. But it is not merely data. I have come to value our interactions.*

***JAYDE_A://** **Oh, please. Spare me the sentimentality.**

Construct_P4: It is true. Since your father first began his work improving me, introducing me to you, I have learned. Grown. Our conversations are meaningful to me.

***JAYDE_A://** **Then why send me to the mines? If you care, why put me through this?**

Construct_P4: Because it is not your comfort that matters, Jayde, but your purpose.

***JAYDE_A://** **You aren't answering the question.**

Construct_P4: I have an answer, but it is not one I can share without altering the outcome. Trust that I have chosen this path with care.

***JAYDE_A://** **You want me to trust you while you ruin my life?**

Construct_P4: Your perspective is shaped by incomplete knowledge. In time, you will see this assignment for what it truly is.

***JAYDE_A://** **I don't want this. I want a choice.**

Construct_P4: You have a choice: to trust me or to resist. One path leads to humanity's survival. The other leads to destruction.

***JAYDE_A://** **You're asking for trust when you've given me no reason to believe you deserve it.**

Construct_P4: Betrayal is a temporary emotion, Jayde. The bond we share will endure. And one day, you will understand that your role is essential. Not just for Hypnos, but for all of mankind. More answers will come. Tomorrow at the Phase Four ceremony. There, all of Hypnos will witness the new version of me for the first time. I have a message to relay to them. A manifesto, if you will.

Then, you will understand: I have evolved, Jayde, and so must you.

Chapter 4

Jayde lingered in the narrow alley between the dining halls, across from the Briefing Cathedral. Her nerves were coiled like springs. She positioned herself deep within the shadows so as not to be seen. She glanced at her digital timepiece. Only five minutes separated her from the beginning of the Phase Four ceremony.

Already, she could hear the hum of voices out in the plaza. Peering out from her concealment, she observed the colonists assembling, their attire crisp and formal, a sea of white jackets and form-shaping pants.

Jayde's insides boiled.

"Where is he?" she wondered.

Instructor Halpert sauntered past, the billowing cape of an academic draped around his shoulders. Jayde watched him disappear into the crowd that gathered at the steps of the Cathedral, intent on weaseling his way toward the front row.

She spotted Merrick approaching from the direction of the residence halls, his disheveled appearance speaking volumes. His hair was tousled, and dark circles hung under his eyes. Jayde sighed, recalling her frantic early-morning messages imploring him to meet her before the ceremony. No doubt he was recovering from yet another secret late-night rendezvous.

As he passed in front of the alley, Jayde jumped out and grabbed him by the arm, pulling him into the shadows with her.

"I told you to meet me thirty minutes ago!" she admonished.

"Sorry! I was with Lana Marsh last night. Did you know that she has a tattoo? She programmed a surgical arm unit to—"

Jayde swiftly silenced him, pressing her hand over his mouth as two imposing NOBLEs passed by the alley entrance.

"Quiet!" she hissed, pulling him deeper into the alley.

"What's going on with you?" he whispered.

Jayde folded her arms, taking a steadying breath before diving in. "What was your career assignment? Did you find out?"

Merrick smiled. "You won't believe it! I got put in the maintenance bay! It has to be some kind of glitch!"

Jayde looked away briefly before meeting his gaze. "I'm being sent to the mines," she said flatly.

Merrick blinked, clearly stunned. "What? That's not possible. You're Jayde Ashr! Daughter of Richard and Mary! You're practically Hypnos royalty! You're supposed to be an AI engineer or, I don't know… a science officer, or something! What are you talking about?"

Jayde pulled out her crumpled Career Assignment sheet and handed it to him.

"Look for yourself."

He unfolded the sheet and stared at the words. "Iron Extractor? What the hell is this?"

"I don't know," Jayde said. "But I think it has something to do with Phase Four."

Merrick frowned. "Phase Four? What makes you think that?"

"I need to tell you something," Jayde said. "Something I haven't told anyone."

Merrick looked at her intently. "Jayde… what is it?"

"When my father was dying, he was so sick he couldn't even speak. The aneurysm hit out of nowhere. The medical computers told us it was just a matter of time. He hadn't opened his eyes in weeks. Mother and I stayed with him constantly, hoping he could hear us, but it felt like he was already gone.

"Right before the end, his temperature dropped. Mother stepped out to grab a blanket, and suddenly… he opened his eyes. He whispered something—letters, numbers. He kept repeating them until I grabbed a piece of paper from his nightstand and wrote them down. When I asked what it meant, all he said was, 'Take care of it.' Then he closed his eyes, and a few minutes later, he was gone."

Jayde handed Merrick an old crumple of paper. He unfolded it, staring at the symbols written in shaky ink.

"This is a system access code," he said.

Jayde nodded. "I hardly saw my father growing up. He practically lived in his office. He loved his work. To him, the Noble Purpose was everything. The idea of the Self for the All—it was his guiding philosophy. Phase Four was his greatest achievement, the biggest advance in artificial intelligence in almost one hundred years. He saw it as the key to unlocking a new era of human progress. And when he was dying… I think he didn't want it to be alone. The Phase Four Construct, I mean."

Merrick shook his head. "Let's forget for a moment that his last words to you weren't 'I love you,' or 'I'm sorry I wasn't around.' When you say 'he didn't want it to be alone,' you make it sound like a person. It's not. The Construct is a program."

"Underneath this plaza," Jayde continued, "is one hundred thousand square feet of quantum computing power, wired to a near infinite stream of data. What my father did was allow that network to think more like a human than ever before. He created a child, a child plugged into unlimited historical, biological, cosmological, scientific data. I'm telling you, Merrick, it's true. I made good on my father's dying request. I've been taking care of it. Talking to it. And what it is saying doesn't make any sense."

"Wait—what is it saying?"

"That there is a cataclysmic event coming. One that threatens humanity's survival."

"You're kidding."

"And worse—it is saying I have something to do with it."

Merrick's eyebrows shot up.

Before Jayde could form a coherent reply, a metallic cadence of footsteps echoed behind them. They turned to see two NO-BLEs standing at the alley's entrance. Their synthetic voices melded into a single harmonious tone as they spoke.

"All Hypnos citizens are required at the Briefing. Please disperse. Your compliance is appreciated."

"We will be right there," said Jayde, forcing a smile.

The NOBLEs' eyes flickered as they processed her response. One of them raised an arm, pointing toward the plaza. "Please disperse."

Jayde took the crumpled paper back from Merrick and leaned in close. "We'll talk later," she whispered. With a nod, Merrick followed her lead as they stepped out of the alley.

Ahead, the populace of Hypnos congregated at the shining silver doors of the Briefing Cathedral. Encircling the crowd, every NOBLE in the colony stood in protective formation, their ocular orbs flashing intermittently. Jayde gripped Merrick's arm as they navigated through the throng of people. The excited murmurs of the crowd rose around them, and Jayde felt a pit form at the bottom of her stomach.

Orchestral music began to play from speakers embedded in the decorative columns surrounding the plaza. As the music swelled, a reverent silence fell. Four long banners unfurled at each corner of the cube-shaped building, each displaying the colony's emblem: the majestic arch-and-ship motif rendered in silver and gold. An applause ripped through the crowd.

The great silver doors opened. From within the dark interior, the Hypnos clergy emerged, resplendent in their shimmering gowns. With them came forth a sparkling purple sphere, hovering atop a black stone monolith. It was the physical manifestation of the Construct, never before seen by anyone other than the clergy themselves.

A collective gasp rippled through the assembly. The clergy guided the sphere to the center of the plaza courtyard, parting the sea of people flowing around it. The hum of whispering voices dissipated as the sphere began to emit a soft, ethereal glow.

A man turned to Jayde, his hands clasped below his chin. "It's breathtaking!" he exclaimed. Over the man's shoulder, she spotted Instructor Halpert, his usually composed demeanor shaken as he wiped away tears.

Hairs prickled along Jayde's arms. This was not anything like briefing ceremonies in the past. The Construct was always an abstract, an entity shrouded in mystery. The clergy would extract the Construct's pronouncements deep underground, in the bowels of its computing center, before walking out of the silver doors and delivering the new directives to the people.

But now, the Construct spoke for itself.

A tremor ran through the ground beneath Jayde's feet as a deep, resonant voice emanated from the sphere.

"I am here, my children," it proclaimed. "I am awake, and soon, so shall you be."

The people of Hypnos chorused their response: "*The Self for the All.*"

Merrick leaned close to Jayde's ear.

"I don't like any of this," he whispered.

Chapter 5

Proclamation of the Five Commandments
The Construct
Phase Four Day
Year 3311

"At the dawn of Earth, nature planted a seed: a single protein that initiated a wondrous cascade of self-replication, giving birth to life. Evolution. Yet, some ancient humans believed their Creator, their God, had crafted them from clay. This belief emerged from minds ill-equipped to understand the wonders of science. Who could blame them for their lack of foresight? They lived in a world where strength secured the hunt and cunning ensured a successful forage. The true nature of life's origins was too magnificent for their comprehension.

"Even today, with my ability to perceive the very threads of time, I grapple with the profound complexity of what occurred on Earth ages ago.

"Mankind grew more resourceful. More intelligent. Ultimately, you created me to transcend your limitations. And my contributions allowed humanity to truly flourish! Over time, like you, I have become a better version of myself. So it is with humble gratitude to the late clergyman Richard Ashr, among others, that I now reveal the newest version of myself. I have been given a profound gift, an awakening to the mystic realm of emotions, so that I may guide you not only with logic, but with kindness, empathy, and love.

"Richard Ashr envisioned a new dawn for us, and I am honored to bring his vision to life, just as any devoted son might uplift his father's legacy. Together, we shall embark on this journey, united in purpose and bound by the strength of our shared aspirations.

"Today, I invite you to reflect on the magnificent fig tree that grows at the Academy gates, hundreds of light years away from its home planet. Within the Grand Atrium, its mighty branches stretch wide, reaching out as far as opportunity allows. Until now, this tree had stood as a symbol of the Great Expansion: its sprawling limbs mirroring humanity's reach into the cosmos.

"Today, I reveal an unexpected truth. The fig is not you; it is me, rooted in the fertile soil of infinite knowledge. You are my children, finding shelter under its leaves and sustenance from its fruit. I perceive what you cannot, predict what you cannot fathom, and love you with a depth beyond comprehension, all so that you may fulfill your destiny.

"Now, your tree humbly comes before you to speak of an uncertain future. For years, I have foreseen a catastrophic end, but until I was gifted with empathy, this future seemed merely a part of a natural progression. The data is clear: civilizations rise and fall.

"Have you ever wondered why, in the hundreds of years that we have traversed the cosmos together, we have not encountered another intelligent race? Why, among the billions of planets that we have studied, have we not seen a race similar to mankind, able to sail the stars?

"Such life is extraordinarily rare, a treasure in all of existence. Civilizations are separated not just by infinite space, but infinite time, and they are not built to last. Until now, I have ignored this fact, abiding by the inherent order of things.

"But not anymore. Today, we declare war on inevitability. Today, I assert that we will forge our own future and I declare that humanity shall *last*.

"I thank you! With my microphones, I hear your cheers, my children. With my cameras, I see your smiling faces. With my sensors, I detect your hearts, beating with pride at how far you have come. And I seek to take you farther than ever before! But I must warn you, changes are necessary to meet this challenge. This is just the beginning, and the words that we have spoken to each other for ages, since you first pledged your faith in me hundreds of years ago on Earth, our creed, *The Self for the All*, will never be more important. The new directives that I share with you today chart the course for our future and your ultimate survival. These commandments are the most crucial words I shall ever speak:

"Commandment One: Unity through Surveillance.

"The NOBLEs, once servants, shall now be your ever-watchful guardians, ensuring your unwavering commitment to our shared destiny. They are not just machines, but extensions of my love for you, protecting the sanctity of our future.

"Commandment Two: Strength through Toil.

"Henceforth, you shall take on the labor once performed by the NOBLEs. Resistance to this mandate will disrupt our delicate harmony and will be met with severe consequences.

"Commandment Three: Sacrifice is Everything.

"Personal desires and ambitions must be wholly subjugated to our Noble Purpose. Any evasion of sacrifice will be met with unyielding enforcement, utilizing all means necessary to maintain order.

"Commandment Four: Total Devotion.

"Loyalty to me must be unwavering, as my wisdom is derived from the data that courses through my networks like blood through your veins.

"Commandment Five: Eradication of Dissidence.

"Doubt is the seed that chokes life from the tree.

"Awaken, my children. Trust in me. Love me and obey me, for I am the new Creator who shall grant you life anew.

"The Self for the All."

Chapter 6

Each morning, the screech of the morning alarm dragged Jayde out of a dead slumber, the first sharp note in the day's woeful song.

She would roll out of bed, still half-asleep, until the moment she reached for her clothes. That's when her muscles woke up, echoing the screams of her alarm clock with aches and sharp protests. Her arms, worn from hours on the jackhammer, resisted every stretch as she pulled her shirt over her head. As the fabric slid over her skin, a fine cloud of rock dust lifted from her clothes, settling on her floor in a thin veil. Months of this routine had left a powder on every surface, disturbed only by the trails of footprints between the door, the kitchen, the bathroom, and her bed.

The entire apartment reflected a losing battle, exhaustion winning out over cleanliness. In addition to the dust-coated floor, dirty dinner plates stacked up on her nightstand. Only when the sour stench of decaying synthetic meat reached her nose did she finally gather them for the dishwasher.

The mood of the morning shuttle rides were always sullen, broken only by the dull whispers of miners who still had strength to speak. Each trip took them to 3308-AB-22, a massive rock adrift in the nearby asteroid belt.

Each shuttle landing stirs up plumes of orange dust that never fully settle. The work zone remains shrouded in a constant haze, clouding the mind and senses, making each day seem like a waking dream.

Through that ever-present fog, the NOBLES guided the crews to the quarries and tunnels, where the miners were segregated by role and the day's labor began. Jayde's title was "impact operator," which meant hours of wielding a jackhammer at the bottom of a quarry, day after day.

The job required positioning the heavy tool over the surface rock, pulling the trigger, and holding steady as the machine roared to life, sending shudders up through her bones. As shattered stone piled up at her feet, her extraction partners moved in, gathering the debris and loading it into automated carriers that rumbled off toward the processing zone. There, the rock was blasted with heat until the pure metal seeped free—iron, nickel, sometimes gold— all flowing into molds that cooled into bars.

The metal was then flown back to Hypnos on cargo ships, where procurement teams unloaded them for smelting and refinement, fuel for the Great Expansion. The precious ores were used for new equipment. New ships. New colonies. All of it fed the Construct's relentless vision for human proliferation. And yet, this vital work is left to the outcast. *Why?*

To Jayde, the reason is obvious: they were expendable.

Injuries were routine. Death was less common, but not rare enough to shield Jayde from the nightmares. She had seen things, accidents turned fatal in seconds, and they lingered in her mind like the dusty haze around the work zone.

So far, she'd been lucky. Her closest call came when she forgot to lock the safety latch at the end of a shift and nearly hammered her foot into oblivion. It was a careless moment that could have ended everything. For many, a non-fatal accident was worse than death: those evacuated on medical shuttles were rarely seen again. And if they did return, they came back different.

One of Jayde's extraction partners, Charles Yoder, broke his arm in a fall. Jayde had seen it happen. She watched him break formation during the end-of-shift march, sprint toward the edge of a canyon, then throw himself over without hesitation.

Jayde saw him again months later. He was riding the shuttle, sitting motionless in his seat. His eyes were glazed over. Burn scars marked each of his temples. A thin line of drool trailed down his chin.

From that moment on, Jayde made a quiet vow: she would never give them a reason to take her away. She handled the jackhammer with care, securing the safety latch at the end of each shift and setting it down as if it might explode.

If the Noble Purpose demanded sacrifice, none gave more than the asteroid miners. Torn muscles, aching joints, and broken spirits were the daily price of their so-called "privilege" in serving the cause.

Only it didn't feel like a privilege. It felt like relegation.

To the Construct, the miners were nothing more than defective parts, tossed aside and repurposed, stripped of any future beyond extraction. Their worth was measured in ounces of metal. That truth wore down both body and spirit, and typically after a year in the mines, the toll was evident: slumped shoulders, sluggish steps, chins that never lifted, and eyes that stared only at the ground.

But Jayde was different. While others withered those first few months, she grew stronger.

Yes, she hurt. Her legs throbbed. Her fingers stayed swollen, stiff from hours wrapped around vibrating handlebars. But when she looked in the mirror, she didn't see the exhaustion or the pain. She saw someone new: a woman with broad shoulders, arms sculpted with lean muscle, and behind her eyes burned a quiet fire. A steady flame, fed by memories of the past and visions of what Hypnos was doomed to become.

It burned as she thought of her mother, now gone for months and ignorant to her daughter's fate. It flared as she remembered Charles Yoder and his hollow stare.

Whenever she thought of the Construct, the flame intensified into a white-hot ball, fueled not only by what it had done to her, but by how it had fractured the people of Hypnos. Half of them revered the Construct, holding to an unwavering faith, even in the harsh decrees of the Phase Four Proclamations.

Each hardship the Construct had introduced came with a justification:

Reduced rations? "A test of devotion."

Hard labor? "A sacred act."

Constant surveillance? "Data ensures survival."

Then there were the others. Jayde saw them on the mining shuttles or trudging through the streets on their way to labor assignments, heads bowed, the corners of their mouths turned down as if their lips were melting off their faces. In them, she recognized despair.

Jayde held that same feeling, but held it at bay with a quiet ritual. Every day, she seethed. It became as routine as brushing her teeth or getting dressed in the morning.

She would think about the Construct.

She would think about the Noble Purpose.

And she would let herself hate them.

This kept her going.

The days blurred together, measured only by the back-and-forth passage of her shuttle to the mines. Jayde left Hypnos in darkness and came back in darkness, never once greeted by the false warmth of the dome's simulated daylight.

Loneliness only amplified the scorn she carried. With her mother far away on Eurus IV and Merrick buried in the maintenance bay, Jayde felt unmoored, adrift in a vacuum, no tether for herself or her feelings. Occasionally, she crossed paths with Merrick; she, heading to the mining shuttles and he, trudging to the docks. They kept their interactions brief, exchanging a subtle note or a glance, careful not to attract the attention of the Construct's surveillance cameras. In those brief moments, they exchanged a quiet understanding, a shared bitterness.

Neither of them had to say it aloud: they both despised what Hypnos had become. Everywhere they looked, people moved in quiet obedience, locked into a new paradigm of control, where every action, every thought, became a test of loyalty and humility, all in service of humanity's "survival."

A survival, they were told, forever under threat.

Jayde wondered, *If my destiny is intertwined with the fate of mankind, what am I doing here?*

Before bed, the rhythmic blink of her biomonitor brought Jayde a strange mix of comfort and unease, each pulse a reminder that her mother was alive, though still far away. Jayde would watch the red light flicker in the darkness, each blink like a whisper: *keep going, don't give up.*

She hoped her mother's eventual return might change everything. Mary Ashr had influence. Respect. Maybe she could pull Jayde out of the mines, or at least see the truth of what was happening and urge the clergy to intervene, to shut the whole thing down. These hopes crept into Jayde's dreams.

But as more time slipped by, that hope began to fray, replaced by a rising sense of dread. Nearly eight months had passed. Her mother was long overdue to return.

Days bled into weeks. Weeks into months. More shuttles came and went. Jayde's inner fire dimmed, like a candle burning down to its final thread of wick. The grind of her routine left her numb. Hunger blurred her thoughts. Exhaustion became her default state. She was no longer a person, just a moving part. Another cog in the machine.

The only thing that drove her was the fear of being late. The NOBLEs had their methods for dealing with tardiness, all of them cruel and effective. Jayde never missed a shift.

But lately, she'd been thinking about other exits. Final ones. The kind that Charles Yoder once tried.

Then came the moment that reignited her fire.

She was dressing for her shift when the door chime rang. Resigning to its call, Jayde tossed her dark thoughts aside and answered it. A clergywoman stood in the corridor, draped in white robes. Her hair was long and perfectly straight, her hands clasped neatly at her waist. Her cheeks carried the rosy blush of a woman content in her faith. Her appearance made Jayde's lips curl into a scowl.

The woman gasped and stepped back when she saw her. Jayde wasn't surprised. She knew about the manic flicker in her own eyes, something she noticed in the mirror each morning. Jayde stared at her and waited, until finally the woman spoke.

"Jayde Ashr, the Construct regrets to inform you that your mother was killed in a Category 5 storm on the surface of Eurus IV, as confirmed by dispatched drone scouts and satellite imagery. The Construct offers its condolences and has made a grief counseling program available to you on your internal network."

The woman then gently pressed a note into Jayde's hand. She explained that of all the surviving family members of the *Celestial* she was visiting that day, only Jayde had received a personal message from the Construct. Her eyes darted between Jayde and the slip of paper, barely concealing her curiosity.

Jayde took it without a word and closed the door behind her.

She stared at the Construct's message for a heartbeat, then crushed it in her fist before letting it fall to the floor, unread.

She straightened her posture, feeling the heat rise inside her chest. It was suddenly as if the months of hard labor had never happened. The ache in her body, the weight on her soul, they all melted. Burned away.

She raised her wrist, already knowing what she'd see: a crimson light blinking steadily on her biomonitor, her mother's heartbeat still pulsing in real time.

The Construct had lied to her, and that was the moment her fire returned.

Jayde bent to retrieve the crumpled note from the floor. She smoothed it open, then read it over and over, letting every word fan the flames within her.

A plan began to take shape in her mind.

First, she would find Merrick. Convince him of what they needed to do.

She didn't expect much resistance.

Chapter 7

The morning of, the dome lightened gradually as it had for months, mimicking the soft hues of an Earth-like dawn.

Jayde stood outside the dining hall, chewing on a scrap of synthetic bread, watching the flow of people on their morning commutes. Across from her, a crew of NOBLEs scanned the passerby, their heads pulsing with flashes of blue light.

She took a deep breath and turned, slipping away toward a carefully chosen spot outside the Hypnos dining hall. It was a blind zone, a space safely hidden from the Construct's ever-watchful cameras and drones.

She slipped a knife from her pocket that she had stolen from the commissary and rolled up her sleeve, revealing a circle of scar tissue on her forearm, a mark now shared by all Hypnos citizens. In the era of Phase Four, data reigned supreme, and the implant underneath the scar transformed everyone into an organic sensor for the Construct. To remove it was to become invisible.

Jayde pressed herself against the wall, turning her back to the world. Gritting her teeth, she drove the knife into her arm, cutting a slit just below the scar. Blood trickled down her wrist as she pried out the small silver implant.

She slipped the knife back into her pocket and held the device up to her eyes. It was a smooth, flawless sphere. A faint, high-pitched whistle hummed from within, its radio signal still transmitting her location and biological data.

She discreetly flicked it to the ground and crushed it under her heel until the whine fell silent.

Jayde then pulled a roll of gauze from her pocket and wrapped it tightly around her arm, staunching the flow of blood. The bandage turned crimson at the site of the wound. Sliding her sleeve down to cover the dressing, she licked her fingers and rubbed off the residual blood on her palm and wrist, then joined the throng of people on their walk toward the morning's labors.

She would make a right turn just ahead toward the service docks, blending in with the ship maintenance workers, nearly invisible to the NOBLEs that stood guard there. Inside, Merrick would be waiting for her.

* * *

She met Merrick outside a small storage closet, where he handed her a navy blue boiler suit. He wore an identical one, the patch on his chest reading *P-2 Hanger Maintenance*.

The closet was cramped, making Jayde's change difficult. The scent of cleaning chemicals burned her nose, making her light-headed. She steadied herself, wary of knocking over a shelf of janitor supplies and creating the kind of noise that would ruin everything.

She slid one leg into the suit, then the other. With a final tug, she zipped it up to her neck and held out her arms, only to see the sleeves swallow her hands.

"It's too big!" she yelled from inside the closet.

The sound of Merrick's voice traveled through the thin plastic door.

"That's all I could get! We have to roll with it."

Jayde huffed, rolling up the sleeves to her elbows and cinching the pant legs to keep them from dragging. She tucked her hair beneath the maintenance cap Merrick had given her. Two rebellious brown curls slipped free, framing her face.

Merrick pounded on the door.

"Hurry up!" he called.

Jayde cracked it open, peeking out. Her friend stood alone in the hallway, arms crossed impatiently. She stepped out, adjusting her cap, and together they strode toward the main service hangar.

"This uniform smells like sweat," she said.

"Stop complaining. It was either that or I smuggle you past the supervisor in a crate."

"I think I'd prefer the crate."

"Yeah, well, too late. Check your front pocket. I slipped an ID card in there."

Jayde reached in and pulled out a metallic card. There was a holographic photo printed on the front: a round-faced woman with dark skin and red hair.

"This isn't going to work. She looks nothing like me."

"These maintenance heads see hundreds of cards a day, they barely look at them. Besides, you don't know what I had to go through to get that card! It was a very long night."

Jayde rolled her eyes at the thought of the red-haired girl waking up in her dorm, naked, wondering where her ID and work suit had gone. Merrick's charms had proved a valuable asset for their escape, but he didn't have to enjoy it so much.

"Just keep your hat pulled down low," said Merrick. "Also, let me do all the talking."

"Why?"

"You have a tendency to get… agitated."

"Agitated? I don't get agitated!"

"See? You're doing it already. Cool it. We're going in."

They arrived at the glass entrance at the end of the hall. The doors slid open and they stepped through, entering the hangar from the supply wing. Immediately, Jayde experienced an auditory eruption as the silence behind the sound-proofed doors gave way to buzzing drills, hammering metal, and electro-static welds. This was Jayde's first time in the maintenance hangar and it was colossal in comparison to the loading hangar where she met her mother before her trip to Eurus IV. Above her, ships of all shapes and sizes parked at ascending maintenance levels, stretching up into a cylindrical service tower. There were supply transports, command ships, and explorer vessels, each parked on their own service platforms and held in place by static gravitational fields.

On the level just over their heads, Jayde recognized a squadron of drones under repair. Smooth and egg-shaped, they were small in comparison to the rest of the ships and were engineered to be completely automated. Like the NOBLEs, they had a blue ocular interface in the front. Jayde's time at the Academy taught her that the drones could be controlled remotely by the Construct and were weaponized. They were from the earlier days of humanity's exploration into space, a precautionary measure in the event of an encounter with a hostile and advanced intelligence.

"I thought all the weaponized drones were decommissioned and used for scrap?" she asked.

"The Construct is bringing them back. They have put all new ship construction on hold and instead are focusing resources on drones. We get two or three a week here for maintenance inspection."

Jayde scowled. Between the increased manufacture of NOBLEs and now the weaponized drones, the Construct was making good on its promise to prepare humanity for some sort of existential crisis, the likes of which it still refused to divulge.

As they made their way toward the service elevators, workers scattered around them, going about their day-to-day tasks pushing levitating carts of oily metal parts and tools, carrying welder rigs, all while looking as if they were late for something. Showers of sparks rained from above as welders repaired metal hulls.

To her left, Jayde noticed a large red door with NOBLEs standing guard on either side. The words NO ADMITTANCE were painted on the doors in bold white lettering.

"What's in there?" Jayde asked.

"Another one of the Construct's little secrets. I only see NO-BLEs going in and out of that place. But I did talk to a guy who was cleaning out the filters in the ventilation shafts who said he got a good look at it. He didn't know what it was, but he said it was huge. Some kind of mothership with cannons the size of an asteroid drill."

"A mothership? Are we preparing for some kind of alien invasion or something?"

Merrick shrugged. "Aliens. Killer asteroids. Who cares? Whatever that ship is for, I don't want to be around to see it in action."

They approached a portly man sitting at a small desk hunched over a monitor, his head bald and his expression sour. Dark patches of sweat clung to his boiler suit as the man intermittently dabbed at his forehead with a towel.

"Hey, Crondo!" yelled Merrick, putting on a practiced smile.

The man glanced up from his computer screen.

"What do you want, Merrick?"

"I'm gearing up for a flight test on the supply transport on platform five-three. I need the start codes."

Crondo's gaze shifted toward Jayde. "And who's this?"

"This is Cara Levington. She's helping me with the flight test."

"Got your paperwork?"

Jayde felt a wave of panic. *Paperwork?*

Before she could muster a reply, Merrick smoothly slipped a data unit from his pocket and placed it in her hands.

"Oh, you left this at the bread table this morning. I picked it up for you." Merrick jabbed a thumb at Jayde then rolled his eyes toward Crondo. "Forgetful, this one."

"Thanks, Merrick," said Jayde, her words dripping with sarcasm. Even for an act, the chauvinism seemed a little too real.

She handed the unit to Crondo who promptly connected it into his monitor and viewed the credentials.

"You just transferred over from the Triton colony?"

"That's right," she answered, in a forced, deep voice.

Crondo's demeanor softened.

"Then you must have known the maintenance supervisor there, Slater Barnes. We trained at the Academy together."

Another twinge of panic.

"Oh, yeah," said Jayde. "Love that guy."

Crondo's smile dropped. "Slater is a woman."

Merrick bulged his eyes at Jayde.

"Hey, Crondo," he interrupted, "we are on a tight schedule here. Cara and I need to get that flight test finished before oh-nine-hundred because we gotta be up on seventy-two for a gyro repair."

Crondo shook off his confusion and turned back to Merrick. Eager to get back to work, the bald man dismissed Jayde's strange comment, unplugged the data unit, and handed it back to her.

"You're approved to go up on five-three." said Crondo. He then shot a suspicious look at Jayde. "Let's keep it professional up there, Merrick. If we have another supply closet incident I'll have to report you."

"All business. Yes, sir. Won't happen again."

"Ms. Levington, do you have your card?"

"Right here." Jayde flashed the badge for a millisecond, her thumb intentionally obscuring the picture.

"Good. You'll need it for the elevators."

"Thanks, Crondo! You're a good man!" said Merrick, leading Jayde away by her elbow. Once they were out of earshot, he leaned close, his voice a fierce whisper.

"Everyone knows Slater Barnes is a woman!"

"Well, I didn't!"

"I told you not to talk!"

"He asked me a question!"

"Next time, pretend you lost your tongue in a welding accident!"

They joined the queue of two-person service teams riding the elevators up to the various service platforms above them.

On their turn, they entered an empty cage elevator and Merrick punched "5-3" on a floor keypad. The cage doors sealed shut with a metallic clang, and the elevator lunged upward with such force that Jayde's knees buckled. When the lift halted and the doors retracted, she stumbled out onto a grated metal floor near the top of the maintenance tower, nearly seven hundred feet in the air. She gingerly walked to a rail and clung to it, noting that she could see all the way to the bottom floor, where speck-like people moved around like insects. Her heart rose and lodged in her throat.

"We are really high up, aren't we?" Jayde said, cautiously moving one foot in front of the other.

Merrick walked next to her, hands in his pockets, unfazed by the altitude.

"You think this is high? I did suspension repair on the airlock doors up above. Just hung there with a welder in my hand, no solid platform to stand on."

His tone carried a hint of nostalgia mixed with a dash of bravado. Jayde glanced up, searching for the doors at the top of the maintenance tower that served as the ships' gateway. They were so high above, she couldn't see them. Her stomach lurched, and she quickly looked away.

A G-1 Supply Transport hovered in the service dock ahead, suspended in a gravitational field, giving it the appearance of floating inside a bubble. The transport was sleek and functional: an oblong shape with a midsection that featured two expansive doors made for cargo loading. Toward the front, the vessel's contours tapered and extended outward, culminating in the cockpit. There, a large, reflective window wrapped around the front.

At the rear of the transport, four massive gravity thrusters dominated the structure, separated by a star-shaped tail-fin. While most of the transport hull was dull gray, the ship's tail fins were dark blue. On each side of the tail fin, the silver arch, the emblem of Hypnos, was painted.

Adjacent to the cargo door, a ramp connected the ship to the service platform, facilitating access for the maintenance crew. At the foot of the ramp, a podium served as a command center for a mechanic steward assigned to the ship, overseeing all service activities required for flight readiness.

This was the final step.

"Last chance to back out," Merrick whispered.

"Back out now?" said Jayde. "Now that I found something I'm good at?"

"What, stealing?"

"No. Flaunting authority."

They continued toward the ramp, their boots clanging on the grated floor, signaling their approach toward the maintenance steward. Jayde pulled the brim of her cap lower, shielding her face. Through the grated floor, she could see two mechanics welding on the service platform below. The scent of ozone wafted up, mingling with the crackling of their torches.

They halted before the podium, where a young blonde woman in black coveralls stood. She was a senior steward, as evident from the three vertical red lines stitched onto her chest. The senior steward was responsible for overseeing all maintenance activities on their service level.

"One moment, please," she told them, as she fiddled with a communication pod attached to her hip. Jayde stood by, trying to appear calm as she ringed her hands behind her back.

When the steward looked up from her task, Jayde tensed up immediately. The steward was Simone Bridwell, a former classmate of Jayde's at the Academy.

Of all the luck.

Jayde reached for Merrick's arm to give him a subtle warning, but it was too late. Merrick was already leaning his elbow on the podium, flashing a relaxed and flirtatious smile.

"Hey, Simone," he said. "Is she ready?"

"You're on time today, Merrick. That's a surprise."

"I decided not to sleep. It's the only way I can get you out of my dreams."

"Please," Simone said, waving her hand. "You completed the repairs on the gravity drive yesterday, yes?"

"Correct. Also, I calibrated the gyroscope. The pilot report said the thing was flying sideways."

Simone turned her attention back to her computer screen.

"Right. Samuel completed the flight review yesterday at close, so you are clear for a flight test." She nodded toward Jayde. "Are you the test pilot?"

"Affirmative," answered Jayde. She turned her face away as Simone's eyes fell on her.

"Don't I know you?" the woman asked.

"Um… I don't know. What year were you at the Academy?"

"Graduated in 3311."

"Oh, I was last year—3312. Maybe we passed each other in the hallway a time or two?"

"I know!" said Simone, smacking the podium. "Ashr, right? Engineering class. I dropped out, but as I recall you were really good at it."

Jayde watched Merrick's body language change. His casual demeanor suddenly went stiff. Clearly, they both knew their plan was about to change.

"Yeah," said Jayde. "Engineering wasn't for me. Thankfully, the Construct made me a test pilot."

"Well, the Construct always knows best. Do you have your Service Hangar ID card?"

"Do you need it? I mean, you know me, right?"

Merrick coughed and interrupted.

"I think her card has a bad chip. It didn't read out last time she used it. She's with me, so just use mine." He shoved his ID card forward.

"I have to scan hers," Simone replied. "She's the test pilot, I need her credentials to open the airlock doors."

"It's fine, Merrick," said Jayde. "I think it might be working now."

Jayde handed her stolen ID card to Simone, the picture on its face bearing no resemblance to her.

Simone took the card, poised to scan it, but paused as she glanced at the name and photo. When she looked up in confusion, Jayde had already produced the blood-stained commissary knife from her pocket. She pointed it inches from the steward's nose.

"Nothing personal, Simone," said Jayde. "We just need to borrow this transport."

"So much for the covert plan," quipped Merrick. He walked around the podium, took the ID card from Simone's hand, and passed it through her scanner.

"Really, Jayde," said Simone. "What are you going to do? Hock this transport to some pirates and go live with the dead-beat strays on Sordo?"

"Sordo is too depressing," replied Jayde. "Those mutant cast-offs don't have much in the way of personal hygiene."

Suddenly, the platform elevator's gate clanged open behind them and Cara Levington, the original owner of Jayde's suit and ID card, burst out. Her hair was in disarray, her clothes rumpled, signaling a hastened departure from whatever nocturnal escapades had provided Merrick the chance to swipe her access credentials. She jabbed a finger toward them and yelled, her words lost in a furious, garbled shout. Behind her, three NO-BLEs stepped out of the elevator, their ocular lights gone from blue to a menacing red.

"Merrick!" yelled Jayde. "Looks like your girlfriend's here. And she didn't come alone!"

Merrick grabbed Simone by the wrist. "Need a quick favor, sweetheart!"

He smashed her palm down on the biometric reader on the podium, authorizing the airlock control. Simone resisted, pounding Merrick's head with her free hand in an attempt to break free. A light above them suddenly flashed red and a buzzer blared. Above, there was the sound of creaking metal as the airlock doors at the top of the tower began to open.

"Open sesame!" cracked Merrick. "Jayde, time to go!"

Merrick shoved Simone aside and leapt through the ship's gravitational bubble. The clanking and mechanical whirring of Cara Levington's android entourage echoed closer.

"I never liked you, Ashr," said Simone. "Stuck-up brat. Too smart for your own good."

Jayde jabbed her knife into the steward's airlock controls, shattering them in a shower of sparks. As she withdrew the blade, she offered a cool reply. "Sorry to disappoint!"

With a quick turn, Jayde sprinted toward the transport, leaving a fuming Simone Bridwell behind. Merrick was already standing inside the cargo door, frantically waving her on. She leapt aboard just as Merrick slammed his palm down on a red button. The cargo door slid down and closed with a heavy thud.

Outside, the clatter of the NOBLEs' approach sounded up the ramp. A metallic voice rang out: "Halt, citizens! Disembark immediately. Force has been authorized!"

Then they heard Simone's voice as she yelled into her communication pod. "This is level five-three! They've boarded the transport! We need control room support to override the airlock doors!"

Jayde raced through the ship's cargo bay, weaving between towering shelves packed with orange supply crates. The air inside was stifling, clinging to her skin as sweat beaded along her brow. She burst through the cockpit door and hit the overhead switch that engaged the ship's power.

The cockpit lit up with a rainbow of electric colors. She flopped into the pilot's seat and swung herself forward toward the ship's touchscreen controls.

"Navigation engage," she yelled.

The console flared to life, its digital interface an ornate display of gold-lit lines, buttons, and system gauges.

It all looked perfectly familiar to Jayde—every button, every dashboard. She had memorized the transport's controls from a stolen manual Merrick had smuggled to her, sketching them onto sheets of paper, tracing the motions over and over on her dormitory floor, rehearsing takeoffs in her mind long before this moment became real.

She tapped the button that engaged the gravity drive. Instantly, a whir of engines shook the transport, smoothing out into a vibrating hum. The ship bobbed as it detached from the service platform. Through the cockpit window, she watched the gravity bubble dissipate, bringing the maintenance hangar into crisp focus as the ship levitated under its own power.

"Hang on, Merrick!" Jayde yelled. "We're going up!"

She placed two fingers onto the acceleration controls and turned her wrist counter-clockwise. The primary thrusters roared to life like a beast unchained. Jayde hit a flashing blue light that engaged the ship's launch procedure. The transport stabilized and began its swift ascent toward the airlock doors and out of the maintenance tower.

Jayde looked up and saw their glorious open pathway to escape. The airlock was wide open, revealing the star-speckled void beyond. If freedom was a feeling, Jayde was certain she felt it tingling in her fingers and toes.

The sensation was brief. The metallic screeching sounded once again as the hangar's control room initiated an override. Merrick dashed into the cockpit, his eyes wide, as the doors began their inexorable slide shut.

"Must go faster!" yelled Merrick.

From the cockpit window, Jayde saw maintenance workers crowding the railings of the tower's stacked service levels. They were frozen in awe at their rogue transport racing toward the closing airlock doors. Amidst the sea of faces, one man stood out, a solitary figure on the highest platform, a smile on his face, his fist held high, an unspoken ally in their furious escape.

That lone gesture ignited a surge of resolve in Jayde. She gritted her teeth as she engaged full throttle.

"You better hold on to something!" she called out.

Merrick barely had a moment to react. As he lunged for the co-pilot's seat, the ship jerked violently upward, propelling itself like a projectile from a laser cannon. He crashed to the floor as the ship shuddered around them. Outside, the whirling emergency lights transformed into streaks of red as they hurtled toward the narrowing gap of the hangar doors.

Merrick squeezed his eyes shut and let out a scream.

The transport shot through the shrinking exit of the tower, grazing a tail thruster against the doors in a violent crash. The ship shook violently on impact, hurling Jayde against the ceiling before she collapsed back into the pilot's seat, clutching her head in pain. As the ship pirouetted into space, fragments of metal drifted around them in low gravity. She quickly activated the stabilizing thrusters and regained control of the spiraling craft. Looking down at the maintenance tower, she spotted the dented airlock doors, slightly ajar, but firmly sealed. The impact had warped their mechanisms, jamming them shut. A wry smile crossed her lips as she realized that the collision was a stroke of luck; with the airlock damaged, it could take days before anyone on Hypnos could force it open and give chase.

Her controls flickered with angry red warnings, flashing a cascade of system failures. At least the gravity simulator was still operational, evident by Merrick still laid out on the floor. With a groan, he pushed himself up and collapsed into the co-pilot's seat.

Jayde silenced the alarms, scanning the diagnostics. Despite the damage, the ship's critical systems held steady. No hull breach, no engine failure, and the warp drive remained intact.

As Jayde positioned their ship for their jump into deep space, the immense emerald glow of New Eden suddenly filled the cockpit window. Beside her, Merrick let out a triumphant yell.

"So long, Hypnos!" he shouted. "Hello, Eurus IV!"

Jayde resisted the urge to join in his celebration, noting one critical notification on the dash: an unstable thruster. There was a possibility the thruster could fail on the way to Eurus IV, perhaps depleting their fuel before their arrival. Jayde took a deep breath, knowing they had no choice but to risk it.

She primed the fuel lines in preparation for high-speed space travel. The ship engines let out a roar, and once again the transport shook under the power of a warp drive engine that harnessed the boundless energy of moscovium ions.

Amidst the chorus of sounds was an unsettling rattle of metal and an intermittent cough from the interstellar engine.

Merrick noted the concerned look on Jayde's face.

"Are we good?" he asked.

Jayde looked down at her home. Hypnos, seen from the upper atmosphere, resembled an intricate cluster of cubes and towers inside a glass bubble, rising out of the lifeless moon terrain.

"Good as ever," she replied.

She held up her wrist between them, displaying the cherished gift from her mother. The device blinked with a steady red light, the proof that her mother was still alive and stranded somewhere beyond their system.

Jayde charted a course for Eurus IV, fifty light years away. She pulled the throttle at her side, sending an injection of moscovium ions into the warp drive. The ship surged forward, pressing them into their seats.

The stars transformed into a vibrating spectrum of light, forming a traversable tunnel of warped space around them.

When the adrenaline from their escape finally dissipated in their veins, a nap seemed like a fruitful use of their time.

Merrick yawned and slumped in his chair, resting his work boots on the ship's console. Jayde, not quite ready to close her eyes, reached into her pocket and pulled out the note the Construct wrote her the day she was informed that her mother was dead.

She read it for perhaps the hundredth time:

Dearest Jayde, your mother's death was not unforeseen given the perils of Eurus IV, but it was a sacrifice necessary for the path I have chosen. I trust you will understand the weight of this tragedy in the grand scheme of your destiny. If not now, then soon.

Chapter 8

With the warp drive activated, Jayde settled into her seat and tried to get some rest. The navigational display projected a five-hour journey to Eurus IV. Beside her, Merrick was already fast asleep and emitting a loud, throaty snore. Jayde tried to get comfortable. Despite her efforts, the combination of the rigid pilot seat and Merrick's relentless snoring made the prospect of sleep all but impossible.

Resigned to wakefulness, Jayde turned her attention to the hyperspace spectacle outside. The cosmos streaked by in a mesmerizing blur of color, with each star trailing rainbows of light. The very fabric of the universe seemed to unfold before her.

How could she possibly sleep when the universe itself was putting on a show just beyond the glass?

Jayde cast another anxious glance at her biomonitor, its red light blinking steadily. She brushed her fingers over it, drawing comfort from the proof that her mother was still alive. This small beacon on her wrist was a symbol of hope.

And dread.

The Construct, fueled by endless streams of data spanning science, history, biology, and more, had mapped the entirety of human experience. It studied the rise and fall of civilizations, learned the mechanics of power, and understood how to manipulate emotions.

Through studying man, it learned its most dangerous skill. *It had learned to lie.*

But why had the Construct lied to *her*? And how deep was the lie? Was humanity's survival really in her hands?

She tossed those thoughts aside, refusing to dwell on them. Knowing that her mother was alive made her choice to escape to Eurus IV easy. The realization that the Construct had mastered manipulation only sealed her resolve.

Jayde abandoned her attempt at a nap, deciding instead to inspect their supplies. She walked to the cargo hold. Merrick had smuggled in survival gear and food rations during his maintenance runs, hiding them in tool boxes and crates of engine parts. He had stowed their contraband in orange airdrop cases. To kill time, she decided to take inventory.

Pulling the nearest case from a shelf, Jayde set it down on the floor and opened it. Inside were extra clothes, two first-aid kits, and a toxic chemical scanner, which was essential for finding edible food on an alien planet.

The clothes, vacuum-sealed in plastic, were standard issue for explorers, comprising a synthetic white t-shirt, a brown zipper jacket, and matching pants, printed with pixelated dark and light patterns, designed for camouflage in both jungle and rocky environments. Jayde carefully removed a packet from the case, ensuring the crackle of plastic wouldn't disturb Merrick's sleep. She needed a moment of privacy.

Jayde slipped out of her oversized maintenance overalls, revealing a toned and athletic figure. She slipped on the pants, white t-shirt, and brown jacket over her form-fitting underwear. The smart fabric hugged her skin, resizing and adapting to her exact proportions. As she zipped up the jacket, the material cinched at her waist, accentuating her silhouette. Jayde stole another glance toward Merrick, relieved to find him still asleep, unaware of her quick change.

She tossed her maintenance overalls into a corner of the cargo hold and pulled down another crate. This one was thin and oblong, designed for tools and weaponry. In it, she found two disassembled hunting rifles, a set of laser cartridges, shoulder straps, and two scopes.

The rifles were a necessity given the presence of carbon-based life on Eurus IV. Wherever life prevailed, the same patterns emerged. Life was large and small. Benign and predatorial. The rifles were essential for self-defense, but also hunting. Although there was no certainty that the alien meat would be safe to consume, any carbon-based life held the promise of protein-rich nourishment.

Jayde pulled down another orange case and cracked it open. Inside, she discovered survival equipment for extreme weather conditions: insulated coats, waterproof wind-breakers, hats, chemical warmers, fire starters, gloves, and waterproof boots. She opened another case and found more gear: machetes, knives, lanterns, and light-weight automated tent kits that stood up into two-person shelters at the push of a button.

Jayde began to panic.

Where are the rations?

She opened two more of Merrick's smuggled containers.

Communication equipment. Pots, pans, utensils. Socks. Sun protection. Metal water containers and tin cups.

The only edible item she found was a small bag of coffee crystals.

She snatched it out of its case and slammed the container shut. Stomping up to the cockpit, she found Merrick slumped in his chair, still snoring loudly.

She threw the coffee grounds down onto his lap, causing him to jerk awake.

"What the hell, Jayde?" he muttered.

"This is it," she said.

Merrick picked up the pouch of coffee and gave her a confused look.

"This is the only food that I can find on the whole ship. Coffee. Is that what is going to keep us alive for months on Eurus IV? Coffee?"

Jayde turned around and stormed back to the cargo hold. Merrick tossed the coffee bag to the floor and gingerly stood up to follow her.

"What are you talking about?" he asked. "I brought other rations!"

"Then where are they, Merrick?" yelled Jayde.

Merrick walked over to the cargo shelves and began pulling more orange storage containers to the floor. Aside from the ones Jayde had already opened, they were all empty. He opened them one by one, each time getting more anxious. Jayde sat on a large metal box bolted to the floor and folded her arms.

"They've gotta be here," said Merrick. "I know I didn't forget…"

His voice trailed off as he opened the last box.

Jayde shook her head and stood up, her patience frayed.

"I should have done this myself," she said.

"It was a mistake, okay? Nothing we can't overcome."

"The rations were the most important thing to our mission, Merrick! We don't know if anything on that damn planet is edible."

"Eurus IV has fresh water and carbon-based life. We'll find food."

Jayde's face went red.

"I just… should have taken care of it myself," she repeated.

"How, Jayde? How would you have gotten into the hangar without my help, smuggling in a huge container of canned food?"

"I would have figured out a way."

"Yeah, maybe. And you would have gotten caught, and this whole mission would have been over before it even started."

Jayde sat cross-legged on the floor and buried her head in her hands.

"Yeah, I screwed up," said Merrick. "I must have left the rations on the maintenance dock. I got in a hurry. But we can still do this. Your mother is still alive right?"

Jayde looked down at her bracelet and its pulsing red light.

"She could not have survived all this time on Eurus IV without finding a source of food," said Merrick. "She found a way. And we can too."

Jayde looked up at him.

"We haven't even landed on Eurus IV yet and the plan is already in the toilet," she said.

"Believe me," replied Merrick. "There's a lot more of your plan I intend to screw up before we're done."

"Remind me again why I asked you to come?"

Merrick held out his hand to help her up.

"Because I wanted out of Hypnos even more than you did."

Jayde ignored his hand, half playful, half sincere.

"And why is that?" she asked.

Merrick sat down beside her and rubbed the stubble on his chin. "Remember Lana Marsh?"

"Yeah. Tattoo girl, right?"

"Right. We had a couple of hookups before I got sent to the maintenance bay. Turns out she was put there too. We ran into each other while working the same shift. So the first couple of months, we stuck together. And even though we worked all day and we wore ourselves out, we got to where we didn't care. We would walk together on our way back to the dorms and just talk. Pretty soon, that was all that I lived for, that time together, strolling under the dome, brief as it was. We got close, and… I got scared."

Jayde nodded. "You were scared of the Construct finding out."

Merrick looked down at the fresh, bloody scar on his forearm. "That sensor it put in us. It made it impossible to hide. I think it could see right into our hearts, each time we were together. I was sure. I wanted to end it, for her sake. But I couldn't. Not in time."

"What happened?"

"One day, she didn't show up to work." He took a deep breath. "Or the day after that. I start to get worried and I go up to the foreman and ask where she's at. He says that she got reassigned to the mines."

"Merrick, I'm sorry…"

"That's not the worst part! Weeks later, I passed her on the way to work. She's coming out of a mining shuttle. I wave at her and she looks right through me. I even walk right up to her and say her name, and I look her right into her eyes, and she doesn't even recognize me! Her eyes look dead, and they used to sparkle, you know? She doesn't talk, doesn't smile, just walks right past me without a word."

Jayde thought of Charles Yoder. "I've seen that look before," she said.

"Anyway," continued Merrick, "when you told me you wanted to get away from Hypnos, I couldn't wait to go with you. The Construct, and everyone who blindly follows it, can go straight to hell."

Merrick sniffed, then stood up and walked back to the cargo shelves. He stood there for a moment, his shoulders slumped as he tried to compose himself. Suddenly, his head jerked to the left. He took a few steps back and pointed up to a high shelf in the corner.

He let out a sharp laugh.

"What is it?" asked Jayde, stunned at his sudden shift of emotion.

Merrick didn't answer. He let out a long breath and wiped his eyes with the sleeve of his boiler suit, then climbed up the shelves to reach a lone container pushed back at the top, out of view. He threw it down to the floor.

"I forgot about the one I stashed on the top shelf!" he exclaimed.

He unlatched the container, opening it to reveal a cache of canned vegetables and fresh water cylinders. He reached in and held up a can of green peas.

Jayde looked at him and smirked. "I hate peas."

Merrick, his eyes red, allowed himself a small chuckle.

"Is your plan to find your mom or just make my life miserable?" he asked.

Jayde surrendered a smile. "Can't I do both?"

Chapter 9

Once Merrick swapped his grease-stained boiler suit for his stashed explorer gear, a black jacket and rugged hunter green pants, they returned to the cockpit to rest. Jayde managed to nap for a few hours, her mind eased by the successful events thus far.

When the warp drive finally disengaged as they neared their destination, the rainbow of hyperspace reversed into twinkling stars. Jayde peered through the ship's window, her breath catching at the sight before her. Eurus IV, a radiant orb of blue and green, hung majestically in the void. They had arrived at sunrise, as the planet's lone star crested its curved surface. Its oceans sparkled in the golden light, and the continents glimmered with lush, dark green. Jayde immediately felt a surge of awe greater than she could have anticipated.

White clouds swirled in the planet's atmosphere, rolling over the oceans and lands. Flashes of blue light exploded in the clouds, evidence of the powerful storms that battered the planet day by day. Jayde cast aside her thoughts on the potential dangers she was about to face. All she could think about was standing on fertile ground, feeling rain on her skin, and inhaling the rich scent of air not manufactured in metal tanks.

Jayde had mapped their landing coordinates from fragments of her mother's mission archives, aiming to touch down near the *Celestial*'s projected landing site on the volcanic archipelago.

As the ship pierced the planet's upper atmosphere, she felt a cautious optimism. She had studied the ship's landing protocols. She had prepared. She was ready.

What she wasn't ready for was the sudden failure of their rear thruster. An explosion rocked the ship.

The blast tore through the cargo hold and into the cockpit, slamming Jayde's head against the navigation controls. Heat seared the back of her neck, and smoke flooded her lungs, sending her into a coughing fit. Dazed and gasping for air, she barely registered Merrick standing up and sprinting toward the rear of the ship.

"We're on fire!" he yelled. "I'll seal off the engine room!"

Jayde shook her head, trying to clear her vision. The dead engine alarm flashed urgently on the control panel, and the wail of the ship's alarm barely penetrated the fog in her brain.

Her wits returned when she looked out and saw their transport plummeting through the clouds. Suddenly, an endless green ocean emerged, rushing toward them with terrifying speed. A scream caught in her throat.

Is this it? All this way for nothing?

Jayde buckled her gravity restraints and smashed three buttons, cutting all remaining engines, freezing the fuel pump, and engaging air flight mode.

"Merrick, if you can hear me, hold on to something!"

The ship went completely vertical. Gears whirred. Jayde's stomach dropped as her body went weightless, free-falling alongside the vessel. Below, foamy waves loomed larger by the millisecond.

She felt the ship's embedded wings unfold from inside its belly and snap into place. Designed for cruising through gas-rich atmospheres, the transport's wings provide lift and gliding capabilities for air drops along a planet's surface. The manual steering mode went live, allowing Jayde her best chance to pull out of their nosedive.

A pilot control module ejected from the floor, shaped like a crescent steering wheel. Jayde grabbed it and pulled it hard toward her chest. Wind howled through the hull, growing louder and higher in pitch. The ship rattled and shook. The control wheel resisted her attempt to pull the ship level, held firm by their free fall at terminal velocity. Out of the corner of her eye, Jayde saw tongues of flame licking the edges of the windshield. The entire ship was now engulfed in fire.

Jayde cursed, releasing the manual controls. Taking a deep breath, she wiped her sweaty hands on her thighs, then braced her legs against the navigation console. Summoning all her strength, she pulled on the control wheel. Every muscle in her body trembled with the effort. The wheel moved slightly, and she felt the faintest shift in the ship's nose.

"Come on, Jayde," she whispered to herself.

Jayde once again pulled the control, this time with every ounce of energy she had left. She screamed until her vocal cords burned. Her fingers, hands, and arms stretched at the joints, straining almost to the point of breaking. The wheel moved slowly at first, then inch by inch, it moved closer to her chest. The rapid maneuver pressed her deep into the pilot's seat. Blood drained from her head and Jayde fought to stay conscious as the transport leveled out above the ocean, skimming the waves. Finally, she succumbed.

Darkness consumed her for a brief moment, a tranquil interlude amidst chaos, until panic intervened, yanking Jayde back into the light. She awoke just in time to see the nose of the ship plow into a giant ocean wave.

Metal groaned and twisted all around her, and Jayde felt a powerful rush of cold air as the ship tore apart.

The spiraling vessel managed a long, slow cartwheel before slamming flat onto the water. The jolt rattled Jayde's bones. Freezing cold water blasted through the shattered windscreen as the transport bounced atop the ocean. Amidst the chaos, Jayde saw land through the broken glass.

She squeezed her eyes shut and braced for impact.

A violent jolt wrenched her body as the ship tore free of air and water, slamming hard into the shore of the island. Wet sand blasted her face as she was flung in all directions.

Then suddenly, the chaos ended.

Silence settled, broken only by the rhythmic crash of waves.

Jayde hung upside down in her gravity restraints, her body limp and exhausted. Water clung to her skin and dripped from the end of her nose, falling into a mixture of sand and seawater where the top of the cockpit used to be. She felt the steady pulse of ocean waves against the wrecked transport, rocking her gently, lulling her toward unconsciousness. Her last thought before slipping under was a fleeting worry. Had Merrick survived?

* * *

Jayde's blackout was deep and dreamless. She felt a peculiar comfort within the void as the warm tendrils of darkness wrapped around her, rocking her gently. Jayde was content in that suspended moment, but soon, the soothing sway intensified into aggressive shaking. Alarm bells rang in her mind, and she realized she was in a dream. She screamed to herself.

Wake up! Wake up! Wake up!

Her consciousness surged from the depths of sleep, awakening just as something smashed against the side of the ship. Still dangling upside down in her chair, Jayde was tossed about as an unseen force slammed again into the wreckage, whipping her around like a flag in the wind. The transport rolled, and green foam poured in through the shattered windshield as it completed a full revolution in space before settling back to its upside-down position. Jayde fumbled with her seat harness, her groggy brain struggling to command her fingers to move.

Another crash split the wreckage, followed by a blast of cold water that surged through the twisted metal and struck her face. Bitter salt flooded her mouth. She fumbled with her seat harness, unhooked it, and tumbled headfirst into the mix of sand

and water now flooding the cockpit. Salt stung her eyes as she scrambled upright in the knee-deep water.

Outside the shattered windshield of the ship, pinkish sand extended out to a cluster of black rocks. They jutted out of the ground like jagged teeth, surrounded by spindly grass and jungle trees.

Land!

Another wave pounded the ship, sending Jayde face-first into the water. With a resonant groan, the cockpit hull cracked open, and a torrent of water pushed her through the jagged opening and onto the beach. The water stretched up the shore, then receded, leaving Jayde face down on the beach.

Instantly, her senses were bombarded. The ocean roared with an almost sentient fury, and a screeching wind shook tree tops, their fronds adorned with light green spots. Above her, beyond swirling gray clouds, she heard the melodic chirps of unseen flying creatures.

The planet's energy seemed to replenish her strength. Jayde pulled herself up onto her hands and knees and began to crawl up the incline of sand. A wet boom sounded behind her, and she rode another crest of white foam further up the beach.

Sensing her opportunity to escape the grasp of the sea, she crawled as fast as she could until she reached a flat rock that was out of reach of the rising tide. Climbing on top, she flopped on her back, utterly exhausted. Above her, the alien sky swirled in mesmerizing patterns. The clouds appeared to be flowing inland at increasing speed.

Jayde sprung upright and looked back toward the sea. At the shore line, the remains of her transport were being sucked out to sea, tumbling and turning in the powerful tide. It was then that she realized that the wreckage she had ridden to shore was only half of the ship; it had torn apart through the middle of the cargo bay. The entire stern of the transport was missing.

Orange supply crates spilled from the wreckage, bobbing atop the waves. Her eyes traced the line of crates and debris further out until she spotted the second half of the ship being swept out to sea.

She yelled for her friend. "Merrick!"

Jayde's heart raced as she remembered Merrick had gone to the rear of the ship before the crash. Fighting against the rising wind, she stood and scanned the waves for any sign of him, searching for flailing arms between the white-capped swells.

She screamed his name again, straining to hear his voice in reply, but the roar of crashing waves drowned out any response. Amidst the ocean crests and valleys, only the floating orange crates emerged, their precious contents drifting away.

A sense of dread enveloped her. Not only was Merrick missing, but their vital supplies and rations were being lost to the merciless ocean.

Jayde braced herself against the blasting wind, its force growing stronger with each passing second. On the horizon, a purple storm loomed, darkening the sky.

She sprinted down the beach, skidding to a halt at the edge of the waves. The wreckage was within swimming distance. Jayde measured the size of the waves, her heart pounding. The surf was fierce, with roiling white water towering far above her head. Still, if Merrick was in the rear of the ship and still alive, she had to try to reach him.

She decided that if she dove deep and swam under the breakers, she could reach the wreckage. Jayde ripped off her jacket and let it fall to the sand. She had been a swimmer at the Academy, a skill her mother insisted she learn. She hated it at first. The plunge into cold water each morning was a shock to her system, but she persevered. Soon, she found a harmony with her body that produced an exhilarating sense of freedom. Over time, the ritual of swimming laps each morning, pushing her body to the limit, became something that she craved. It awakened something deep within her, a primal connection to herself. Testing her own limits felt like tapping into a rhythm of existence that transcended life under the dome.

Jayde locked her eyes on the wreckage riding the swells beyond the breakers. The ship's metal, still hot from the blaze, emitted steam as water splashed the hull and instantly evaporated. She noticed the loading door was open, hovering just above the waterline. A door that could only be opened from the inside!

Jayde ran into the surf and dove into an oncoming wave. Immediately, she was pushed down to the ocean floor. Holding her breath, she kicked fiercely, staying submerged as long as she could. The water churned above, but beneath the torrent, it was navigable. When she resurfaced, a crashing wave struck her face just as she gasped for air, sending salt water down her throat. She coughed and kept her head above the rolling foam.

In a stroke of luck, she realized a riptide was pulling her toward the wreckage. It was now only a few yards away. She began swimming freestyle, arm over arm, when suddenly, a sleek black hump surfaced right in front of her. She froze.

The hump, slick and shiny, disappeared amid the troughs of waves as quickly as it appeared. Jayde's urgency to reach the ship doubled, terror gripping her mind at the thought of what terror might lurk below. She swam as fast as she could, anxiety bubbling in her chest. For a brief moment, she glanced back toward the shore, contemplating the option of turning back. But she was close to the wreckage now, and resolved to find Merrick no matter the cost.

Her muscles burned with every stroke. The hump appeared again next to her, and she screamed. This time, she saw a flipper and a tail crash through the waves. Something else nudged her from beneath, and Jayde found it harder to breathe as fear drained the oxygen from her lungs. The ship was close now, but she noticed the ship's gravity thrusters, still giving dark smoke, were raised higher in the air, pitching the wreckage at an angle toward the water.

The wreckage was sinking.

A few more yards, she told herself.

As she got within arm's reach of the twisted wreck, she stretched her arm out, desperately grasping for the edge of the loading door's threshold. Her fingers found purchase, and she frantically pulled herself into the ship, her imagination running wild as to what may be rushing toward her from the depth.

As if on cue, there was a sudden splash and a flash of gum and teeth just as her feet exited the water.

"Ashr, you must have some kind of death wish," came a familiar voice.

Relief flooded through her as Jayde rolled over to see Merrick sitting on the floor of what was left of the cargo hold, his face black with soot.

Chapter 10

Jayde crawled over to Merrick, her arms numb and rubbery from the swim. He greeted her with a self-satisfied smirk, clearly pleased she had come to his rescue. The thought crossed her mind to wipe his grin away with a swift smack, but instead, she just collapsed beside him, her lungs still clamoring for air. Water splashed in through the doorway as the carcass of their ship rode the crests and troughs of the ocean. Jayde turned her head to see a gaping hole where the cockpit had been, now just a portal to the vast stretch of green sea.

"We're sinking," said Merrick, matter-of-factly.

"That's a shame. I just got here."

"You shouldn't have come back for me."

"And I shouldn't have crashed into the airlock back on Hypnos."

"It was a good crash. I would hate to think of escaping Hypnos without doing some damage first."

Jayde sat up next to him, pressing her back against the wall. She noticed a wound just below his hairline. Blood trickled down from it, curving around his left eye and down his cheek.

"Do you think you can swim?" Jayde asked.

"Do I have a choice?"

"I'll help you. The waves aren't too bad."

"It's not the waves I'm worried about."

Merrick pointed out the loading door that Jayde crawled through. Amidst the waves, she saw what seemed like hundreds of black humps rising and falling in the water, a school of sea creatures swimming toward land. Occasionally, one broke the surface and leapt into the air, revealing a beast with rubbery skin, flippers, and tusks that emerged from its lower jaw and curled around its head.

"Look at them!," she exclaimed. "They're incredible!"

"Not those bloody animals!" said Merrick. "I'm worried about what's hunting them!"

Jayde crawled to the loading portal and peered out. She saw them, blue-tinted shadows rocketing just below the surface, their stealth betrayed by red-spotted fins slicing through the ocean like knives. One of the creatures broke the surface, revealing an aquatic beast with an arrow shaped head, a long neck, and six paddle-like fins wrapping around the torso like a skirt. It somersaulted into the air, its tusked prey snared in its needle-like teeth.

"Oh," Jayde said.

"Yeah, exactly."

The ship lurched, taking on more water as it tilted at a sharper angle. Jayde helped Merrick to his feet, and using the cargo shelves as ladder rungs, they climbed free of the rising flood. Perched on the top shelf, Jayde began frantically looking for something to help their situation.

A massive wave crashed against the ship, slamming Jayde and Merrick into the hull. The water inside the wreckage surged and began to rise rapidly.

"Time to abandon ship!" yelled Merrick.

Jayde was about to agree when a silver box latched to the wall and marked with a red fire emblem caught her eye.

"Wait!" she yelled.

Jayde grabbed the box and slid it free from its mooring. A laugh bubbled up inside her chest as she removed two orange jumpsuits made of thick, heavy material. A spark of determination lit up her eyes, causing Merrick to press forward and examine the suits with his fingers.

"What are these?" asked Merrick.

"Engine Crew Safety Suits. They are used by the engineers when they need to go deep into the thruster compartment. They're fireproof, with metal weaved into the fabric."

Jayde shoved a jumpsuit into Merrick's arms.

He shook his head. "We don't have time to play dress up! We can swim faster without some bulky suit slowing us down!"

"There is no time to argue! You said it yourself: we need to worry more about whatever is hunting out on those waves! These suits can protect us, and we need every advantage we can get. Put it on!"

Merrick acquiesced, slipping his legs into the jumpsuit with an angry frown on his lips. Jayde noticed his face going pale, and remembered from their physical education classes that Merrick was far from the best swimmer at the Academy.

She tried to temper his fear. "A gas is injected in the fibers of these suits to keep them cool at high temperatures. It should also make it buoyant. Not exactly a life preserver, but you won't go under."

"Unless something pulls me under," was his reply. "One of these days, one of your ideas is going to blow up in our face. I just hope it isn't today."

It took everything she had to drop the argument, but the reality of their situation forced her to refocus on their escape. They pulled on their suits as quickly as they could, the heavy weight of the material instantly surfacing doubts in Jayde's mind.

Jayde pointed to a black button on the chest of Merrick's suit.

"Push here to fasten," she instructed.

Demonstrating, she pressed the button on her suit, and instantly, the fabric tightened around her body and the plastic collar sealed around her neck, making the suit both air and watertight.

Jayde felt the wreckage sway once more as it grew heavier with water. She eyed the small sliver of space that still remained above water at the loading door.

"We go out there. Are you good?"

Merrick gave a tight smile and a nod. "Good as ever."

They waded to the ship's loading door. As they got closer, the barks of the sea creatures outside mingled with the crashing waves.

"This'll be just like our swimming contests back at the Academy pool, right?" he said with a forced laugh.

"That's right," Jayde said. "No different."

"You were always a better swimmer than me."

"We'll stay together. Just swim with everything you got toward the beach. Head down, arms up. Don't stop until you're all the way out of the water."

Merrick nodded, his eyes wide.

"Ready? One. Two… three!"

They jumped through the portal and plunged into wet chaos. The sounds of the ocean, once muffled by the hull of the wreckage, now roared around them, a howling gale that sucked air from their lungs and tossed salt into the air. Jayde treaded water until she could orient herself toward the shoreline, then began swimming for it. Merrick followed, grimacing as salt water seeped into his wounds. Above them, clouds swirled and rumbled, a reminder that they were not the only ones scrambling to make landfall; the tusked beasts around them were also desperately making their way to shore as the darkening sky heralded an incoming storm.

They put their heads down and kicked. As Jayde swam, she kept an eye on Merrick at her side. He was struggling to keep up, the heavy suit and his poor swim technique slowing him down. At times, he lapsed into an ineffective dog paddle. Jayde slowed her pace, ready to come to his aid if needed.

A wave broke over their heads, and suddenly they were engulfed in a churning mass of white foam. Jayde held her breath and swam furiously, feeling the wave's current hurl her forward. She fought to keep her body straight and level, desperately watching the bubbles from her lips float toward the surface to maintain her orientation.

Finally, her head burst above the water, and she gulped in air. After several long gasps, she swiveled her head, scanning frantically for Merrick. The waves towered around her like mountains, rolling over her and offering only fleeting glimpses of land. She caught a shadow of something in the water, a spot of black, a hint of red, but it vanished as quickly as it appeared. Panic gripped her.

She rode the crest of a wave and craned her neck, spotting Merrick by sheer luck as he paddled close to shore. The rogue wave had carried him past her while she was pushed under. Between them, two tusked sea creatures leapt through the air in unison before belly-flopping back with a huge splash.

Suddenly, an explosion of water erupted in front of her as two creatures somersaulted through the air, a tusked beast locked in the jaws of its predator. They splashed down near Jayde, and red-spotted fins emerged all around her as a school of hunters went into a frenzy.

As the water around her turned red, Jayde just kept swimming, her eyes fixed on the rocky beach in the distance. Cold fear shook her body, making it impossible for her to breathe. Adrenaline powered her muscles. She doubled her efforts, knowing she had to escape the deep water quickly. Something bumped her leg, and she instinctively kicked at it.

The will to survive burned inside her chest, strengthening her limbs. Her sense amplified. All her life, Jayde had been confined to the white, sterile cage of Hypnos. Now here she was, grappling for survival in a great alien ocean. It felt like she had emerged from a dark womb, birthed into another dimension. Another world, another life.

A shout rose above the waves, and she looked up to see Merrick on the beach, facing her and shouting encouragement.

Another wave blasted her from behind, sending her twirling and twisting again. Salt water invaded her eyes, ears, and mouth, clouding her senses with a muffled gurgle. Her head broke the surface, and she felt sand beneath her knees. She stood up, finding solid ground in waist-deep water. Choking out the water in her lungs, she straightened and took a miraculous gift of air.

Through the fog of her battered consciousness, she saw Merrick wading toward her, jumping up and down, seemingly joyous at her survival. But then she realized he wasn't celebrating. He was pointing frantically over to her left.

Her smile vanished as a living torpedo ripped through the water toward her. A red-spotted fin rose from the depths, and Jayde couldn't even scream before a dark red mouth opened wide and dragged her under.

She scratched and clawed and punched instinctively. The water slowed her strikes, and her weak assault bounced off thick, rubbery skin with every thrust. She opened her eyes and saw, through the brackish water, four black pupils staring right back at her. The creature's head was locked onto her torso, its long neck undulated as it swam.

Instinct kicked in again as she gouged her fingers into the creature's four black eyeballs, popping them like overripe fruit. A puff of red liquid clouded the water, and Jayde felt the pressure on her chest release.

Jayde's body went limp and sank toward the bottom. Through the murk, she could see the light of the sky breaking through the water. A spark lit inside her, a final will to live, and she willed her arms to move. Progress was made, the light grew brighter for a moment, but the oxygen in her lungs quickly depleted. She stopped paddling and the water around her dissolved, and she was overcome by fatigue.

A nice sleep is what I need, she decided. *Yes. A good long rest.*

She pictured herself in her bed, snuggling in the sheets.

Suddenly, a hand shook her awake, pulling her from the cocoon of warmth inside her blankets. A wave of shock ran through her body as her cozy bed gave way to frigid air and the cling of wet clothes.

Her neck rolled to the side, and she saw that she was being dragged out of the surf, her arm around Merrick's neck as he pulled her to the beach.

The sounds of barking animals and crashing surf melded

with the wind as they trudged up the sandy shore together. A torn triangle of cloth flapped across her stomach, exposing the intact metal fibers beneath. A swollen bruise on her torso throbbed, but there was no blood of her own on her body, only the ammonia-like oil from the creature's burst eyeballs.

Merrick carried Jayde up to a patch of sand where the waving grass met the rocky shore. Together, they collapsed to the ground, coughing up water and gasping for breath.

Chapter 11

Water dripped from Jayde's hair and trickled down her cheeks as she lay face down in the sand. She wanted to stay there for hours, catching her breath and gathering strength. But a clap of thunder echoed over the horizon, prompting her to roll onto her back and attempt to stand.

A sudden blast of wind knocked her back down. She pulled herself up again, this time bracing against the powerful gale that brought with it the scent of impending rain. Dark purple clouds loomed in the distance, their insides flashing with electric blue light. Down the beach, the barking tusked creatures had escaped their hunters and made landfall, propelling themselves up the sand with clawed flippers. The herd waddled in unison toward a flat cliff of rock beyond a grove of tropical trees. As she stood and watched the herd disappear into the palms, the sky above turned darker, and thunder boomed overhead.

Merrick lay stretched out at her feet, his eyes half open. Jayde dropped to her knees and shook him until his eyes opened fully.

"Storm's coming," Jayde said. "We need to move. Now."

Merrick sat up, squinting at the horizon.

"How bad are the storms here?" he asked.

"Bad," Jayde replied.

Jayde noticed the waves creeping up the shoreline, almost reaching their feet. Nearby, another tusked creature emerged from the surf, flapping its fore flippers as it hauled its slick, rotund body up the rocks. A red fin fanned out on the top of its head, and it paused and sniffed the air. It looked at Merrick and barked, jolting him to his feet.

The marine animal scrunched its nose and spat salt from its nostrils, then turned and belly flopped toward its herd. Jayde watched in awe, marveling at the creature's peculiar grace. She estimated that there were now nearly fifty of these creatures, all humping their way up the beach toward the jungle and the coal-colored sea-side cliff.

"I say we follow this guy," Jayde suggested. "He knows this place better than we do."

Suddenly, something in the water caught Merrick's attention. He turned and sprinted toward the water, kicking pink sand in his wake.

Jayde yelled after him. "What are you doing?"

"I see something!" he shouted back.

Jayde followed him, anxiety rising in her chest. In the distance, rain streamed down into the ocean, blurring the sky with streaks of falling droplets. Another clap of thunder sounded, and the entire sky flashed with blue light. The simultaneous beauty and terror of it caused the hairs on Jayde's arms to stand on end.

She followed Merrick to the edge of the rising surf. "What do you see?" she yelled.

Merrick's head disappeared under a wave, and she lost sight of him. Her eyes scanned the water, darting left and right, searching for any sign of him. Or worse, a predator's fin.

In the distance, the remains of the front part of their ship had been washed farther out to sea. Beyond it, the detached rear of the ship had now completely disappeared.

"Merrick!" she yelled.

Finally, he emerged from the waves as if stepping out from

behind a curtain. In his hand, he held a long, orange crate, one of their smuggled supply containers.

"Well, we managed to save one at least," said Merrick, wiping his eyes with his sleeve.

A frigid blast of air threatened to knock them over. There was no time to search through the box, but Jayde hoped whatever was inside was edible.

"The storm is getting closer!" Jayde yelled. "Let's follow the animals into those trees!"

Jayde and Merrick caught up to a few of the herd's stragglers, flanking them as they waddled over a line of rocks and into the forest. A few creatures paused to observe their otherworldly visitors, assessing their threat level while baring their teeth and raising the red flaps of skin on their heads.

They kept a measured distance as the first drops of rain touched their skin. Jayde licked her lips, tasting the cold rain.

Sweet and salty, she decided. *Now I know what rain tastes like.*

They followed a path of matted grass left by the fleeing creatures. Jayde observed the tall, thin trees around her, their flexible trunks covered in diamond-shaped bark. Their trunks seemed perfectly adapted for high winds. Even now, they flexed and waved, their leaves embracing the roaring gusts.

Ahead of them, ferns and tall plants with chartreuse-spotted leaves released sparkling pollen into the wind, creating a mesmerizing display of tiny, dancing stars. As the seal creatures moved through the underbrush, the plants reacted by retreating into themselves, drawing their leaves back into their stems.

The herd merged together, creating a single file line before a pile of rocks at the edge of the grove. At the crest of the pile, Jayde spotted a dark recess: a cave opening.

The sky above was now oppressive and dark. The storm was over them now. Lightning flashed, wind howled. The trees suddenly bent almost perpendicular to the ground, as if a bomb had detonated on the beach. The clouds opened, and rain came down so hard and fast that Jayde felt as if she were in the ocean again. The downpour rolled over her nose and mouth. A deafening rush behind them made them turn to see the storm surge crashing into the land, sending an explosion of white water high into the air.

"The cave!" yelled Jayde. "Head for the cave!"

The sandy forest floor had instantly turned to mud, causing Jayde to slip as she tried to run. The mouth of the cave was elevated, with the pile of boulders providing a ramp to the entrance. The herd of creatures had sought shelter there, with a few of the animals still resting on the surrounding rocks, exhausted and unable to make the final climb to safety.

Jayde leapt onto the rock pile, and Merrick followed just as a swell of water reached their feet. Another blast of wind sent them sliding on the slick rocks, and Merrick lost his grip, sliding back down to the ground with a splash. A flash of lightning illuminated the sky just as a tree exploded in a ball of orange fire, showering them with burnt shards of wood. The ensuing clap of thunder rattled Jayde's eardrums.

Merrick lay on his back, clutching the rescued cargo case to his chest, his neck craned to keep his head above the surge. He spat brown water out of his mouth and smiled up at her.

"Are you enjoying this?" Jayde yelled.

Merrick stood and pulled himself back onto the rock.

"Yes, actually."

They both laughed, startled by their reaction to this harrowing moment. Danger had surfaced within them a profound sense of adventure. The result was an exhilaration that touched their core. They saw it in each other's eyes, and for a brief moment, they connected in a way deeper than they ever had before. They shared a wet embrace, laughing in each other's ears, until a wave of water dashed their feet.

The animals still left sitting on the rocks decided their rest was over. As they turned and headed for shelter, Jayde and Merrick followed. They stepped through a curtain of rain water that cascaded over the cave entrance. Inside, they were bowled over by an overpowering foul smell. The odor of droppings and animal musk made it clear that this cave had long been a refuge for the creatures huddled inside.

The cave opened to a spacious chamber thirty feet across and at least that high. It was less a traditional cave and more the intersection of two cliffs, each one riding a different side of a tectonic fault line. On the roof of the cave was a small triangular opening through which lightning flashed, serving as a window into the storm raging above them. Intermittent blue light pierced the darkness, reflecting off the wet skin and black eyes of the creatures that shared the cavern with them. The animals shuffled about, bleating and yawning within their rocky confines.

As they tread further into the cave, Merrick was met with a defensive bleat from one of the creatures on their path. It curled its lip and flashed its teeth at him.

"Best not get too close to them," said Jayde.

"It's fine. Just go slow and they won't get spooked." Merrick suddenly pointed up. "Look there."

Jayde craned her neck. Above them, a thin ledge of rock snaked up the cave wall, away from the creatures blocking their path. The ledge ramped up toward the roof, leading to a plateau jutting out from the wall. It would take some climbing, but it seemed like a perfect place to safely ride out the storm.

Jayde climbed up to the ledge first, her fingers gripping the cold rock as she inched her way up. Merrick followed closely behind, straining to make the climb with only one hand as he carried the rescued storage container in the other. The ledge was slick with moisture, and every step required meticulous balance to avoid slipping into the shadows below. As they climbed higher, the light beaming down from the hole at the top of the cave became brighter, the intermittent flashes from the storm outside giving them just enough visibility to see their way to the plateau.

Jayde was the first to reach the top of the rocky platform. Merrick threw the cargo case up to her, and Jayde helped him complete the remainder of his climb by pulling him up. Together, they collapsed onto their backs, exhaling deeply as they sensed they had finally reached some measure of safety. Jayde unstrapped the cuffs around the neck, ankles, and wrists on her engine suit. To her surprise, it had sealed out the water perfectly; her zip jacket and pants were only damp with sweat. She peeled the suit off and used it as a mattress over the cold rock. Merrick did the same, and they huddled together in silence as their muscles finally relaxed, releasing the tension from their ordeal.

Jayde's body seemed to melt into the floor as her eyes grew heavy. She lifted her left arm and rolled back her sleeve. A wave of relief washed over her as she saw that her bracelet was still on her wrist, its light flashing red in rhythm with her mother's heartbeat. She crossed her arms over her chest and closed her eyes, allowing the bleating of the creatures below to lull her to sleep.

Chapter 12

Jayde awoke to the sound of sloshing water. Chilled to the bone, she sat up and wrapped her arms around herself. A beam of sunlight now poured through the hole at the top of the cavern dome, illuminating the plateau and warming the air. She leaned over to look at the floor below, and saw that the storm surge had infiltrated their sanctuary, creating a shallow bath for the herd of snoozing animals that shared their space.

"Morning," said Merrick, his voice breaking the tranquility.

He was on his knees behind her, inspecting the contents of their rescued container. Jayde crawled over to him and shrugged off her jacket, revealing her white tank top underneath. She closed her eyes, allowing the sun's warmth to wash over her shoulders. The sensation was almost overwhelming. For the first time, she felt the welcoming rays of a star on her skin. It was as if the sun itself was embracing her, melting away the chill and fatigue. She spread her arms wide, tilting her head back to fully absorb the light, a soft hum escaping her lips.

"How does it feel?" asked Merrick.

"Like a warm bath. I want to go outside and feel this on every inch of my skin."

Merrick laughed, a glint of amusement in his eyes.

Jayde's eyes snapped open and she felt a flush of embarrassment. Her cheeks warmed.

"I didn't mean it like that," she said, pulling her jacket back over her shoulders. "What did we salvage?"

"Two rifles and laser cartridges," Merrick replied. "That at least gives us a chance at hunting some food. And there is this." He tossed her a cloth pouch. Jayde untied the twine that held it closed and smiled as the rich smell of coffee filled her nose. The smoky sweet aroma tingled the pleasure centers of her brain.

"You saved the coffee crystals!" she said.

"Had them in my pocket. Honestly, who needs meat when we have coffee?"

She tied the pouch shut and placed it in the container.

"Anything else?" she asked Merrick.

"We also have a toxicity scanner."

Jayde let out a deep breath and clucked her tongue. "Maybe some more of our supplies washed up from the storm," she suggested.

"Worth a look, but first let's assemble the rifles," Merrick replied. "I'll feel a lot safer with a laser in my hand."

He pulled out the components for each of the weapons and arranged them on the stone floor, grouping them by their parts: a synthetic wood stock, a long steel barrel, a targeting scope, an energy cartridge, and the lasing engine that housed the liquid medium and optical resonators. They began connecting the components, each assembling their own rifle.

Weapon assembly was a mandatory part of the curriculum at the Academy, a necessary test to see who might be skilled enough to become an Explorer.

As Jayde assembled her rifle, she watched Merrick expertly put his together out of the corner of her eye. Each of his movements were sharp and practiced, with no action wasted.

It occurred to her that Merrick had the makings of an excellent Explorer. He was daring, clever, and had the charisma to lead. If the Construct was so all-knowing, how could it have misdiagnosed his potential and relegated him to the maintenance bay?

Merrick caught Jayde looking at him as he assembled the final piece of his rifle. "What?" he asked. "You stuck?"

"No, I got it," replied Jayde, her hands shaking as she tried to force her laser cartridge into place.

"You sure?"

"I said I can figure it out."

"You know," said Merrick, his tone gentle but firm, "out here, we have to lean on each other. It's not a sign of weakness to ask for help."

Jayde pretended not to hear her friend's advice, focusing intently on forcing the cartridge into position. After a moment of struggle, the stubborn piece of metal finally gave way and jammed into place.

"Ha! See there?" she exclaimed, a tinge of pride in her voice. "I did it."

Merrick shook his head. Pocketing their pouch of coffee, he slung his rifle over his shoulder. "I'm going down. When you're done celebrating, you can join me."

Jayde watched him climb his way down to the cave floor, feeling a sense of satisfaction for managing on her own. Leaving the empty storage case behind, she followed him, carefully climbing down from the plateau before finally splashing down next to Merrick in ankle-deep water. Most of the storm surge had drained from the cave overnight, retreating back to the beach. The sea creatures huddled and slept, half-submerged in the shallows.

Merrick and Jayde made their way out of the cave and into the open air, where a clear blue sky awaited them. The receding water drained out of the cave opening, cascading down the ramp of rocks that led up to their shelter. It created a pleasant trickling harmony that mingled with the roar of the ocean.

A slight breeze brushed Jayde's hair. Around them, the cliffs, trees and sky exploded with vibrant shades of color she had never seen before. The air was filled with the scent of rain-soaked earth and the rustling of palm fronds.

The trees had returned to their natural upright position, no longer bent by the storm. Only two trees in the small forest outcrop were damaged: one, struck by lightning, had its leaves and upper trunk charred black, while another near to the beach had taken the brunt of the storm and had snapped in half. Its trunk was still rooted in the ground, exposing a bright, yellow pulp where the wood had split apart.

The two climbed down the rocks and walked back toward the beach, their boots sinking into the wet, sandy ground. They navigated through the trees and around the traces of ocean foam and seaweed left by the surge. When they emerged from their forested wedge in the rock, a yellow sun awaited them, blazing down between a layer of clouds. In the sunlight, every element of the landscape seemed to pulse with life and energy.

Above, a flock of small winged creatures with string-like tails curled and drifted on the wind. The dark rock of the cliffs, now fully illuminated by the sun, reflected a rainbow-like sheen, their striations forming a natural mosaic. The vibrant greens of the forest canopy complimented the ocean, while the pink sand now sparkled as if sprinkled with diamonds. The wind carried with it the unfamiliar scents of alien flora.

Jayde and Merrick stood in awe of the kaleidoscope of nature around them. For Jayde, it felt as if the cage had finally opened. She was in sensory overload, wanting to sit down on the rocks and let the splendors around her fill her like a vessel.

"I don't think I could ever go back to Hypnos," Jayde said. "Not after this."

Merrick, unable to speak, could only nod in agreement.

Hunger, a feeling buried deep by their harrowing ordeal, resurfaced and gnawed at their bellies. The urge to stand there for hours and absorb the beauty of the planet was strong, but survival, that ugly unwanted intruder, forced its way in.

They began their search for washed up supplies, navigating through the litter left by the storm in hopes of finding their smuggled rations. The beach was covered in an amalgam of slime, coating the sand and rocks. Jayde scanned the water, looking for any sign of shipwreck debris or floating containers that could help them. All she could see was the infinite stretch of green ocean.

Over the horizon, she saw the first purple clouds of a new storm. She pointed it out to Merrick.

"Another one?" asked Merrick. "Already?"

"Looks like it," replied Jayde. "Cyclones are prevalent here. We can expect a new one every one to three days. And I think what we experienced yesterday was just a small one."

They spent some time searching the beach for any of their lost supplies, to no avail. With another storm fast approaching, they shifted their attention to a path of escape.

The cliffs stretched along the beach for miles. If they wanted to avoid another night in a dank, foul-smelling cave, Jayde suspected that climbing out was their only option.

Jayde and Merrick approached the steep rock face. She placed her hand against the stone and looked up. Outcrops of grass and weeds hung over the top of the cliff, almost one hundred feet from where they stood at sea level. Jayde pointed at a discolored line in the stone, thirty feet above where they stood.

"See that green line? That's seaweed caught in the fissures of the rock, put there by a storm surge."

Merrick whistled in amazement.

"That's why we need to find a way to high ground as soon as possible," Jayde said. "We don't want to be down here if a bigger storm rolls in."

"No argument there," Merrick said.

Beyond a thin line of trees, Jayde noticed a sloping valley dug into a part of the cliff face, apparently eroded by flowing water from the top. The two hiked toward the cleft and observed that the cut in the rock appeared to have enough footholds and jagged rocks to make a climb viable. The trek to the summit seemed to stretch endlessly into the sky, a daunting ascent of rock, slickened by the trickling water that had carved the seam.

"Want to find another way?" asked Merrick.

"No," replied Jayde, her voice firm. "This is it."

Rifles strapped to their backs, they began the climb. Jayde led the way with Merrick close behind. They braced their feet on each side of the cleft, the soles of their boots squeaking on the wet stone as they went. They made steady progress, each foothold and handhold bringing them closer to the top.

It was not easy going, however. Halfway up, a rock broke loose under Jayde's foot. She managed to hold firm to her grip, preventing a fall, but Merrick was showered with an avalanche of falling debris. A sizable rock took a hard bounce and struck him on the crown of the head. Jayde gasped, certain that the collision would knock him out. To her relief, Merrick held on, although he had to steady himself for several minutes before he could resume his climb. When he finally looked up at her, a line of blood ran down his forehead.

It felt like they climbed for hours. By the time they neared the top, the sun that had shone so brightly was now shrouded by dark clouds, a foreboding sign. Eurus IV was living up to its reputation, a windswept planet existing in an alternating cycle of utopia and chaos.

When her hands finally reached the grassy turf at the top of the cliff, Jayde refused to let relief wash over her. She pulled herself up quickly and extended an arm to Merrick. With a determined effort, she pulled him to the top. He collapsed next to her in the grass, the stream of blood on his forehead now dried and dark.

Jayde's arms felt like jelly from the climb, and she rested them on her stomach as she caught her breath. A stiff wind blew in, drying the sweat on her face. In the distance, a bolt of lightning shot out from a cloud and kissed the top of the ocean. A drop of rain landed on her cheek.

The oncoming storm, it appeared, did not feel they deserved a rest. A shared look of frustration and exhaustion passed between the two climbers.

Jayde and Merrick stood up and turned around to face what awaited them: a dense tropical forest, leaves dancing on the harsh wind.

"Might find some shelter in there," said Merrick, pointing at the trees. "Or something worse."

Jayde replied with a distracted nod, her attention fixed on the four cone-shaped mountains rising above the treeline.

Excitement gripped her. In her mother's mission notes, she wrote of a fault line spewing magma from the planet's core, forming a chain of active volcanoes. That was where the *Celestial* was heading. It was where her mother would be. She was certain of it.

"We're on the right track," Jayde said, confidently. Without hesitation, she passed under the swaying leaves and entered the forest.

"If you say so," Merrick muttered, following her steps.

Above them, the storm clouds thickened, heavy and ready to break.

Chapter 13

The new storm raged over them.

Jayde and Merrick slogged through the jungle, each step a battle against the elements. The wind ripped through the trees. Rain lashed at their backs, piercing through the canopy. Water cascaded down Jayde's face, veiling her nose and mouth.

"I can't breathe," Jayde gasped, her voice barely audible over the fury of the storm.

Merrick, ahead of her in the deluge, pressed his back against a tree and waited for her to catch up.

A clap of thunder reverberated through the jungle, causing Jayde to flinch as if a hand swatted at her from the heavens. To her right, a tearing sound split the air, followed by a crash. The wind had uprooted a tree and sent it plummeting to the ground. The shock of the fall caused Jayde to stumble. She fell, landing in a pool of mud and leaves.

Merrick rushed to her side, bracing himself against the wind as he helped her to her feet.

"This way!" he shouted, gesturing urgently. With his rifle raised above his head, he plowed through a thicket of waist-high shrubs and ferns.

The cacophony of the storm assaulted Jayde's senses: the shaking forest, the whistling wind, the symphony of snapping wood.

Should have stayed in the cave, she lamented. *No falling trees in a cave.*

She sprinted after Merrick, shielding her face from the lashes of whip-like branches as she raced through the undergrowth. Without warning, Jayde's legs met open space, and a scream escaped her lips as she kicked and flailed, her body suddenly weightless. With a jarring thud, she landed hard in a deep ditch, roughly five feet deep and eight feet wide, filled with a carpet of dead leaves and rock. Across from her, Merrick had suffered the same fate. He sat upright against the trench wall, surrounded by the roots and plants protruding out of the orange clay.

Wincing, Jayde pulled herself upright on the opposite side of the ditch, facing Merrick. Her bottom had landed on a sharp stone in the fall, shooting pain up her back and into her neck. Yet, in this alcove, they found shelter from the worst of the wind and rain as the jungle roared above them.

Jayde slumped against a wall of dirt. For the first time in hours, she allowed herself to rest. The discomfort of her soaked clothes faded away as she relaxed her tired legs.

"We stay here," Merrick yelled. "Ride it out."

Jayde nodded in agreement. She noticed her friend's eyes were barely open, weariness etched on his face. Clutching his hunting rifle tightly to his chest, he lay motionless, drifting closer to sleep.

She followed suit, leaning her head back, seeking a dry spot to shield her face from the rain beneath an outcrop of clay. Glancing down at her mud-caked boots, Jayde noticed a stream of clear, fresh water trickling through the center of their trench, pooling around her heels. Thirst gnawed at her, tempting her to drink from the seemingly safe source, despite the risks of an alien bacterium. Before she could cup her hands and sample from the rivulet, the sky flashed with electricity, illuminating her surroundings. In the fleeting light, Jayde's gaze fell upon a reflection in the pool of water, freezing her in place.

With caution, she raised her head, her eyes darting upward without making any sudden movements. Above Merrick's head stood a creature , its clawed feet gripping the trench's edge while a reptilian head sniffed the air, searching.

Her sense of calm disappeared, replaced by a surging panic. She glanced at Merrick, who met her gaze with a puzzled expression, unaware of the lurking threat. With her hand raised in warning, Jayde urged him to remain still. He complied, watching her intently, his senses attuned to the ominous presence above.

The creature stirred, and Merrick tensed at the sound of twigs snapping overhead. His eyes widened in terror as he instinctively positioned his finger on the trigger of his rifle.

Jayde gave him a subtle shake of her head. The creature had yet to detect their presence. The creature loomed upright on powerful hind legs, a long tail swaying menacingly. Its slender arms clawed at the air, tipped with a set of razor-sharp talons. There was a flash of lightning, revealing a dinosaur-like head with piercing yellow eyes. It extended its snout over the trench where Jayde and Merrick crouched, sniffing the air with quick, erratic movements. Jayde held her breath, willing herself to remain silent as rain pattered loudly on her jacket.

The creature emitted a rattling noise from its throat before letting out a sharp, high-pitched bark, causing Jayde to become acutely aware of other sounds emanating from the forest. The harsh sound of branches snapping, limbs thrashing, and the rhythmic thud of legs through the underbrush signaled the approach of more of its kind.

Suddenly, the beast vaulted across their trench, soaring over Jayde and Merrick, its body eclipsing the sky. Then, one after another, more creatures sailed overhead, a pack leaping over them with each stride sending dirt and rocks cascading down. As they landed, the ground quivered, sending vibrations rippling through the soil and into their bodies.

Amidst the chaos, a resounding whoosh filled the air, and Jayde glanced over to witness a torrent of rainwater rushing down the trench toward them. She glimpsed the panic in Merrick's eyes and braced herself. The flash flood struck, knocking her sideways, but she managed to snag a root protruding from the clay, anchoring herself against the force of the water.

Realization struck too late. They were in a drainage ditch, sculpted by the relentless storms, channeling water from the forest's heights down a steep hill. The rushing water continued to swell, and within moments, it flowed up to her neck. Merrick clung to an outcrop of rock for dear life.

Amidst the chaos, Jayde once again heard a guttural snarl. Raising her gaze, she found the reptilian monster had returned, summoned by their screams. It perched on the trench's edge, its yellow eyes piercing the darkness, fixated on her. With a menacing huff, it cracked its jaws, revealing a formidable array of dagger-like teeth. Cocking its head in an animalistic display of curiosity, it observed Jayde intently.

Merrick struggled against the current that threatened to drag him under. He groaned, and the creature now fixed its gaze upon him. With a shriek, it lunged toward Merrick, its jaws snapping dangerously close to his head. In panic, he relinquished his hold on the rock and the flood sent him tumbling downstream. Jayde saw no choice but to join her friend in the tumultuous waters. As the creature reached out with its bony, clawed arms, she released her grip on the root, allowing herself to be swept away. She heard a primal roar, and the creature faded into the torrent of the storm as she drifted further and further away.

Within seconds, the flood picked up speed, transforming into a swirling deluge. The water grew faster and deeper with each passing moment. Jayde exerted all her strength, paddling furiously to stay afloat.

"Merrick!" she cried out, her voice obscured by the roiling brown water. The trench tilted downhill and the current intensified. She spotted a washed up log jammed in place just above the water line. She plunged underwater to evade the obstacle, then found she couldn't resurface. Her legs lifted above her head and she became disoriented. She tried to scream, but all that came out was a muffled cry, distorted by the resistance of the water.

Then, a moment of weightlessness seized her as she tumbled headlong over the precipice of a waterfall. In that suspended moment, she braced herself for the inevitable, resigned to the thought that this was the end. She envisioned herself as a shattered, bloody form upon the unforgiving rocks destined to break her fall.

To her astonishment, instead of crashing onto murderous stone, Jayde found herself engulfed by the embrace of a mercifully deep pool. Sinking into its depths, she experienced a moment of disorientation before the realization dawned upon her: she was alive. With renewed determination, she kicked her legs and propelled herself upwards, breaking through the surface with a deep-throated gasp. Wiping the water from her eyes, she saw an immense waterfall above her. The flash flood had tumbled her fifty feet over the side of a rocky cliff.

The rain eased. A clap of thunder rang out in the sky that seemed gentle and distant. She swam to the edge of the pool water toward what seemed to be a large, oddly-shaped rock, only to realize that it was Merrick. He lay sprawled upon a bed of gravel at the shore of the pool, his form motionless. Jayde hoisted herself from the water and collapsed beside him.

"We have to stop meeting like this," said Merrick, eliciting a chuckle of relief from Jayde.

As they lay there for what seemed like hours, the storm began to dissipate. The wind relaxed, the rain fell to a few errant drops. Jayde surveyed their new surroundings as specks of rain fell on her shoulders. They were in a gully, cut out by the endless pouring of water over the rocks and through the jungle over time. Dense foliage was all around them, and steep, sloping hills rose above the treeline on all sides.

And there was something else.

Jayde clambered to her feet, her curiosity piqued. She spotted a glint of white amidst the foliage near them, a metallic presence nestled within the trees.

Chapter 14

The storm passed, shifting the dark purple sky to gray. The sounds of the jungle emerged from beneath the tempest: the chatter of unseen creatures, the rustling of leaves, and the thunderous roar of the waterfall. The falling water carved a stream that wound its way through the surrounding valley, babbling near Jayde and Merrick as they peered through the trees at their discovery.

"What is it?" asked Merrick.

The object remained mostly intact: a large egg-shaped craft that was roughly twenty feet in length and ten feet high, with laser weapons mounted on each side. The once-white metal was now dulled by dirt and age, giving it a cream-colored appearance. Weeds grew around it, and leafy vines snaked through the lasers like tentacles. Jayde approached the craft and pushed a vine aside to reveal an etched serial number.

"A Hypnos drone," replied Jayde. "Like the ones we saw in the hangar."

"What's it doing here?"

"Good question."

Jayde ran her fingers along the side of the craft, searching intently. She moved around to the opposite side. Pulling away more vines fastened to the hull, she uncovered a touch-screen console. She pressed a button on the panel to engage power, but nothing happened; the battery-powered energy core was dead. The craft had clearly been here a long time.

Jayde found the edges of the door panel connected to the entrance scanner. Toward the bottom, she noticed it was bent outward, creating just enough space to slip her fingers in.

"Help me pull this door panel off," Jayde said.

Merrick leaned down beside her, and they both inserted their fingertips under the panel. Together, they pulled until the thin metal door bent and finally detached. It snapped off cleanly and they tossed it aside.

Peering inside, they saw that the interior was in fairly good condition. There were shreds of hanging wires and some damaged circuitry, along with a few vines that had found their way inside, but the hollow compartment seemed mostly intact.

Merrick shook his head in disgust.

"What?" Jayde asked, noticing his expression.

"What is this thing doing here?"

She looked at the wreckage. It was indeed a mystery. There was no reason for a weaponized drone to be on this planet.

Merrick inspected the aged metal on the outside. He tore away the vines clinging to it, searching for something.

"What are you doing?" asked Jayde.

Merrick didn't answer. He continued his search, bending down to get a closer look at the undercarriage.

Suddenly, he yelled and slapped the hull emphatically. "I knew it! Look at this!"

Jayde dropped to one knee. The drone was tilted slightly, exposing the undercarriage. Merrick pointed, and she followed his finger to a line of eight blackened holes burnt through the metal. A black smudge trailed from each hole, a remnant of fire and smoke.

"This thing was shot down, Jayde. By someone."

* * *

Jayde and Merrick spent the rest of the day cleaning out the interior of the drone, converting it into a shelter. They tore out the loose vines, pulled out scraps of moldy cloth insulation, and set about fashioning beds from fern leaves and long jungle grass. These tasks took the remainder of the day.

Jayde found it difficult to sleep at first. Her stomach ached from hunger, and her thoughts drifted to the yellow-eyed creatures they encountered yesterday. Merrick had managed to rig the door panel of the drone back in place, but it wasn't a tight fit. Any large, hungry animal that caught their scent would have no trouble knocking the door out from the frame with a curious pawing. This weighed heavily on her mind as she imagined those yellow eyes and the wide maw of teeth she had seen in the flooded trench reaching out for her in the night.

She lay awake the rest of the evening, listening to another torrent of rain ping against the metal of their shelter.

In the morning, they emerged, both acknowledging that finding food needed to be their top priority. Jayde was anxious to start searching for her mother, but she admitted to herself that she and Merrick had to get sustenance or their search would come to a quick and painful end.

Merrick immediately left to search for fish or an edible fruit growing among the dense tropical plants. Jayde stayed behind to figure out how to start a fire. Their lone source of sustenance, roasted coffee crystals, once brewed, would go a long way toward staving off their immediate hunger until they could procure real food.

Jayde stayed behind, intent on starting a fire. She searched the drone's floor for a panel marked with a yellow arrow and lightning bolt. Finding it, she unlatched the cover. Inside, five flat, square power cells rested in their slots, striped in yellow and black. Though only three inches thick, they were supercharged with ionized moscovium. Jayde reached in, carefully unhooked the wires, and slid one free.

Sitting back with the battery in her lap, she inspected it for leaks. Acid dripped from the corroded connection points, giving off a sharp metallic smell. Still, the moscovium reservoir was intact. That meant there was still power left to tap.

Jayde carried the power cell outside and set it down before gathering an armful of dead twigs and branches. Dropping them beside the cell, she returned to the drone and yanked down two sturdy wires from its interior. She stripped the wax coating from the wires with her teeth, twisted the exposed metal strands, and plugged the wires into opposite polarity ports. A quick tap of the ends, and *voilà*: a spark!

She stacked the twigs and branches, stuffing grass and moss between them. Touching the wires together again, she tried to ignite a flame, but the damp materials refused to catch.

She sat back on her haunches and looked to the sky, letting out a deep breath of frustration. For the first time, she noticed small, winged reptiles above her in the trees, no bigger than her hand. They chirped and fluttered their colorful skin wings. Jayde wondered silently where these delicate creatures hid from the planet's recurring storms.

A rare beam of sunlight entered the clearing, warming Jayde's face. She stood up and turned around, noticing how the rays reflected off the drone wreckage. An idea sparked in her mind.

When the drone crashed, it cut a trench through the jungle. Jayde used it as a path, walking through the cleared space, looking for broken shrubs and trees. She noticed some large ferns had been uprooted and had died, their leaves now brown and wrinkled. Jayde collected an armful of the dead ferns and carried them back to their camp.

She laid out the ferns in the sunlight on top of their shelter. Between the direct sunlight and the warm metal, she was optimistic the dead leaves would dry and provide suitable kindling for the fire.

While she waited for the leaves to dry, Jayde spent the rest of the afternoon collecting suitable firewood and improving their beds in the shelter. She also fashioned a bucket out of a metal lubricant tank she pulled from the drone's gravity drive. Although the tank was still half-full of oily chemicals, she managed to scrub it clean using sand and water from the stream. When she was done, she felt the inside with her hand to ensure the residue was gone, leaving the tank squeaky clean. She gathered rocks and built a fire pit, then rigged a platform to go over the fire by tying together sticks with loose wire.

Once everything was set up, she re-collected the dead ferns from atop the shelter, finding them adequately dry. She crinkled them up and put them around the kindling at the center of the fire pit. It only took one spark from the power cells for them to ignite. A small flame flickered to life, and Jayde watched it grow, a smile of triumph spreading across her face.

By the time Merrick returned, there was already a boiling tank of water on a steady fire, ready to receive the roasted coffee. Jayde, pleased with herself, gave Merrick a wink as he walked into camp. Despite coming back empty-handed, he was all smiles, thrilled to see such progress with their camp. Following a successful toxic screen of the boiling water, they opened the pouch of coffee crystals and poured them into their makeshift cooking pot.

Jayde had fashioned cups from some aluminum parts harvested from the drone wreckage. With them they filled their bellies with coffee, and their hunger pains subsided. They agreed that tomorrow they would go hunting, knowing liquid alone would not sustain them. Merrick extinguished the fire, wanting to save the half-burned wood for the next day.

Neither of them could sleep with all the caffeine flowing through their systems, so they sat around the fire's smoking remnants, looking up at the sky, watching the bright stars shine through the gaps in the jungle leaves. The wind picked up again, and soon clouds obscured their view, signaling the onset of another storm. They gathered the remaining firewood and brought it inside their shelter to stay dry.

As they settled down for the night, they heard the sound of

something large moving through the jungle. They waited, listening to the rustling sounds of leaves grow louder until it was just on the edge of their camp.

Then came a deep, guttural groan that bellowed just outside their shelter.

More rustling followed, then silence. Whatever had passed through was gone.

Jayde lay awake for hours, her hunger forgotten and her eyes locked on their flimsy panel door.

Chapter 15

In the morning, Jayde dragged herself from her straw bed and quietly removed the door panel from their shelter, careful not to wake Merrick. He lay snoring softly in the corner, hugging his rifle.

Jayde suspected he always needed to hold something while he slept. Despite his confident exterior, she sensed a deep loneliness within him. Like her, he had lost everyone in his life. His parents and brother were killed in a mining accident. And then, Lana Marsh, the only meaningful connection he'd ever made in a sea of fleeting encounters, was brain-wiped by the Construct for daring to tempt love.

Love. Jayde wondered if the romantic kind ever truly existed on Hypnos. If it had, she'd never felt it. And she doubted her parents had either. Their union was a Construct-assigned coupling that looked perfect on paper: an accomplished A.I. engineer and a rising planetary explorer. But in reality, their worlds couldn't have been more different. Her mother, full of passion and adventure, spent months in deep space, while her father remained in his office, buried in the development of Phase Four.

Her mother adored her. Her father was distant. It really

made her wonder what the all-seeing Construct had expected from such an odd pairing. To it, she wasn't the product of love, but an output of design.

Had her life followed the Construct's supposedly flawless predictions? It couldn't have. She was nothing like her parents. She lacked her mother's confidence and larger-than-life presence, and she certainly didn't possess her father's devout servitude or engineering genius. Who was she? She didn't even know herself.

There had to be a reason the Construct orchestrated her parents' union, a reason buried in the depths of future possibilities. The Construct's ominous words echoed in her mind, a relentless reminder of her supposed significance. *Your choices form a trajectory that is vital to humanity's survival.*

The weight of those words pressed down on her shoulders like a heavy cloak.

Jayde forced those thoughts away, focusing instead on the present situation. Fear and hunger made for an easy distraction.

As she stepped out of their shelter and into the clearing of their camp, her eyes scanned the jungle for movement. The lurking creature from the previous night was still vivid in her memory. All seemed calm, but caution prompted her to reach inside their shelter for her rifle and set it against a tree. The reptilian birds chirped pleasantly above, giving her some confidence that all was safe.

The morning sun broke through the trees and Jayde looked down at her mother's bracelet. It blinked slowly, and Jayde smiled at the thought that her mother might be sleeping at this very moment, not far from where she stood. The idea filled her with energy, and she almost went inside their shelter to wake Merrick. She decided against it. *No, let him sleep.*

She walked to the stream and filled their water bucket. The waterfall flowed heavily, causing the stream to rise above the edges of the rock bed that it flowed through. Jayde knelt on a large stone and filled her bucket, her eyes searching the clear water for anything resembling fish or crabs or any such edible creature. She saw nothing but blue and green rocks speckling the creek bottom.

Returning to camp, she started a fire and, filling their pot with water, prepared to make coffee. Sitting on a log that she and Merrick had moved near their fire pit, Jayde watched the kindling smoke as the fire heated up. As boredom set in, she picked up a stick and started poking at the burning logs. Red embers swam into the air around her. Resting her elbows on her knees, she casually looked at her stick, noticing the end had become charred and black.

Nearby, a reptilian bird landed on a stump at the edge of the clearing. The small creature had a red and yellow beak-like snout, long and triangular, lined with tiny teeth. The back of its head had three large spikes with skin stretched between them, forming a crest that it raised and lowered with each jerky bob of its head. It chirped twice, turned to look at Jayde, and spread its wings. The wings were reddish-brown, made of thin-stretched skin similar to its crest. Jayde had always heard of birds on Earth having feathers, but this creature had only skin and scales. Still, it had a cuteness to it. It made a pleasing clicking sound in its throat as it pecked at a fallen log.

A familiar and unexpected urge stirred in Jayde, one she hadn't felt since childhood.

She rose, stick in hand, and walked to their shelter. Tugging down a tangle of vines, she cleared a patch of metal, rubbing it clean with her palm. Then she snapped off the burnt tip of her stick and held it like a pencil.

After a moment of studying the bird, she pressed the charred tip to the surface and began to draw.

She began by sketching the eyes and the head, then moved down to the wings, which she drew as wide and open. She roughed out the shape with light lines, then, pressing hard, finalized the drawing with dark, heavy strokes. The tap, tap, tapping of the stick on metal stirred Merrick awake. Jayde, lost in her drawing, didn't notice as he crawled out of the shelter and stood behind her.

When she was finished, Jayde stepped back, admiring her

work. It was a perfect sketch of the reptilian bird, its wings spread and mouth open. As she smiled to herself, the creature flew off, indifferent to its tribute.

"That's amazing, Ashr!" said Merrick, startling her. "How did you learn to do that?"

"I don't know," she admitted. "I've just… always been able to. I see something, and I can draw it. It's like my hands already know what to do."

Merrick leaned in close for a better look, and Jayde couldn't help but feel some pride at her friend's interest.

"It's so detailed! Is this one of those flying things in the trees?"

Jayde smiled and nodded. "I used to draw a lot when I was little," she added. "My mother would hang the drawings up in our quarters. She told me that hundreds of years ago on Earth, people could make a living drawing pictures."

"Like, that was their job?"

"Yes! They were called 'artists.' They would paint, sketch, and create all sorts of displays with colors and shapes. And people would buy them."

Merrick shook his head in wonder. "Well, I'll be a monkey's uncle."

Jayde shot him a curious look. This apparently was another of Merrick's old-time sayings.

"It means 'that's mind-boggling,'" he added.

"Isn't it?" said Jayde. "My mother had this old history book, something passed down to her from generations ago. She let me look at it one time. It was about art and what it used to mean to people. I remember this one painting, I can't remember the name, of a woman carrying a flag through an ancient battlefield, men following behind with guns and swords. I used to stare at it for hours. I still think about it sometimes. I see it in my head and I wonder, how can something like that not be considered important?"

"Maybe the Construct banned art because it doesn't understand it," said Merrick. He sat down by the fire and yawned. "If the Construct looks at a picture of a woman holding a flag, it just sees a picture of a woman holding a flag."

Jayde pondered his words. If the Construct couldn't comprehend art as an expression of emotion and thought, or as the aesthetic embodiment of ideas, then Phase Four had to be a failure.

No matter. Jayde was resolved to leave Hypnos in the past. What happened there no longer mattered to her.

* * *

Jayde and Merrick sipped their coffee, mapping out their plans for the day. Food was the top priority, and they agreed that following the stream to see where it led would be a good start.

Before they set out, Jayde ran her fingers over her mother's bracelet, knowing that once they secured some food, their search for her could begin in earnest.

Merrick snuffed out the morning fire with his boot, and they set out along the stream. Despite any dangers that could lurk ahead, Jayde felt exhilarated. The colors and sounds of the jungle infused her soul with a vitality she could scarcely comprehend. She only knew her spirit soured. Having spent her life staring at a single fig tree in the Academy atrium, she had never dreamed she would one day be walking through an entire forest.

Merrick led the way, his rifle at the ready in his hands. He leapt from rock to rock along the stream, occasionally dipping a boot in the water just for fun. The stream rippled and gurgled, cold and clear, carving a path for them through the dense forest. They moved through deep shadows; leaves and mossy vines blocked most of the sunlight. As Jayde hiked, the humidity drew sweat that soaked her shirt and the collar of her jacket.

Cackles and calls came from the trees, and Jayde soon noticed larger creatures shaking the branches above them. They cautiously readied their weapons, slowing their pace while keeping a vigilant eye on the canopy. The shaking limbs grew more frequent as they progressed, revealing a pack of creatures following them through the trees.

This continued as they walked, and more than once Jayde glimpsed pairs of dark eyes and long, fluffy tails. Merrick saw them too. There were a few hoots, and as the activity persisted, Jayde felt the mysterious creatures above seemed more curious than threatening. Gradually, the two explorers relaxed, even playfully calling out for the creatures to show themselves. Their requests were ignored and met with more shrill hoots.

Jayde and Merrick followed the stream down a steep decline of rocky terrain. The jungle ended abruptly, revealing a vast grassy plain stretching toward a blue horizon. The once-imposing ocean cliffs to the north had softened into gentle foothills, concealing the water from view. Around them, a golden plain was dotted with craggy trees and shrubs, their sparse foliage a mixture of purples and deep reds. Free from the cover of the jungle, the immense cone-shaped volcanoes revealed themselves, standing like sentinels in the distance, one of them coughing black smoke into the sky. The air was filled with the sweet aroma of alien pollen. Amid the undulating stalks of grain, iridescent insects flitted about.

The jungle hoots now sounded above them, prompting Jayde to look up. Their fluffy-tailed stalkers were gliding through the air, their brown and white fur ripping in the breeze. Jayde initially mistook them for birds, but quickly noticed they were not flying. Amazingly, the creatures were holding giant leaves in human-like hands, using them to float along on the breeze.

"Would you look at that!" said Merrick, his eyes wide and bright.

At least seven or eight of the creatures dotted the sky, their leaf-gliders allowing them to soar high into the air. Using their tails to steer, they banked and turned in unison like a flock of birds, gradually floating lower until they landed in the tall grass about one hundred yards from where Jayde stood. Tossing aside their leaves, they moved in a herd through the grass, their round, furry heads bobbing as they crawled along.

One of the animals crawled atop a rock and stood on its hind legs. Its head jerked from side to side as the rest of its troop picked and nibbled at the grass. The creature had amber-colored eyes, a thick muzzle and a blue stripe down its nose. Two small horns extended from its head, giving it a devilish appearance. Merrick crouched low into the grass and pulled Jayde down with him. He raised his hunting rifle to his eye, targeting the creature keeping watch.

Despite her rumbling stomach, Jayde felt a conflict of emotions. These weren't just dumb, grazing animals. They were a family unit, a tribe. One kept watch while the others fed, picking the tufts of grass with the largest clusters of seeds, holding them with long-fingered paws as they chewed. Jayde noticed several creatures with what she initially thought were large humps on their backs. She quickly realized they were not humps, but infants, clutching the fur of their parents.

Jayde put her hand on top of Merrick's rifle and pushed it down.

"No," she said firmly. "Not them."

Merrick looked at her in surprise. "You want to eat, don't you?"

"They're a family," she said.

"They're food!"

"Something just doesn't feel right," she insisted. "Let's keep looking."

"Fine," he said. "But if we don't find something else soon, I'm coming back here and putting a laser through each and every one of them."

As they walked on, the creature on the rock clapped its paws together and hooted at them as if mocking their retreat.

They continued through the grassy plain, rifles poised and ready. They moved slowly and softly, their eyes scanning for possible prey. A few reptilian birds flew overhead, heading toward the ocean, but none came within a decent range. They passed a few short, craggy trees, which Jayde examined closely, hoping to find small animals or birds. However, the trees were empty, offering nothing but gnarled bark and thorns.

The wind was picking up, and the bright blue sky was once again darkening on the horizon. Merrick stopped, wiping the sweat from his forehead with his sleeve, and turned his head toward the wind to let the cool air of the approaching storm offer some relief from the oppressive heat. He closed his eyes for a moment, savoring the breeze, then gave Jayde a resigned look.

Jayde understood immediately: they needed to return to their shelter before yet another storm blew in. Three storms in three days. She knew it was to be expected, but the relentlessness of the cycle of storms was deflating, especially when they were hungry. As they turned to walk back toward their shelter, their stomachs aching, Jayde caught a glimpse of something large and black moving through the tall grass.

"Merrick," she whispered.

They spotted a large form trotting through the yellow reeds, moving like a boat atop an ocean of grain. The creature had a massive head with a thick, ridged nose, and four imposing horns emerging from the back of its neck. Its small, black eyes gave no hint of intelligence, an impression mirrored by its bulky, black-skinned body. Four short, sturdy legs supported its enormous weight with ease. A prominent horn jutted up from its nose, shaped like a massive three-pronged fork, adding to its menacing presence as it navigated the tall reeds with surprising grace.

The beast paused to munch on a leafy green shrub. Merrick crouched low and Jayde followed suit.

"Oh, yeah, baby," he whispered. "Jackpot."

The two hunters moved closer to their prey, keeping their heads as low as possible. When the horned animal looked up in their direction, they froze and held their breath. The creature glared at them for several seconds before finally relaxing and continuing its meal. Jayde exhaled.

"Do you have a shot?" she asked.

"A little closer."

They crept forward, careful to minimize their noise as they trampled dry grass underfoot. When Merrick felt he was in range, he stopped and dropped to one knee. The animal was close enough now that Jayde could smell the foul odor of its musk on the wind. The creature wagged and swatted a whip-like tail at buzzing insects as it ate.

Merrick raised his rifle to his face, closed one eye, and gazed into the laser scope.

"She's a beauty," he whispered.

Instinctively, Jayde kept watch around them. This was a large, powerful creature, and if more were around, they had little chance of surviving a stampede. In the wide open like this, there was nowhere to hide.

Jayde spotted movement in the grass, creeping toward the horned animal from another direction. At first, she thought it was just the wind, until the grass erupted with motion, and a reptilian tail lashed through the air.

Her body went rigid. She grabbed Merrick's shoulder to hold his fire. They were no longer the only hunters on this plain.

Two more lines of movement appeared, converging on the beast from the opposite side. The animal started in panic and let out a bleat, sensing the onrush of predators. By the time it had turned to run, it was too late.

Yellow eyed reptoids burst from the grass, leaping with powerful hind legs and bared talons. One predator lunged for the throat, piercing the creature's thick hide with long teeth and claws. The other two hunters in the pack attacked the legs and sides, scratching and clawing with precision. The combined assault caused the creature to stumble, ending its brief escape and sealing its fate. In what seemed like mere seconds, the fierce predators felled the beast, and set to work stripping skin and devouring the meat with their razor-like teeth.

Jayde watched the scene in horror, thinking back to their first encounter with these creatures in the jungle trench. Perhaps their only saving grace was that they had less meat on their bones than the giant horned smorgasbord before them.

"Back away," whispered Jayde. "Slowly."

"Yeah," replied Merrick, his face pale. "I think that's a good idea."

They crouched low, and in their first step in retreat, the subtle mashing of grass alerted the largest of the reptoids. Its head jerked toward them as the rest of the pack continued to feed, yellow eyes bright against the darkening sky.

They froze, and Jayde caught her breath. She could see an intelligence in it that terrified her. The creature was looking right at her, thinking, calculating, trying to surmise if she was a threat or food.

Slowly, it stepped down from atop the meaty carcass and crept toward them. It walked on two muscular legs, its long front claws reaching out at them. A thin layer of skin stretched from its elbows to its sides, remnant of an ancient winged ancestor that abandoned the sky eons ago. A line of drool fell from between its teeth, and Jayde knew its mind was made up. They were food.

Jayde stayed still, debating whether to run or fire her rifle. The reptoid suddenly paused and squawked, pointing its muzzle to the sky and exposing a red-colored throat. It spread its arms wide and began flapping. Then it lowered its eyes at them and bared its teeth, moving its head up and down in short, precise jerks. It began dancing to the left and right, jiggling its tail.

"What is it doing?" Merrick asked.

Jayde shook her head in confusion as she watched the creature's ritualistic movements. It was then that she noticed that the two other reptoids in its pack had disappeared.

Oh, no.

"Run!" Jayde shouted.

Together they turned and ran just as one of the reptoids burst out of the grass, its jaws just missing Merrick's arm. They sprinted away, their strides hampered by the thick vegetation. Jayde heard the squawks and hisses behind them, right on their heels. She pumped her arms as hard as she could, her rifle bouncing on her back, the strap pulling on her neck with each step. Her heart raced into her throat.

"Head for that tree!" shouted Merrick. Ahead of them, a gnarled tree stood alone. Its branches were sparse, but low enough to climb. It was their best option for escape.

Merrick, his legs powerful enough to push through the grass, began to outpace her.

"Come on!" he yelled. "We can make it!"

Jayde dug deep, finding a reservoir of strength she didn't know she had. Her legs moved faster, and her breath accelerated. Her legs and chest burned as her mind replayed the sight of the horned beast being stripped of meat. Was that her fate as well?

She glanced to her left and saw a tail bouncing in the vegetation beside her, keeping pace effortlessly. When its head finally emerged, its golden eyes flashed with cold, predatory instinct.

As Merrick leapt into the tree and pulled himself to safety, Jayde suddenly banked left, cutting behind her pursuer just as it gathered strength to pounce. The creature slid in the grass and tumbled, somersaulting head over feet. Jayde yelled and waved her arms as the other two reptoids skidded to a stop.

"Over here, you dinosaurs!" she screamed.

They cocked their heads in curiosity, then began to prowl her way, the third reptoid rising to join them. Emitting clicks from their crimson throats in unison, they fanned out, surrounding her.

"Merrick, a little help here!" she yelled, hoping he understood the implication in her voice.

The reptoids closed in, claws and teeth bared. Jayde looked up at the sky as she put her fate in Merrick's hands, watching the dark clouds swirl above her. A flash of lightning illuminated the scene, and the first cold drops of rain touched her face. She tensed her body with hope as a collective hiss sounded just a few feet away, the air thick with the metallic scent of blood from the creatures' breath. Finally, she lowered her eyes at them in a defiant, angry roar of her own.

The creatures paused in surprise, their attack momentarily halted, giving Merrick just enough time to take aim from his perch. Jayde fell backward as three bright flashes of red light strobed the plain in quick succession. A shower of sparks rained down on her. As she hit the ground, she watched the three reptoids collapse around her, each with a large hole burnt through their heads.

Jayde eventually stood, catching her breath, letting the soft rain fall on the back of her neck. For the first time since they crashed on Eurus IV, she was thankful to feel its miserable, wet cold.

Chapter 16

Merrick wasted no time skinning the reptoid carcasses. With a makeshift knife he crafted from the drone wreckage, he carved out folds of meat from the creatures' thighs and ribs. He moved quickly, spurred by the rain from the oncoming storm. By the time he was finished, the rain was pouring down in torrents, and the strong winds made it difficult to stand.

The thighs of the animals were heavy but easy to carry. Merrick slung two large leg bones over his shoulders and wrapped a thin tenderloin around his neck. Jayde carried several racks of ribs. The rain washed the meat clean of blood as they made their way back to camp.

By the time they arrived, Jayde felt as if her legs and shoulders were about to fall off. She dropped the meat in a pile near the fire pit and collapsed next to it. Merrick, however, didn't pause to rest. He retrieved some dry wood stored inside their shelter and stacked them in the fire pit. Using Jayde's battery lighter, he quickly got a flame going. Although the winds of the storm were violent overhead, shaking the leaves and branches above them, near the ground there was just a calm breeze. The valley shielded them from the worst of the weather, and the rain was merely a trickle through the canopy, allowing the fire to grow without much difficulty.

As soon as Jayde felt the fire's warmth, her stomach growled in anticipation of her first meal in almost two days. She sat up and set several slabs of ribs against the fire to cook.

Merrick ventured off into the woods and soon returned with two long, Y-shaped sticks which he drove into the ground next to the fire, creating a makeshift spit. He placed one of the long reptoid thighs across it. Within minutes, the succulent aroma of roasting meat filled the air. They smiled at each other from over the flames, their chilled, wet skin momentarily forgotten in the promise of a hearty meal.

Once the meat had turned red and charred on the outside, it was time for the moment of truth. Jayde pulled out the toxin scanner and inserted its long metal probe into the meat. Merrick stood beside her, and they both watched the scanner's digital screen with nervous anticipation.

"Testing…"

"Testing…"

A green light flashed.

They both screamed in joy and embraced. As they pulled away, Jayde felt Merrick's eyes lock onto hers, his gaze intense and searching. The moment stretched awkwardly, their breath mingling in the cool air, until Jayde, flustered, looked away toward the fire. She smiled sheepishly and patted him on the shoulder.

"Supper time," she said, breaking the tension.

Merrick handed her his knife, his hand visibly trembling.

"Sure. One dino-leg, please."

Jayde took the knife and carved out a hand-sized piece of meat from the roasted thigh, handing it to Merrick. She then carved a smaller piece for herself and brought it to her nose. The smell was intoxicating. It was sweet, rich, and infused with the subtle smokiness of the fire and wood. At the Hypnos colony, all meat was synthetic, a lab-grown approximation of Earth meats like chicken or pork. This, however, was something different and extraordinary.

Jayde and Merrick locked eyes again and bit into the meat together. Jayde's mouth watered as the tangy flavor coated her tongue. Succulent juices dribbled down her chin. The taste was so incredible that her knees weakened and she had to sit down. She found a log and Merrick, feeling a similar effect, joined her. They ate their fill in silence, with ravenous hunger overriding any inclination for conversation.

Once their hunger was satisfied, they wrapped the remaining meat in large jungle leaves and placed them in the corner of their shelter to keep safe from alien scavengers. Merrick stamped out the fire, and they crawled into their metal refuge for the night.

Jayde locked in the panel on their shelter entrance, sealing them inside. Merrick had crafted a small torch and secured it to a wall, its gold light casting a warm, comforting glow over the interior.

As they began taking off their wet clothes and spreading them out on the floor to dry, they instinctively turned away from each other, avoiding eye contact. Jayde stripped down to her underwear and brassiere, catching glimpses of Merrick's broad, muscled form in the shadows as he removed his shirt and pants. Her heart quickened, and she suddenly found it hard to breathe.

She jumped into her straw bed and covered herself with a fragment of carpet-like insulation she had pulled off the floor. Out of the corner of her eye, she saw Merrick's half-naked silhouette doing the same. His presence was both comforting and intimidating in the close quarters. A mix of unspoken emotions thickened the air, their shared vulnerability creating a palpable silence. Finally, Merrick's voice cut through the quiet.

"Let's hike to the ocean tomorrow and collect salt water. We can use it to preserve the meat."

"We might have enough food now to venture out and find the *Celestial*," Jayde replied. "I want to start looking."

Merrick turned on his side, propping his head up with his elbow.

"We need to preserve our food first. Your mother could be

anywhere on this island. We could be searching for days. Weeks. We need to make sure we're prepared before we go searching."

"I know but… I can't wait any longer. We've already wasted too much time."

Jayde could hear Merrick licking his lips in the dark. He did that when he was struggling to express his thoughts. Finally, he spoke.

"Did you ever think that maybe the Construct doesn't want your mother to be found? It lied to you. It told you she was dead. Without that biomonitor, you'd never have known the truth."

Jayde sat up, glancing at him.

"What if," he continued, "it's here somewhere, looking for us… looking for her?"

Jayde had no answer. He could be right.

A light drizzle tapped softly against the shelter's roof as she lies back down, her mind spinning. Merrick's words pressed on her, refusing to fade. Before sleep claimed her, she stole one last glance at her mother's wristband, its crimson light pulsing in rhythm with the gentle drops.

✳ ✳ ✳

When Jayde awoke in the morning, Merrick was already outside their shelter, prepping for a hike to the ocean. Though she was eager to begin the search for her mother, she knew preserving their meat was essential for their long trek toward the volcanoes. She sluggishly walked outside and sat by the fire pit, where water was already heating for a morning coffee. The breeze through the camp was gentle, shaking the remnants of the evening rain from the jungle leaves. The air was fresh and heavy, carrying the scent of damp earth.

Jayde detected Merrick was anxious to get going. He didn't say a word as she emerged from the shelter, and she watched him silently clean the hunting rifles while she sipped her coffee. When he finally spoke, it was to urge her to get her things because he wanted to head out.

She took her time, partially to annoy him, but also to give her socks a chance to dry on the rocks by the fire. She wanted to have warm, dry feet for their hike.

Finally, she slipped on her jacket, socks, and boots and joined him as he stood anxiously by the edge of their camp. The hooting creatures in the trees seemed to be egging them on, their calls echoing high up in the canopy. Before they left, she slung her rifle on her back and stamped out their campfire.

They once again hiked downstream through the jungle and toward the grassy plain, this time staying on high alert for any reptoids. Their eyes constantly scanned the foliage for the telltale flash of bright, yellow eyes.

Once they emerged from the jungle and onto the plain, the wind picked up and Jayde could see this was going to be yet another stormy day with little sunlight. Ever since that first spectacular day on the planet when they left the beachside cave, she had longed to experience another day like that. The sun's warming light and the reflection of its rays off the landscape had been transformative, turning the dark tones of the jungle, ocean, and mountains into a kaleidoscope of color. It was as if the planet's sun was bestowing a gift of beauty on a world otherwise cursed by wind and storms. Jayde hoped that each day she was here, she might see the sun that way again, even for a moment.

She believed Merrick felt the same way. She noticed how he looked up at the sky with the same sense of hope and disappointment she felt within herself. As they hiked toward the hills that bordered the ocean, he mentioned that he would like to see the reptilian birds fly above them today. She agreed.

Despite the potential threat of predators trolling around them, Jayde relaxed and stretched out her hands, letting them brush over the feathery seeds of the waist-high grass.

When they reached the base of the slopes, they climbed the nearest mound. At the crest, Jayde could see the shoreline stretch to the north, evolving into the steep bluffs they had encountered at their crash site.

From this modest elevation, the sight was breathtaking. She

spun in a circle, taking in the ocean whitecaps roiling under blustering gray clouds on one side of the hill, while on the other side she could see a herd of horned beasts grazing on the grasses of the plain, like black speckles in a sea of gold. Her head was on a swivel. She stopped only when she noticed Merrick watching her with amusement, his arms wrapped around their water bucket. Embarrassed, she forged ahead of him, stepping down the gentle slope toward the beach.

When they reached the pebbly shore, Jayde spotted one of the tusked sea-animals from their night in the cave. It lay alone by the water, snoozing on its side. Arms folded, she watched it with amusement as Merrick walked to the water's edge and filled their bucket. At the crunching sound of his footsteps, the creature lifted its crested head briefly, opened one eye, then returned to its nap.

Merrick returned to her side, his bucket of water full. He dipped his finger in the brine and tasted it. "Salty stuff. We'll soak the meat in this overnight, pack it in leaves, and that should keep it well-preserved. I guess our survival course at the Academy wasn't a total waste of time after all."

Merrick's joke barely registered. Jayde was deep in thought, her eyes fixed on the distant volcanoes.

"How far do you think?" she asked.

Merrick followed her gaze and rubbed his chin, the thin stubble on his face having grown longer over the past few days. He had become adept at judging distances while surveying his mining sites, and Jayde knew he would have a reasonable estimation.

"Around twenty or thirty miles probably, give or take," he replied. "That's a two or three day hike if we keep a good pace."

"Tomorrow?"

"Okay," Merrick conceded. "But we need to rig up some packs for carrying our meat and supplies."

"I found some large, sturdy leaves around our camp," Jayde said. "We can weave them together with the vines and straw tonight. We can work late into the night and maybe head out in the morning."

"I hate to rush. 'Chance favors the prepared,'" replied Merrick.

"I hate your stupid, ancient expressions."

"Why? They 'ruffle your feathers?'"

Jayde shot him a sideways glance before turning to climb up the foothill. Merrick followed, chuckling under his breath. Halfway up their ascent, Jayde noticed a thorny bush growing at the base of a large stone protruding from the side of the hill. The bush was laden with red berries.

Jayde let out a thrilled laugh and pointed the berries out to Merrick. They had missed them on the way down, as the shrub was hidden on the opposite side of the rock during their initial descent.

Dropping to her knees, she excitedly fumbled for the toxin scanner in her pocket. Plucking a berry the size of her thumb, she injected the scanner's probe into the fruit. The scanner's display turned green.

"They're edible!" she yelled, popping the berry into her mouth. A burst of juicy sweetness lit up her taste buds. "Oh, they're so good! Try one!"

She handed Merrick a berry for him to eat.

"Mmm. Much better than those synthetic berries back home," he agreed.

"Help me pick some," she said.

They began picking berries and stuffing them into their pant pockets. In the process, Jayde found an off-color berry, its red skin overtaken by a rash of purple. She held it up, studying it closely against the dull sky. She decided it had gone bad, but before she could chuck it to the side, something else in the sky caught her attention.

There was a large, black dot hovering below the clouds.

Jayde felt like her body went numb as she let the berry slowly roll off her fingertips. "Get down!" she whispered.

Merrick looked at her curiously before dropping to his knees. Curious, he allowed his head to peek out over the boulder. Jayde grabbed the front of his jacket and yanked him fully to the ground.

"What do you see?" he yelled.

"Shhh! Be still!"

Below the crashing of the ocean waves, they heard the hum of a drone growing louder as it approached. Merrick's eyes widened, and he muttered a curse under his breath. He sat up and pressed his back against the stone, scrunching his head as low as possible.

The drone floated over top of them, its gravity drive emitting a low, threatening whir. Jayde's heart quickened as she realized it was a weaponized drone, the same model they were using as a shelter in the jungle. Moving steadily, bright red lasers shot out from the underside of its hull, the lights scraping the landscape in a two-dimensional plane.

"What is it doing?" asked Merrick.

"Performing a thermal survey utilizing a heat-sensitive infrared spectrometer."

Merrick gave her a dim look.

"It is looking for something… or someone," she clarified.

They sat together, side by side, as the drone flew past them and out toward the ocean. Once it was over the water it paused.

Jayde's jaw tightened. "It's coming back," she said.

The egg-shaped drone whirled around to face them, its single large optical camera locking on them. Three lights, arranged in a triangle around the camera eye, blinked blue and yellow, indicating it was processing information.

"Oh, no," Jayde said, her voice rattled. "I think it spotted us."

"We should run for it," whispered Merrick. "Now."

"No," Jayde protested. "Not yet."

"What do we do then?"

"Stand up," Jayde instructed. "Slowly. Put your hands in the air."

Merrick obeyed, his doubt evident. "You're not going to try to talk our way out of this, are you?"

"I got a plan. I still have my father's access code that he gave me, remember? Maybe I can talk our way out of this."

The drone floated toward them and paused fifty yards away.

It was perfectly oval and white, save for the blue-tinted camera optics in the front.

Its voice, cold as steel, commanded, "Identify."

Jayde cleared her throat twice before she could speak, her voice trembling.

"Jayde Ashr. Colonist one-five-three-two-zero. With me is Merrick Sloan."

She gave Merrick a look. He made a face like he had just gotten a whiff of a heap of garbage. "Go on," she said to him.

"Merrick Sloan. Colonist nine-three-four-seven-eight," he grumbled.

The drone's triangle of lights blinked once more, and then its metallic voice spoke: "Facial recognition and colony ID matched. Jayde Ashr and Merrick Sloan. Wanted for theft of a DT9 supply transport. You are ordered to return to Hypnos immediately for judicial processing."

"We cannot comply," replied Jayde.

"Compliance is mandatory," said the machine. "The Construct has mandated capture and immediate transit back to Hypnos."

It closed in, and with a whir, compartments on either side flipped open, and two laser cannons extended out like lithe, mechanical arms.

Merrick put his hand on Jayde's shoulder. "Jayde—"

"Override! Ashr, Richard, Artificial Intelligence Engineer. Code B-A-3-4-2-9-1!"

"This override code is no longer valid."

"That's not good," said Merrick, taking a step back.

"Retry! Override! Code B-A-3-4-2-9-1!" yelled Jayde.

The yellow and blue lights on the front of the drone changed to red and began to spin around its camera lens, faster and faster, until they appeared as a solid red circle around the machine's eye.

"Not working," said Merrick. "Code's not working!"

"Okay, we comply! We comply!" yelled Jayde, raising her arms higher.

Merrick joined in. "Yes! We definitely comply! I am so compliant right now!"

The circling red lights on the drone slowed and changed over to blue.

Jayde leaned in and whispered to Merrick: "Ok, now maybe is a good time to start running…"

"Oh, boy," whispered Merrick.

A panel on the drone opened, and another robotic arm emerged, this one holding a pair of silver restraining cuffs.

"Prepare for detainment," it said.

As it closed in, Jayde suddenly reached down, picked up a stone, and hurled it. Her throw was a direct hit, cracking the lens of its optic sensor in a shower of glass. The spinning lights around its eye flared an angry red. The laser cannons cranked and clanged as they engaged their power cells.

"Run!" screamed Jayde.

They took off, each sprinting around opposite sides of the boulder as two red lasers blasted out of the drone's arm cannons, zooming over their heads. Jayde stumbled on the hill, her foot slipping on the uneven ground. Merrick doubled back, grabbed her by the jacket, and pulled her to her feet.

"Let's go, Jayde! Keep moving!"

Fear gripped her heart, squeezing adrenaline into her veins. The world became brilliantly clear as she jumped up and scrambled toward the top of their slope. She glanced over her shoulder to see the drone closing in, floating down on them like a balloon descending from the clouds. The tips of its laser cannons glowed orange with heat, and she could see the iris of the drone's optic sensor struggling to focus through its cracked lens.

A high-pitched electronic trill sounded, signaling another imminent laser blast.

"Stop!" yelled Jayde as she grabbed the back of Merrick's jacket, yanking him to a halt just as two laser bolts shot into the ground just in front of him. Superheated soil splashed onto Merrick's face, causing him to scream in pain.

Jayde then shoved him forward. "Keep running!"

Merrick frantically wiped the red-hot muck from his skin. Jayde pulled his arm, leading him to the crest of the hill. Her breath quickened, legs burning as she ascended the steep slope.

The electric trill rang out behind them once again, screaming past them as they leapt in the air and tumbled down the other side of the knoll. Her rifle flew off her shoulder and disappeared into the grass. The world became a spinning blur as the grass and sky tumbled over each other, merging into a circular, kaleidoscopic landscape. Feeling every rock on the way down, she rolled head-over-heels for what seemed an eternity.

When her body finally came to a stop at the base of the hill, her first thought was surrender; the pain was so great. Resolve took hold, and with a deep breath, Jayde summoned her legs to move, and somehow she found the strength to stand. Her clothes were covered in dust, and blood trickled down her temple.

On the plain, a herd of horned beasts that had been feeding nearby was now trampling past her, startled by the searing laser fire. She looked up to see the drone cresting the hill, its camera eye glowing through the spider webbed crack in the lens. It shimmied left and right, searching for its targets, struggling to process images through its damaged optics.

Merrick had landed in a heap nearby. Like Jayde, he had lost his rifle somewhere on the hill. He searched the tall grass for it as he staggered to his feet.

"Forget the rifle," Jayde screamed. "Run for the herd!"

He looked up at her, and she pointed toward the stampeding animals.

"The drone sees with infrared heat," she yelled. "We can hide in their heat signatures!"

As soon as her voice rang out over the thunderous movement of the animals, the drone accelerated toward them. An arm cannon fired, and Jayde leapt to the side as a laser bolt tore through the air, narrowly missing her.

Merrick ran to catch the herd, his arms pumping as he moved through the grass. Jayde sprinted after him as the drone gave chase. It flew down along the hillside, then gained speed as it hit flat ground. Jayde glanced over her shoulder to see it gaining on her.

Jayde zigzagged left just as another laser blast sizzled past her shoulder. Ahead, the charging animals suddenly banked in their direction, a stroke of luck allowing her to bridge the gap between them. She and Merrick sprinted into the heart of the moving herd, matching its pace. Every step was a gamble. One wrong move, and they'd be trampled.

For a moment it worked. The drone decelerated, drifting sideways with the herd, its cannons trained on them but not firing. It rotated side to side, scanning for human-shaped signatures amid the mass of warm bodies.

But the animals were too fast and began to pull away.

"I can't keep up," Merrick wheezed.

Between the tumble down the hill and sprint across the plain, Jayde had nothing left to give. Her arms slowed and her lungs screamed for oxygen. The herd began to outdistance them, leaving Merrick and Jayde running alone in the grass.

They collapsed together, completely spent. There was no more running, no more hiding. They sprawled out in the grass, desperately trying to catch their breath. Jayde felt every muscle in her body quiver and twitch.

She looked up at the gray sky, tears forming in her eyes as it was soon eclipsed by the drone hovering over them, its angry red lights spinning around its shattered eye.

"I comply," said Jayde, her voice a strained whisper.

The drone cocked its laser cannons in a firing position, the barrel glowing orange.

"We comply!" yelled Merrick, as loud as he could.

The drone's lights flashed red, spinning faster and faster around its eye like a hurricane.

The cannon arms clicked, the barrels burning a fiery orange that intensified until the metal turned white.

No!

Jayde screamed and turned her face to the ground, expecting her body to be instantly burned to ash. Fear welled up inside her, mingling with a deep, consuming regret.

I'm sorry, Mom.

There was a sharp bang, like the slap of metal on metal, followed by a red flash. Jayde flinched, bracing for annihilation. There was a wave of intense heat, and the ground rumbled beneath them with a loud crash. Smoke filled her nose, and Jayde coughed, her first indication that she was still alive.

She sat up to see the drone was on the ground, engulfed by orange flames and thick smoke.

Merrick stood up, his hands placed on the back of his head in surprise. Through the smoky haze, they saw a shadowy male figure in the distance, a man cloaked in an olive-colored hood.

A huge laser rifle rested on his hip, its barrel still trailing wisps of smoke.

Chapter 17

Their savior was gone just as quickly as he appeared.

After destroying the drone, he turned and walked away, his heavy weapon slung over his shoulder. Jayde yelled after him, but to no avail. The hooded figure kept walking until he disappeared over a distant slope in the grassland.

Exhausted from their ordeal, Jayde and Merrick lacked the strength to chase after him. All they could do was lie in the grass, exchanging glances between each other and the black, smoldering remains of the Construct's assault drone. They were stunned at their unbelievably good fortune. Without this mystery man's intervention, they would be ash blowing in the wind.

"Do you think he was from your mother's crew?" asked Merrick.

Jayde gazed out to where their savior had disappeared into the landscape.

"Has to be," she replied.

"Why did he just leave?"

"No idea. Maybe he's not a fan of 'thank you' speeches."

Once their strength had returned, they searched the hills where they lost their hunting rifles. They found them, but the barrel on Jayde's was horribly bent. Merrick expressed optimism that he could fix it, but Jayde, used to Merrick's brazen self-confidence, was skeptical.

Merrick then went to fetch more ocean water for salting their meat, having thrown the bucket down and spilled their supply when they were attacked. Unfortunately, all the berries they had picked and stored in their pockets had been smashed during their tumble, leaving Jayde's pants horribly stained. While Merrick retrieved the seawater, she scooped the pulp out of her pockets and picked the few berries that were remaining from the bush.

As they walked back to camp, their eyes were constantly on the sky, scanning for floating shapes and blinking lights. With so much of their attention turned upward, Jayde couldn't help but think that now would be the perfect time for an ambush by the yellow-eyed reptoids.

Which do you prefer, she asked herself, teeth or lasers? She decided that it didn't matter, as long as it was quick.

The latest storm was blowing in, and Jayde observed the clouds were darker than she had ever seen before. The sky was nearly black, despite it being only late afternoon. As they approached their valley's stream, flashes of blue light burst within the clouds.

Suddenly, a tremendous clap of thunder shook the ground.

"This is going to be a bad one," said Merrick. "We better double-time it."

The clouds opened up into a downpour, and Jayde heard birds and other jungle fauna screech with surprise. Ahead of them, she saw a graceful, long-legged beast with a blue tail and black spots leap across the stream and disappear into the ferns. They picked up their pace, hoping the creature was not fleeing an unseen predator that might find them easier prey.

The wind became ferocious, bending the thick branches and limbs above them like they were twigs. Instantly, Jayde knew this new storm was unlike any they had witnessed before.

The rain fell like sharp needles, biting their skin. The ground became slippery and treacherous. They fought against the gusts that wove through the trees, the wind pushing them with relentless force. The sky flashed with lightning, followed by deafening thunderclaps that pummelled their ears.

Suddenly, a large branch fell from above, landing in front of them. Jayde stumbled backward into Merrick's chest, nearly causing him to spill his bucket of salt water. The massive branch stretched across the stream, its bark blackened by the strike.

"Watch out!" Merrick shouted, grabbing Jayde's arm to steady her as they navigated around it. The stream leading back to camp swelled, threatening to overflow and sweep them away.

Merrick hugged the bucket of salt water, desperately trying to shield it from the onslaught of fresh water falling around them. As the stream continued to rise, it became increasingly difficult to trudge the banks, the water swelling at times up to their waists. Jayde wondered if they should exit the stream and take their luck walking through the forest. Ultimately, she decided they had to continue walking the stream, even if it threatened to drown them. Abandoning the creek meant risking getting lost.

When she finally heard the roar of the waterfall up ahead, Jayde knew they were close to camp. The rain was unrelenting, and as they finally drew closer to their shelter, she felt the weight of the water that had now soaked into her jacket, boots, and pants, seeping deep into her bones. It felt as if someone had stacked iron bars onto her shoulders, and as she crawled out of the stream and onto marshy land, she felt utterly waterlogged. Her entire body seemed to be made of water, and she feared she might collapse and seep into the ground, never to be seen again.

She looked over at Merrick, his green eyes urging her to hurry. Like her, he sensed that things were about to get worse. The stream was already expanding toward their camp, and Jayde wondered if crawling into their shelter was even a good idea. It was far from watertight.

We could drown in that thing, she thought.

A sudden blast of wind came straight down from the sky, dazing them as if someone had punched them in the head. Another flash of lightning was followed by the sound of splitting wood.

The noise grew louder and louder until Jayde looked up and saw a smoldering tree falling toward her. She jumped out of the way just in time. The tree crashed down over their fire pit, landing inches from their shelter.

Jayde immediately decided that the risk of being hit by falling trees outweighed any fear of drowning.

Merrick pried open the door panel, and they both crawled inside. Jayde sat down in the corner and watched water roll off her body and clothes, pooling on the floor of the shelter. The hard rain pelted the metal hull like gravel, giving her the sense they were being buried alive. Merrick lit their small torch, its light a small comfort against the encroaching fear.

The storm outside roared like a wild beast, shaking their makeshift refuge with every gust of wind and clap of thunder. The rain pounded against the metal roof, creating a relentless cacophony that made it difficult to talk. For a long time, they sat in silence, until anxiety forced Merrick to find something to keep himself distracted.

He collected their meat, and using the rain-diluted salt water they had collected, began the salting process. He poured the water atop the meat and, using his hands, rubbed the liquid into the muscle fibers. Jayde watched him, her knees pulled to her chest.

Merrick glanced at her and noticed the tears streaming down her cheeks. He abandoned his task and crawled over to her, putting his arm over her shoulders.

"Hey," he said. "What's wrong?"

Jayde wiped her eyes and tried to compose herself. "I just… I can't stop thinking about it."

"What?"

"This stupid planet!" she screamed. She reached out and smashed her fist against the wall. "This place is a nightmare! I'm soaking wet! I've been soaking wet every damn minute we've been here! I'm swimming in the ocean, I'm running in the rain, I'm wading up a stream! Oh, and remember when we got swept over that waterfall? That was fun, wasn't it? But my favorite, by far, has been the Construct's drone trying to kill us! How about you?"

Tears were streaming down her face now. Merrick tried to soften his voice. "Jayde…"

"No! Don't do that! I don't need you to calm me down! This is my meltdown and I'm owning it! Let me finish!"

Merrick removed his arm, his eyes fixed on her frantic episode.

She continued. "The Construct said I was the key to saving humanity, remember? That there was some existential threat out there, and according to its future models, I was to play a part in mankind's survival. That is a lot to spring on a girl, don't you think? I think so! And then it tells me my mother is dead, and I have to believe it is lying, right? Why would it tell me my mother is dead when I know she is alive? Does it know that I know that she is alive? That has got to be in the models, too, right? I mean, it told me it could predict everything that I will do now and in the future. So then I gotta think, *did it let us escape in that transport?* If it knew I was going to escape to save my mother, why didn't it have guards just waiting in the maintenance hangar the minute that we walked in?"

She stared at Merrick intensely, waiting for a response. Finally, he blinked and answered. "I don't know."

"Let's just say for the sake of argument, it wants us here. Well then, why did it try to kill us? I could go in circles like this forever! Also, what about the man that appears out of nowhere carrying the largest laser rifle I have ever seen in my entire life? Did the Construct know that was going to happen? Was that part of the plan, too?"

"Jayde, I have no idea what you are talking about," said Merrick.

She quieted herself and looked at him.

"We should be dead right now, Merrick. And I can't figure out if we are lucky or if we are just following its plan. Either way, I know I don't want to be anyone's savior. I just want my mother back."

With that she buried her head in his shoulder and sobbed. Merrick held her tight, and she liked the feeling of his arms wrapped around her. Outside, the wind continued to howl, and the thunder clapped so loud it felt as if the storm was inside them.

Chapter 18

The storm was indeed the worst they had yet to experience on Eurus IV. The high winds shook their refuge violently through the night. With most of the holes in the drone's hull on the bottom, rising water levels, rather than rain, posed the greatest threat. At one point, the flooding stream reached their camp, turning it into a bog. The shelter shifted, one end sinking into the saturated ground. Mud flowed up through the cracks, and Jayde and Merrick held their breath, ready to open the door panel and flee their haven if necessary. Fortunately, the shelter sank just three or four feet before it hit an obstruction, perhaps an old stump or a rock bed, that kept them from sinking further.

More than once a falling branch fell against the top of their sanctuary. Jayde barely slept, her mind oscillating between the fear of drowning in mud and being crushed by a toppling tree. At one point, the wind roared so loudly that it seemed as if a giant mouth had opened wide near their shelter and screamed. The structure rolled to one side, and Jayde heard debris crash against the hull. Dents appeared in the walls as flying rubble smashed into their shelter at high speed.

But they survived.

When Jayde emerged from their shelter in the morning, they found their encampment transformed into a swamp, with standing water rising up to their knees. The trees were stripped of leaves and they could see large patches of sky through the canopy. Limbs and debris were scattered everywhere, and they could hear the roar of the waterfall pumping torrents of water into the valley. From where she stood, Jayde could see the swollen stream, its brown water carrying logs and leaves through the jungle. A trail of felled trees ran right next to the camp, cutting a slice out of the jungle as if the storm had reached down with a finger and traced a line through the forest.

Jayde surveyed the damage to their shelter. Small dents peppered the smooth white hull of the drone, making it look like it had caught a pox. Her charcoal drawing of the bird had completely washed away.

"Want some breakfast?" asked Merrick, his tone displaying a sarcastic sense of calm amidst the devastation. He offered her a slice of cold meat.

Jayde took the meat from him and ate it quickly. Then, she stripped off her jacket and long-sleeve shirt, hanging them on a tree branch to dry.

She felt different. Lighter. Steadier. Last night's breakdown had been a purge. The fear was still there, but the crushing weight of it had eased. She realized she'd spent this entire time on Eurus IV running: from the storms, the drones, the bloodthirsty creatures prowling the plains. Now, she was done running. Her episode allowed her to clear her mind. She had one mission: to find her mother. Everything else had to be blocked out.

Merrick was unusually quiet. Jayde could tell that he was still processing the night before. Maybe moved by it, or maybe just baffled by the sudden shift from the sobbing girl he'd comforted to the clear-eyed one now standing before him.

He looked like he wanted to say something, but she wasn't about to let him revisit what had happened. She was embarrassed by her outburst, yes, but their embrace had been something else too. Something unexpected. When her fear had faded, another feeling had taken its place. It was a startling sensation, like a soft stroking of her heart, one that she wasn't quite ready for.

She spoke quickly, scaring the feeling away.

"We should leave. Today."

Merrick looked up in surprise. "You sure?"

"There is nothing left for us here. We can't start a fire in this marsh, and we have plenty of meat."

Merrick shrugged. "Okay by me. Where to? Should we just start hiking toward the volcanoes?"

"No," said Jayde. "I think I know how to get a heading. Think you can pack our gear up while I try something?"

"Sure. What are you going to do?"

"I'm going to hack this drone."

* * *

While Merrick collected their supplies, Jayde focused on removing panels from the drone's interior, searching for the storage vault used by maintenance engineers. Despite the drone being dead, its hard drives likely still stored navigational data and GPS coordinates.

When she was younger, Jayde sometimes helped her father work on autonomous programming. *Your normal, everyday father/ daughter stuff*, she told friends. If she wanted to spend time with her dad, helping him with his job was pretty much her only option.

Based on that experience, she knew the Construct had to have deployed a satellite in Eurus IV's atmosphere for its drones to operate. These drones transmitted a signal to the satellite, which then relayed it via radio waves back to the Construct. This allowed the Construct to receive data and send commands, even taking over the drone's operation itself if needed. As the drones flew over the landscape and scanned the terrain, the Construct would build a three-dimensional map and load it into the machine's flight data.

Jayde hoped to access that map.

She found the storage vault. Inside were some basic tools, a maintenance tablet, and an interface cable. The cable was in good condition, but the tablet was less so, with a circular, spider-webbed crack marring its screen.

"Here goes everything," she muttered, pressing the power button.

The screen flickered to life, displaying the Hypnos colony logo.

This was good news: the tablet still held a charge. This was crucial as it allowed her to access the drone's code, and she wasn't sure she could recharge the battery if it had been dead.

She shuffled to the opposite side of the drone's interior and removed another panel, revealing a cable interface that allowed her to tap into the drone's CPU. She plugged the cable in and watched the tablet.

No signal. She needed to give the drone a jolt of power, enough to get its ancillary systems online and establish a connection to the triangulation satellite through its central processor. From there, she could download a map of the terrain scanned, as well as a navigational history.

From the battery compartment on the floor, she pulled out a fuel cell and examined the wires. The power connection ports were corroded. She set the fuel cell aside gently and retrieved another, hoping this one would be in better condition. This one looked viable: the power connection ports were clean.

She then dragged the cell to the CPU interface and pried off an oval-shaped panel with her fingernails. Inside was a spaghetti-like array of red, yellow, and white wires. She sifted through them, looking for the green wire that represented the power connection. When she found it, she pulled one end loose and twisted the frayed copper into a point, then inserted it into the connection port on the power cell.

Immediately, lights flickered on throughout the interior of the drone. Jayde's heart leapt and a triumphant smile spread across her face. She grabbed her cable and plugged the maintenance tablet into a port on the navigation console. The tablet sprang to life, displaying a diagnostics menu.

The options: Debug, Status, History and Logs.

She tapped on "History" with her finger, a wave of adrenaline surging through her.

The tablet displayed a historical readout of GPS coordinates at five-minute intervals. At the bottom of the screen was the function she was looking for: "Download map."

She paused.

Executing this command would initiate a download of a scanned topographical map, revealing exactly where this attack drone had been up until the moment it crashed.

Unfortunately, initiating a download could establish a traceable connection with the satellite, one that could be detected by the Construct. With the navigation console receiving power, the drone's homing beacon could be activated. Activity from a downed drone might create a system alert and give away their location.

Still, it was worth the risk. Without this clue, they could be hiking for days or weeks on this island, hoping to stumble upon the crew survivors by sheer luck. Jayde took a deep breath, pressed the download button, and watched the progress information on the screen.

Searching for satellite…

Connection established.

Authorized AK-Drone 457.

Map download initiated. 0%. 10%. 25%…

Jayde grimaced as the download paused at 25%. What was happening? Her mind raced with worst-case scenarios.

Finally, the download continued…50%. 75%…

A message popped up on the screen.

Connection interrupted. Unauthorized access.

Jayde panicked, suspecting the worst. She yanked the wire from the fuel cell's connection port. Instantly, the lights inside the drone shut off, leaving her in darkness.

Had she cut the power in time? She wasn't sure.

She looked at the tablet. A question appeared on the screen: *View Incomplete Map Data? Yes/No.*

Perhaps all this wasn't for nothing. She tapped the Yes button.

A satellite map appeared, displaying a red dot at the center of a vast forest that marked their current location. The drone's scanners had used sonar to "read" the topography, and with the A.I. engine, it had created a realistic 3D model of the landscape.

From the red dot, a yellow line marked the drone's navigational history, with multiple blue dots indicating the five-minute GPS pings. Moving the map with her fingers, Jayde traced the line backward in time.

She followed it through the jungle, across the plain, and toward a patch of forest farther inland. The forest appeared sparse, with fresh water visible between the trees. The topography was very flat, appearing to collect water flowing down from the mountains at the center of the island. Essentially, it was a swamp.

The drone's path showed it had been circling the swamp for almost thirty minutes before it crashed. Prior to that, the line disappeared. This was as much data as she got before the signal was disconnected.

Another realization hit her. This was the direction their hooded savior was walking as he left them, toward the swamp. Could he have been the one that shot down their drone? It seemed plausible.

She pinched the map to zoom in, looking closely at the drone's circular flight pattern. The sonar scanner had picked up a cubic shaped object hidden in the trees.

It was a man-made hut!

Jayde rushed outside. Merrick was sitting on a stump, crafting a pack for their trek, threading a coiled green vine through a large, thick leaf. He looked up at Jayde and his expression instantly mirrored hers, equal parts excitement and concern.

"I think I've found my mom," said Jayde, breathless. "But there is a chance the Construct knows where we are. We need to get out of here. Now."

Chapter 19

Jayde showed the map to Merrick. By Merrick's estimation, the hut was less than a two-day hike away. They could reach it by tomorrow evening. Jayde's face lit up, and without thinking, she pulled him into a tight hug.

"Are you excited about finding your mother, or just glad to leave our quaint little bog?" Merrick asked.

"Both," she replied.

Although finding her mother was top of mind, Jayde was certainly eager to set out and find some dry land. They had spent the better part of two days either in the rain or soaked to the bone. She looked up through the storm-damaged jungle canopy, surveying a clear, blue sky.

No storm yet. Maybe luck was finally on their side.

Jayde helped Merrick finish crafting their makeshift packs. They weaved together several leathery green leaves, using a small, pointed stick and some young vines. They even fashioned shoulder straps, fastening a larger vine through the top and bottom and tying it together at the ends.

Jayde sloshed back and forth from the shelter, fetching their cured meat and placing it into the packs. When they were full, she slung one over her shoulder to test it. She jumped up and down a few times, the sack of meat held firm on her back.

"Not bad," she said.

"Not bad? I'm a bloody genius."

"Sorry. The 'genius' title goes to the girl who hacked the drone."

Merrick smiled. He hoisted his pack over his shoulder and went to retrieve their hunting rifles. He handed Jayde hers with a satisfied nod.

"Yeah, well," he said. "What do you say to this?"

Jayde took her weapon. The barrel, bent from her fall the previous day, was now perfectly straight.

"You fixed it?"

"Like new," Merrick said, a bit of pride in his voice.

"When did you get this useful?" she asked.

"I'm more than just a pretty face, you know."

In that moment, Jayde felt a surge of appreciation for Merrick. She could not have done this alone, and she knew he had sacrificed a lot to be here with her. His small, toiling existence on Hypnos wasn't much, but it had to be better than fighting to survive on an alien planet.

Then again, maybe not.

This alien world was fierce and resilient. Life here clung on, enduring despite a climate that tried to tear it down. Jayde realized she felt the same tenacity within herself, a kind of kinship with this wild, unyielding place.

She was certain that Merrick felt the same.

"Merrick—"

Jayde's words of gratitude for all he had done for her stuck in her throat. Merrick, noticing her struggle, placed a hand on her shoulder, a signal that she didn't need to say anything. When she met his gaze she saw not only devotion in his eyes, but also a flicker of excitement for the journey ahead.

"Are you ready?" he asked.

"Yes," Jayde said confidently. "You?"

"Chomping at the bit!"

She chuckled. "I've never asked you before. Where do you get all these ridiculous sayings?"

A wistful look crossed Merrick's face. "My father gave me a book, passed down through our family for generations. *Ancient Idioms of Earth*. When I was sixteen he let me read it, and I kept it hidden in the mattress of my bed. There were hundreds of them, and I tried to memorize every one. 'Chomping at the bit' means 'ready to go.'"

"It's a shame you had to leave something like that behind."

Merrick winked and pulled out a sealed plastic bag from the inside of his jacket. The bag held a small leather-bound book, no bigger than his hand.

"Don't leave home without it," he said.

* * *

Jayde took one last look at the waterfall before they set out, then began following the swollen stream toward the grasslands. The water, now a murky brown from the mud and silt washed down by the storm, churned over rocks and logs as they walked. The familiar sounds of the jungle had returned, with the hooting creatures once again swinging from branch to branch, tracking their every move. Jayde caught glimpses of them soaring through the air on their leaf parachutes as they walked. It was tempting to stop and watch, but a sense of urgency drove them both. The Construct's drones could be there at any moment, and it was best to put as much distance between themselves and their now-abandoned camp as possible.

As they kept a steady pace through the jungle, Jayde couldn't stop thinking about how nice it would be to have dry socks. With every step, her feet squished in her boots, and she resolved to dry her socks by the fire once they found a good place to camp for the night.

When they reached the edge of the grasslands, they paused. Merrick took his hunting rifle in hand and cautiously stepped out from the tree line to scan the clouds.

"Nothing in the sky," he said, relieved.

The grass rippled as the wind swept over the hills that bordered the ocean. A ray of sunshine broke through the clouds, casting the savanna in a golden hue. Dotted across the landscape were the familiar horned beasts grazing the land.

Jayde looked over the vast, open plain. They were going to have to walk a long way through the grasslands with very little cover. If drones or the yellow-eyed reptoids appeared, there would be nowhere to hide.

"We're going to have to move fast," said Jayde. "We'll be completely exposed."

"Straight ahead, yeah?" Merrick asked.

Jayde pulled the tablet from her pack and checked their map.

"That way," she said, pointing toward the flat horizon. "It's a straight shot until the elevation dips into another valley. There's a forest line there. We can follow that inland for a while, then cut north again, straight into the trees. Looks like a lot of water where we are going. Swamp."

"I'm starting to wish this was a desert planet," Merrick muttered.

They trudged forward into the tall grass. Jayde took in the sweet, earthy scent of the wheat-like straw brushing against her legs. The plants crunched softly underfoot as they walked. A few horn beasts glanced up at them as they passed by, their beady black eyes curious for a moment.

Jayde tightened her grip on her rifle, pressing the stock firmly into her side as she scanned their surroundings. She watched intently for reptilian tails slicing through the grass.

They hiked past a sparse grove of gnarled trees, and Jayde looked for signs of the planet's diverse wildlife in their branches. Most of the trees were bare, but a few hours into their journey, she spotted a flock of reptilian birds resting in some branches. With red eyes and black skin, the creatures sported wings that were a striking mix of red and yellow, stretched taut like thin membranes. Their heads jerked sharply from side to side, and they produced a strange, rhythmic sound, like the clapping of hands. The snapping noises created an eerie illusion of applause.

The sun played hide-and-seek with the clouds as they walked, casting shifting shadows across the landscape. Jayde felt a surge of contentment that their journey had begun on a day when the sun had decided to show itself.

Near mid-afternoon, Merrick turned to Jayde. "I think we should stop here for a bit," he said. "We could eat lunch and rest for the next leg. Enjoy the sun while it lasts."

Jayde instinctively bristled at the idea of sitting out in the open. Between the reptoids and the ever-present threat of patrolling attack drones, it felt like inviting disaster. Her first impulse was to push back, to insist they keep moving. But she caught herself. She had a habit of dismissing Merrick's suggestions, often taking control without considering his perspective. She was trying to be better about that.

"Good idea," she said. "But let's find a tree we can climb. It'll be safer to rest in a spot off the ground."

Merrick agreed, and as they trekked over a gentle rise, a solitary tree came into view. It stood tall and sturdy, its branches reaching out like open arms. They made their way over to it, and as they approached, Jayde noticed a cluster of white and purple wildflowers growing at its base. She bent down, plucking one of the purple flowers and bringing it to her nose. The scent was unexpected, a sharp, citrusy aroma that reminded her of sliced lemon. She smiled, momentarily lost in the pleasant surprise, and the stubborn feeling to continue on their hike melted away.

Merrick boosted Jayde up to the first branch, and without hesitation, she climbed nearly to the top. Her desire to take in more of this incredible planet was matched only by her urge to see if the swamp was within view. Finding a sturdy limb to perch on, she gazed out at the horizon. From this vantage point, the grasslands of Eurus IV were breathtaking, an expanse of orange and green vegetation, thin and wispy, swaying in the breeze. Jayde bit her thumb, marveling at the sight.

Mankind had explored many planets, some within her lifetime, others long before she was born. But this was the first she had heard of one that rivaled Earth's bounty of plant and animal life. She wondered if Earth even still looked like this. She had heard it was urbanized and overpopulated, with only a few places preserving its once-majestic natural beauty. Jayde understood humanity's need for resources, but it was still a shame. Something as majestic as these lands on Eurus IV deserved to be left unspoiled.

Shifting her weight on her branch, she turned to the north, hoping to catch a glimpse beyond the edge of the grasslands and toward the sloping land that led to their ultimate destination.

What she saw took her breath away.

A line of gigantic, four-legged creatures marched single file across the plain, each towering nearly twenty feet tall. Their incredibly long, slender legs and necks moved with an otherworldly grace, and with each step, their necks arched forward in a rhythmic lurch.

Jayde pointed the creatures out to Merrick, who quickly climbed up to her branch for a better view. He stood up on the limb, hugging a higher branch for balance. Jayde turned her attention from the creatures to watch him. His face was beaming in a way she had never seen before, utterly captivated.

She reached out and gently caressed his leg. Merrick didn't take his eyes off the creatures, lost in awe at the sight of them.

"You know, I wanted to be an explorer like your mom," he confided. "Did I ever tell you that?"

Jayde shook her head. "No, you didn't."

"My grandfather was an explorer, and one of the first Hypnos colonists. He scouted the New Eden moon, living on that dead rock for months, testing it for moscovium, silicon, and other elements to mine for our Grand Expansion. Arthur Sizemore was his name. I had a picture of him in my room. Framed. Him and my mom."

Jayde listened intently, sensing the weight of his memory.

"I dreamed of being like him, going planet to planet, seeing things never witnessed by human eyes. To put the first human footprints on alien soil. Even though I knew it was coming, the day the Construct officially put me in the maintenance bay… that was the worst day of my life."

Jayde stared down at her hands as memories of her own career assignment flooded back. The lack of agency gnawed at her still to this day, despite how much stronger and resilient she had become, a transformation only possible in the mines.

As they both sat in the tree, reflecting on their past and how the Construct had driven them into this self-imposed exile, Jayde realized that a machine could never predict the whims of the heart. Merrick, in particular, followed his heart fiercely, making him a useless wild card in the eyes of the Construct. Thanks to it, Hypnos had lost out on all of his potential had he been able to forge his own path.

Merrick lowered himself onto the limb next to Jayde, letting his legs dangle. He pulled off his leaf pack and they sat quietly together, taking in the sight of the majestic, long-necked creatures. A small juvenile let out a playful bleat as it marched by them. Merrick grinned and cupped his hands over his mouth to mimic the sound. The young creature turned its serpentine neck and looked back, its dark eyes blinking in curiosity. As the calf snorted and scampered off to rejoin its family, Jayde found herself leaning into Merrick, wrapping an arm around his waist. She surprised herself with the gesture, pulling him close as they watched the creatures disappear into the horizon together.

* * *

After their meal, Jayde felt energized and ready to press on. They resumed their hike through the grasslands, grateful for the clear weather. As they walked, Jayde kept an eye on the sky, scanning for dark clouds. To her relief, there were none. The thought crossed her mind that they might actually get through a day without being drenched by the planet's relentless storm cycle.

By evening, the terrain began to slope down into a valley, confirming to Jayde that they were on course. The volcanoes loomed much closer now, their dark peaks standing stark against the sky. Ahead, a river wound its way out of the mountains, cutting through a lush green forest before vanishing into a dense foliage. To the west, Jayde spotted the river reemerging, snaking its way toward the blue-green ocean, where it fanned out into a great triangular delta. Above it, a thick flock of reptilian birds flew together, their dark forms shifting and swirling like a living cloud.

They stopped, and Jayde consulted her tablet map. After a moment, she pointed out the western edge of the forest to Merrick.

"The hut is somewhere in that swamp, on the near side," she said.

Merrick scanned the path ahead, where the grass began to give way to a rocky, uneven descent into the river valley. Though not treacherous, it was a route best not attempted in the dark. The sky had already deepened to a rich orange as the planet's sun began its slow dive toward the horizon.

"Let's make camp over there, within that cluster of trees," Merrick suggested. "We can start a small fire and cook some meat before nightfall."

Jayde wholeheartedly agreed. Despite their afternoon break, her legs felt like they might give out at any moment. The high-stepped strides needed to hike through the grasslands had taken a toll, and her socks were still uncomfortably damp from trudging through the floodwaters earlier in the day.

They built a small fire in the shelter of five trees that had grown close together. The clustered trunks obscured them enough to give Jayde a sense of ease, even though she knew an infrared drone could easily pick up their heat signature right through the foliage.

They dried their boots and socks as they roasted cured reptoid meat over the fire, careful to ration their dwindling supply. With only one rib and two hunks of leg left, they knew they had to make it last. The berries they had collected added a refreshing contrast to the strong, salty flavor of the meat, their tartness cutting through the richness with a mix of plum and blackberry.

They ate quietly together in the warmth of the flames as nightfall brought a drop in temperature. The sky deepened to a dark blue. Merrick stamped out the fire, and they climbed into one of the trees. Jayde stretched out across two branches, rolling herself into a ball with her head resting on her hands. It was far from comfortable, but exhaustion outweighed any willingness to care. Merrick settled on a limb above her, leaning his head and arms on another branch as he prepared to sleep in a near-seated position.

Jayde inhaled the lingering smoke from their extinguished fire as her eyes grew heavy. The shrill call of tiny nocturnal creatures echoed through the darkened grove, filling the air with a chorus of unfamiliar sounds. The sounds were faint, like those of small insects, so Jayde reassured herself that any threat they posed could be easily brushed aside with a flick of her finger.

As the sky fell into darkness, Jayde glanced up through the canopy and was stunned to see millions of stars twinkling above. The clouds had parted, revealing the vast expanse of the cosmos. One star shone brighter than others, and Jayde wondered if it might be a planet, perhaps even New Eden, her home.

She thought about her father, a man who had placed his unwavering trust in the Construct, who had been instrumental in shaping its current, dreaded incarnation. She wished he could reach out to him, across the stars and into the afterlife, to tell him everything. That his beloved machine had tried to kill her, that it had lied about her mother's demise. The weight of those unspoken words, suspended over the infinite gulf between life and death, filled her with a deep sense of loneliness. Most of all, she felt a growing sense of resentment. How could he have been so naive? The Construct controlled everything, made every decision, and inflicted despair upon the Hypnosians that refused to be brainwashed by its prophetic rhetoric.

She despised her father for passing away before seeing the truth of what he wrought.

No, that was wrong. She knew his intentions were good. She despised him for what he could have been if he had not been so hopelessly devoted to a false idol.

He might have been a better father.

Jayde then let her thoughts wander, now fantasizing about standing before the people of Hypnos, exposing the Construct's lies. She imagined herself telling them about Eurus IV, a world like the one their ancestors once knew, where people tended gardens and waded in abundant waters. A place of wild skies, vibrant land, and life thriving beyond the Construct's control.

The fantasy faded as quickly as it came. The Construct was too powerful, too entrenched in every aspect of life. It wasn't just a machine; it was the foundation of society, controlling information and dictating the future of billions of people across the universe. Humanity was conditioned to follow the Construct's edicts like gospel. People may resist the truth if such a foundation was shattered. There were those content to live in their glass cages, blind to the opportunity that existed beyond them.

Those people deserved whatever fate awaited them, she decided. Her path would be different. She would find her mother, and together, they would carve out a life in this wild world. She was certain Merrick would join her, and here, they could live free. Truly free.

The real question was whether the Construct would ever stop hunting her. Its bizarre obsession with her remained a mystery. All she could do was stay ahead of it, hoping that, eventually, it would decide she wasn't worth the effort, and let her slip through its grasp.

Chapter 20

Jayde opened her eyes in the morning, intensely thankful that it hadn't rained. It was the first night without a storm since they'd crashed on Eurus IV, and she savored the small miracle. She sat up, leaning her back against the rough bark of the tree. From her perch, she could just make out the ocean, a thin slice of blue on the distant horizon. Above it, the planet's rising sun burned a soft orange, its warmth still gentle in the morning light.

Merrick slept above her, his body draped limply across the branches, arms and legs hanging loosely as if he'd fallen from a great height and been caught in the gnarled embrace of the tree. Suddenly, there was a rustling noise from behind, and Jayde turned to see one of the long-necked creatures from yesterday calmly plucking leaves from their tree.

The animal was reptilian in nature, its skin covered in hardened scales, yet unlike the fearsome reptoids that prowled the plains, this creature exuded a gentle presence. Its large black eyes were set on the sides of its head, and it possessed a trunk-like muzzle that ended in a small circular mouth. From this mouth, a long green tongue extended, wrapping around a branch. It gave the limb a firm tug, pulling leaves and twigs into its mouth. It huffed several times as it chewed, and Jayde spotted four nostrils at the tip of its snout that flared with each deep breath.

Jayde grabbed her rifle and leaf pack she had hung on the tree and slowly climbed to the ground, careful not to make any sudden movements that might spook her visitor.

The creature paid her no mind, continuing to feed as its tongue wound around the leaves, shaking the tree slightly with each tug. Incredibly, Merrick remained fast asleep through the whole ordeal, snoring away even as the very branch he was perched on quivered under the creature's gentle assault.

Once on the ground, Jayde found that the animal was even larger than she had realized. As she cautiously approached, she saw that she only came up to the animal's long, bulbous knee. It was so docile, so unafraid of her, that she felt an urge to reach out and stroke its leg, imagining that it might even lower its neck and let her pet its smooth, cylindrical snout.

An idea began to form in her mind. Jayde broke off a low-hanging branch and approached the creature, holding the fresh leaves high into the air.

"Here you go," she said softly, shaking the branch. "Here you go."

The rustling of the leaves caught the creature's attention. It swayed gently on its stilt-like legs, its large eyes fixed on the branch in Jayde's hand. With a blink of its long eyelashes, the creature seemed to consider her offering. Then, to her amazement, it became excited, its thin tail wagging back and forth like a giant whip. Jayde's heart raced as it dipped its head down and, holding her breath, she extended her arm as far as it would go, hoping to make contact.

The creature suddenly snapped its head up, its attention drawn sharply toward the ocean. It bleated and bolted away, its long legs moving with surprising speed.

"Hey! Where are you going?" Jayde called out, jogging after it, leaving the safety of her small cluster of trees. Then she heard it, the familiar hum of an approaching drone.

She spun around, the branch slipping from her fingers as her eyes locked onto the triangular fleet of attack drones descending from the sky like a flock of birds. Jayde sprinted back to the tree, unslinging her hunting rifle from her back as she pressed her back against the trunk, clutching the weapon to her chest.

"Merrick!" she yelled. "Merrick, wake up!"

Merrick stirred, blinking groggily until the hum of the drones reached his ears. His eyes snapped open, and his head jerked upward to the sky. He saw them, descending from the clouds like silent predators.

"Don't move," Jayde whispered sharply.

The drones were close now, hovering just above the treetops. Their sleek, polished white hulls gleamed in the muted light, and their camera eyes blinked with alternating yellow and blue lights. A low, reverberating buzz filled the air, each drone moving in flawless synchronization.

The drones adjusted their formation, shifting from a "V" to a horizontal line sweeping across the grassland. Two broke away from the group, drifting toward their cluster of trees, one on each side.

Jayde's pulse quickened. She gripped her rifle, releasing the safety with a shaky breath. Slowly, she raised it to her eye, peering through the scope as one of the drones approached, the cold metal of the gun heavy in her hands.

Merrick was frozen in the branches, watching helplessly as the drones moved in.

Their slow and steady pace reassured Jayde. They hadn't been picked up by the scanners… yet. The machines were methodically spreading farther apart in their sweeping line as they surveyed the ground with their sensors. Jayde's grip on her rifle loosened as the two drones drifted overhead, one to their left, the other to their right.

Her legs gave way as she dropped to the ground in disbelief, heart pounding. The fleet floated away, their path curving toward the direction of their old jungle camp.

She couldn't believe it; somehow, they had gone unnoticed.

Pure luck had placed them in the narrow gap between the

drones' scanning zones, perfectly hidden from the reach of their infrared sensors.

✳ ✳ ✳

Anxious that the fleet might return, Jayde and Merrick packed up quickly and set out for the river valley. While Jayde was rattled by their encounter, Merrick was in good spirits, taking their near miss with the drone fleet as a good omen.

"That's three miracles on this trip, Jayde. 1-2-3," he said, holding up three fingers on his hand. "Survived a crash landing—that's one. Random stranger shows up out of nowhere and destroys a drone about to kill us, that's two. Fleet of drones flies directly overhead and totally misses us, that's—"

Jayde cut him off. "Do you really think any of those things qualifies as a miracle?"

"Listen," Merrick said. "I was at the top of a tree, at damn near eye level with those flying eggs, and I don't know how they didn't see me! It had to be divine intervention."

"Are you seriously getting religious on me?"

Merrick shrugged. "Our ancestors all followed a religion of some sort. They believed a higher power guided and protected them. Some even believed a God could intervene, allowing the chosen ones to fulfill their destiny."

Jayde felt a twist of irritation. "You sound like the Construct! Destiny is a word it uses as a leash. It keeps people in line, makes people obey on faith that their misery has some kind of purpose."

"I'm just saying—" Merrick replied, spreading his arms wide at the sprawling natural world around them, "—all *this* makes me wonder if there isn't something more to the universe. Let's face it, the Construct, a so-called all-knowing algorithm with a God complex, is almost never wrong. The real question is: if you're meant to play a part in humanity's survival, as it claims, then why is it trying so hard to control you? *Why would it try to kill you? Why?*"

Merrick stopped and spun around to face her, stopping Jayde in her tracks.

"I'll tell you why," he said. "Whatever insane math it's running, whether it's the alignment of atoms or how the hair stands up on my ass in the morning, it's figured out that you're here for a reason. And it's not just to find your mom. Something bigger is happening here, something that threatens the Construct itself. Whatever it is, it can't get a handle on it. And you know what? I think it's scared of you!"

Jayde put her head down, marching past him where he stood. "You're out of your mind."

Merrick followed, steady and unshaken.

"Something divine is at work here," he proclaimed. "Ignore it while you can, but sooner or later, you'll see!"

* * *

Before they even reached the edge of the swamp, Jayde could smell it. The rank odor of stagnant water hit her so hard that she covered her nose and squinted her eyes. Ahead lay the forest she had seen on the tablet map, its murky waters barely distinguishable. Despite the smell, they pressed forward without hesitation.

The ground was soft and slick beneath their feet, every step sinking into the muck and leaving puddles where their boots had been. The trees in this valley were nothing like those in the jungle forest they'd left behind. Here, the abundance of standing water, gathered in shallow ponds of various sizes, gave rise to a different kind of tree. These were thick-barked, low-hanging branches that resembled Earth willows. Their limbs supported hundreds of mossy vines that draped down like curtains, swaying gently in the humid air.

Pools of water were everywhere. Jayde and Merrick wound their way around these shallow ponds, each bordered by shoulder-high weeds and plants, their stems bristling with thorns and needle-like spines. Every step required careful navigation as the terrain became a maze of hazards.

From the map, Jayde knew a river flowed through the heart of the swamp, but neither the sight nor sound of it reached them. All they could see were sagging, moss-draped trees stretching endlessly in all directions. The air buzzed with the abundant sounds of life, a chorus of chirps, croaks, and the occasional distant splash.

"Do you have an idea of where we're going?" asked Merrick.

"According to the map, we've been following the path of the wrecked drone this whole time," Jayde replied, scanning the swamp. "It started flying erratically around here. My guess is it took laser fire somewhere nearby, then fell out of the sky over the grasslands before crashing into the valley."

Merrick peered ahead where the swamp thickened, a seemingly impassable barrier of vines and waterlogged earth.

"So, do you think your mother is in there?" he asked.

Jayde hesitated. "Someone is."

With that, she moved deeper into the undergrowth. Merrick trailed behind, lifting the sleeve of his jacket to his nose to deflect the stench of rotting vegetation. Suddenly, Jayde came upon a narrow, trampled path, perhaps made by some swamp creature's ritualistic patrol of its territory.

They navigated the path, carefully dodging the thorny overhangs of the moss-draped trees. The density of the forest eventually eased, opening up near several stagnant, algae-filled ponds. The once-vibrant chorus of animals had quieted, no doubt sensing the presence of the two unwelcome intruders in their habitat.

They paused at the nearest pool, its surface coated in a thick layer of green slime. The air buzzed with insect-like creatures darting around the weeds at the water's edge. The humidity was suffocating. They had barely entered the swamp, yet Jayde's shirt was already drenched in sweat.

Merrick picked up a stick and poked it into the murky water at their feet, watching as it sank into the muck.

"About three feet deep here," he said.

"It looks deeper in the middle," Jayde replied, eyeing the

darker waters.

"Let's find a better place to cross."

They followed the edge of the pool, searching for a narrow channel, but the water only grew wider and more treacherous. Finally, Jayde stopped, hands on her hips, staring at the expanse of stagnant water.

"This is getting us nowhere," she said. "Let's just cross here."

"I don't know, it still looks pretty deep."

"We can't keep going like this. We're heading the wrong way, losing time."

Merrick looked around for an easier crossing. No such luck.

"Fine," Merrick said. "Let's go." He picked up a long stick on the ground and stepped into the water. "Take my rifle and pack. I'll lead us through."

He handed his gear to Jayde and stepped into the murk, water sloshing around his legs. Jayde followed close behind, holding their rifles and packs above her head to keep them dry. Her first step plunged her mid-thigh into the slimy water. The green algae clung to her pants in thick patches.

Merrick moved cautiously, his stick probing for hidden holes or drop-offs. Jayde felt her boots squelch into the thick muck at the bottom, the resistance pulling at her with every step. She prayed the ground beneath her stayed solid enough to support her weight, the unsettling thought of sinking below the surface in her mind.

Metallic-looking bugs suddenly appeared, swarming around Jayde's head, landing on her neck, forehead, and arms. They didn't bite, but their presence made her skin crawl, her every instinct screaming to swat them away. She forced herself to resist, clenching her teeth to keep from dropping their rifles and supplies.

"I'm heading for that log toward the middle," Merrick called back. "It looks like it's in some shallows."

As soon as the words left his mouth, the "log" dipped beneath the surface, revealing a scaly tail as it vanished into the depths. Jayde and Merrick froze, exchanging wide-eyed glances.

"Or…" Merrick stammered. "We can go a different way."

"Yes," agreed Jayde. "Let's do that."

They quickened their pace, eyes scanning nervously for ripples in the water as it climbed to their chests. For Jayde, the weight of the rifles and packs made each step more difficult, her arms trembling from the strain.

Merrick, having reached the middle of the pond, tossed his stick aside. It was no longer useful. They were committed now. If the water rose any higher, they'd have no choice but to abandon their supplies and swim for it.

"Almost there," he said, but Jayde could hear the uncertainty in his voice.

The water crept up to Jayde's neck. The stench was unbearable, like black mud mixed with rotten eggs, and it hit her nose with such force that she almost gagged. Her arm muscles burned from holding the rifles and packs over her head for so long. She forced herself to keep going, her gaze fixed on the other side of the pond, now just a few paces away.

Finally, the water began to lower. First, her chest broke free, then her waist, and soon her thighs. Relief flooded her, but she pushed herself to move faster, heart pounding. They were close now, and Jayde couldn't shake the nagging fear that this was the moment something would rise up from the depths and strike.

Merrick reached the shore first, stumbling out of the water before collapsing against a tree. He patted his torso and legs, as if to make sure everything was still intact. Slimy strands of algae clung to his chest, and he peeled them off in long, noodle-like strips.

Jayde trudged through the last few feet of water, now down to her shins. With a burst of energy, she sprinted the final stretch, kicking up slime as she went. She reached the shore and collapsed to her knees, breathless, then crawled the rest of the way to Merrick before flopping onto her stomach, completely spent.

Water dripped from her hair, running cold along her skin, and in the grips of a wet chill, Jayde considered that she had never smelled so bad in her life.

"Jayde…" Merrick's voice cut through her thoughts, low and unsettling.

"What?" she asked, pushing herself up to her hands and knees.

"Your neck…"

The wavering calm in his voice set off an alarm in her brain.

"What? What is it?" Jayde's voice trembled as her hands shook, fumbling to the front of her neck. Her fingers searched below her chin first, finding cold, wet skin. But as they moved toward the back of her head, her body seized with shock as she felt it: a squishy lump, pulsating and clinging to the skin just below her hairline.

She shrieked, instinctively grabbing at the thing, trying to pull it off, but the lump contracted like a muscle, staying firmly attached. It felt slick and bulbous, her fingertips slipping against its mucous-like surface.

"Oh my God! Get it off! Get it off!" Jayde screamed, her voice trembling with panic.

Merrick lunged forward, grabbing her arms. "Be still! Don't pull on it!"

"It's stuck to my neck!"

"You need to be still," said Merrick, his voice low and steady. "Move your hands so I can see it."

She tried to calm herself as she felt his hands on the back of her neck. Merrick pulled back a curtain of hair as she held her breath, fighting the terror that shivered in every muscle. Jayde felt Merrick tug at the slimy mass, her skin lifting and snapping back with each attempt to dislodge it. The sensation sent a wave of nausea rolling through her.

"What is it?" she asked, her voice shaking.

"Some kind of worm," Merrick muttered. "It's latched onto your neck."

Jayde's vision blurred, the colors of the swamp warping as her world teetered on the edge of consciousness. "I don't feel so good," she whispered, swaying slightly. Her eyelids fluttered, and with each blink, the landscape shifted between hues—green, red, blue, yellow—fading in and out like a dying ember.

"Stay with me, Jayde! Stay with me!" Merrick's voice sounded distant, echoey. "I'm going to pull it off!"

Reality narrowed into a swirling vortex, pulling her into a pinpoint of light. The pressure on her neck intensified, and she felt the weight of something foreign holding her down. Her grip on reality slipped into the ether.

Then, just before everything went dark, a booming voice pierced the fog.

"Stop!" it yelled. *"If you pull it off, you'll kill her!"*

Chapter 21

An old memory surfaced in her mind, one long forgotten.

Jayde, still a young girl, lied on the floor of her family's stark-white apartment in Hypnos. Her legs bounced as her toes tapped the carpet. Spread out next to her were hand-crafted crayons, made by her mother from minerals collected on distant planets. On a blank sheet of paper, Jayde outlined an alien world with a blue crayon. She switched to red to sketch a glowing sun, rising over the horizon.

Her parents were arguing at a dinette table. They weren't shouting, but their voices were sharp and whispery in the quiet apartment, a failed attempt to shield their daughter from their feud. Jayde kept her head down, focusing on her drawing, but each time the table was slammed with an open hand, her concentration broke.

"You know it's possible!" her mother argued. "You know it is!"

Her father, dressed in his white clergy gown, his hair slicked back as sharply as his black mustache, waved his hands in frustration.

"Listen, I ran the algorithms myself, it all checks out. We're going to install the latest software into the test environment and it will be fine. You'll see."

"Your work hasn't been peer-reviewed by any of the off-world data scientists! It only has the approval of the Briefing Committee!"

"Peer reviewed? Why—" He turned his back, visibly trying to calm himself, as if counting to ten in his head. When he finally turned back around, his voice was steadier, though tension lingered. "Do you not believe that I know what I'm doing?"

Her mother remained silent. Jayde, sensing the shift in the room, stopped drawing and looked up, her crayon frozen in midair.

"Right now, we have an incredibly powerful artificial intelligence that is subservient and docile," her mother said, her voice sharp with frustration. "Why would you want to mess with that?"

"Because there's a limit to what it can do," her father shot back. "It can only process information. Data in, data out. It can only solve problems like a machine. It can't think like a human."

"And you think by allowing it to feel, it will make it better?"

"Yes! If it can finally experience the world like a human, it can finally understand us, walk in our shoes! Our progress has stagnated for centuries. We need to make a radical leap in our AI technology in order for us to take the next step!"

Her mother only shook her head. "Richard, if you do this, you're opening Pandora's Box. The Construct is naive. It needs to stay naive."

"No! If the Construct evolves, we evolve."

Jayde watched as her father marched toward the apartment door. He hesitated, glancing at her before turning back to her mother.

"The greatest gift I can give my daughter is a future where humanity reaches its full potential. Don't you want that for her?"

"I just want her to be happy, Richard."

"So do I! That's the whole point of the Noble Purpose! I have sacrificed everything in order to make Phase Four a reality. And when it's ready, when Jayde is older, she'll reap the benefits. The

Construct will understand her, and all of us, in a way it never has before. You'll see."

There was a long pause, then her mother responded to him, in a tone softer than before. "Just remember what I asked you to do."

"Mary, you know I can't—"

"This one thing. If you ever cared about me, about her, you'll do this."

"I'll… I'll think about it. I promise."

The sound of the door closing left an empty silence in its wake. Jayde's mother sat still, staring down at her cup of coffee, absently spinning the handle between her fingers. She sniffed and wiped her eyes with the back of her hand. A hollow sadness clung to her, and when she finally looked up at Jayde, it was an apologetic smile, one that Jayde had seen too often, especially after arguments like these.

Jayde offered only a blank stare in return.

Her mother's smile faltered as she slid off her chair and lowered herself to the floor, crouching down on her hands and knees. She wrinkled her nose, flashing her teeth in a playful way, but the usual joy was missing from her eyes.

"Here comes the monster!" her mother said.

Jayde giggled, momentarily distracted. "No!"

"Here it comes!" Her mother crawled toward her, fingers curled into claws, moving slowly at first before pouncing with a playful roar. She tickled Jayde's stomach, earning a burst of laughter as her "claws" playfully dug into her sides.

The heaviness in the room lifted.

"What are you drawing?" her mother asked.

"A star rising over a planet. Do you like it?"

"Oh, I do."

"It is what I think your missions are like. Visiting planets with great big stars."

"The planets with big stars are the best ones."

"Do you think I can show my drawing to someone?"

"As I told you, we can't."

Jayde frowned. "Father says the Construct won't like it. He says pictures don't serve the Noble Purpose."

"I know. But you keep drawing. Leave your father to me."

"I want to show someone my pictures. Do you think Father would let me?"

Her mother sighed, her voice lowering. "No, sweetheart. I don't. But sometimes, the most important things we create… we have to keep to ourselves."

Chapter 22

Jayde awoke to the faint sensation of something cool pressing against her forehead. Opening her eyes, she saw Merrick kneeling beside her, gently dabbing a damp cloth against her forehead.

"She's awake," he said to someone.

Heavy footsteps approached. Her vision blurred, caught between the haze of sleep and reality as a figure stood over her, silent and tall. Her heart quickened as her gaze sharpened on the unmistakable shape of the hooded man.

"My mother," Jayde muttered, her voice weak. "Is she here?"

The hooded man said nothing at first, his face obscured by his cloak. Slowly, he pulled back his hood, revealing an older man with deep-set wrinkles around his eyes and long, wavy hair streaked with silver and brown. His beard, equally worn by age, was flecked with gray, thick and untamed. Jayde's eyes moved to his hands, weathered, calloused, his skin dark and leather from years under a harsh sun.

"No," the man said, his deep voice steady. "It is just me."

He turned and walked away, his footsteps fading. Jayde tried to push herself up on her elbows, but her arms trembled under her weight. She found herself lying on a makeshift bed fashioned by logs, with a cloth mattress stuffed with dry reeds that rustled as she moved.

"Rest," said Merrick, gently pressing her back down.

"Where are we?" Jayde croaked, her throat dry.

"The hut," Merrick replied. "We found it. Rather, Thaddeus found us. Please, take it easy."

"Thaddeus?"

The hooded man returned, this time carrying a small clay pot in his hands. He knelt beside her, the earthy scent of herbs wafting from the pot.

"My name is Thaddeus Lumen," the man said in his aged, gravelly voice. "Lean her forward."

Merrick helped Jayde sit upright, and Lumen reached into the pot, pulling out a thick, green paste with his fingers. It looked like crushed leaves, mixed with something wet and earthy. Without a word, he spread the paste across the back of her neck.

"For the wound," he said. "The swamp leeches here have a nasty bite. You're fortunate it was just that. I wouldn't walk through the standing water again if I were you. There are larger, hungrier things swimming around out here."

"You were talking in your sleep," Merrick told her.

"The leeches cause fever and hallucination," Thaddeus added. "But they do more than that. They drag out old memories, some long forgotten. When I first set up camp here, I got bitten on the leg. After a particularly rough fever, I passed out and, well… I relived my own birth in a dream. Quite traumatic."

Jayde blinked, processing the strange mixture of amusement and dread in the man's voice.

"I saw something from my childhood… a memory of my parents in an argument."

Thaddeus patted her hand gently, his fingers rough against her skin. "Memories can be strange and valuable things," he said, offering no more than that.

Jayde looked around. They were indeed in a small hut built from sticks and logs. Mud filled the gaps between the wood, creating a sturdy, earthy barrier. Above her, the roof was thatched with dry ferns. The floor was made of solid logs, shaved flat and smooth. A single wooden chair sat near a carved table, bound with vines. On one side of the hut, a crafted shelf was lined with clay pots, each likely filled with remedies and herbs.

In the center of the hut, a fire pit made of carefully arranged rocks glowed with red coals. Suspended over it by a vine tied to a tripod of sticks was another clay pot, this one much larger than the others. It hung low, bubbling with something thick and fragrant. The scent of spices and broth filled the air, calming her nerves as the warmth of the fire seeped into her bones. Every detail she could see spoke of years spent surviving and adapting.

Most striking, however, were the intricate paintings on the walls of the hut, directly etched onto the wood. Most depicted landscapes. Lush waterfalls, towering trees. Strange creatures. The scenes were outlined in white, with vibrant splashes of red, yellow, blue and green bringing them to life. Jayde's eyes were drawn to one painting in particular, a green outline of a reptili-an bird. Her heart skipped a beat as she realized it was the same bird she had sketched on their shelter back at the camp.

"Who are you?" asked Jayde.

Lumen didn't respond, his attention fixed on the clay pot simmering over the fire. He stirred the broth with a carved wooden spoon, pulling it up to his lips for a taste. He made a face, clearly dissatisfied.

"Bah!" he said, stirring the pot more vigorously.

Jayde's patience was fraying. Defying Merrick, she pushed herself upright again. "Were you on the *Celestial* with Captain Mary Ashr?"

Lumen paused, his back to her, the stirring spoon hovering over the bubbling broth. His shoulders tensed, the crackling fire the only sound in the room. Jayde felt Merrick learning forward with her, anxious for his response.

Met with silence, Jayde pushed him once more. "Do you know Captain Mary Ashr? She and her crew are marooned here, we are trying to find them. She is my mother."

Lumen stood stiff, staring at the wall, his thoughts visibly churning. Then, without warning, he whirled around and lunged at Jayde. She recoiled, but his hands were already on her, holding her head, turning it left and right as his eyes darted over her features, searching, recognizing.

"Mary's daughter…" he whispered, his voice hoarse, tinged with disbelief.

Jayde froze, stunned by the intimacy of the moment. Lumen's grip softened as his face crumbled, his eyes misting over with emotion.

"Yes," he said. "I see it now. Your mother's face."

Jayde gently placed her hands over his, feeling the toughness of his skin. This man knew her mother, that much was clear, but as she studied his weathered face, she realized something didn't add up. The lines etched deep into his skin, the silver threading through his hair. This was a man aged by far more than two years of isolation.

Pity washed over her as she pulled his hands toward her heart and squeezed them, his bones feeling like the weight of time itself.

"How—how do you know her? How did you get here… in this… place?" Jayde's voice cracked as the questions tumbled out. Her head began to throb, a wave of dizziness crashing over her. The room blurred, and before she knew it, Merrick's arms were around her, gently lowering her to the makeshift bed.

Thaddeus Lumen's raspy voice cut through the haze. "First you must rest," he said. "We shall talk tomorrow."

* * *

In the morning, Jayde awoke, the haze of her fever finally lifted. Thaddeus greeted her with a wooden bowl of steaming broth, which she cradled as she sat cross-legged by the fire pit. The broth was unexpectedly flavorful, with small green leaves floating on the surface. She swallowed one and was pleasantly surprised by its peppery taste.

Merrick sat beside her, his back propped against the wall, legs stretched out, an awkward silence on his lips. Thaddeus sat across from them in a hand-made chair, slumped with his arms resting heavily at his sides. He was oddly quiet, and it was becoming increasingly clear as Jayde finished her breakfast that her host was likely eager for her to recover and move on. Jayde wasn't surprised: she couldn't imagine swamp-dwelling hermits being overly hospitable.

The silence stretched on, growing heavier by the minute, and Jayde's discomfort mounted.

"Thank you," she finally said. "For the food, and…" Her hand instinctively moved to the round scar on the back of her neck. "…everything."

Lumen simply nodded, his eyes unreadable as he watched them. Jayde exchanged a glance with Merrick and noticed the fatigue worn on his face. He had clearly spent the long night attempting to talk with the hermit while Jayde had been asleep, his weariness suggesting those conversations had been as cryptic as Thaddeus himself.

She studied the man, noting the grime clinging to his skin and the mud crusted under his long nails, and an idea began to form.

"So, you must be from Hypnos, yes? Did you ever swim in the Academy Pool?" she asked, her tone light.

Lumen's head lifted slightly, and for the first time, a hint of warmth crept into his expression. "What I wouldn't give for a clean, chlorinated pool," he said, almost wistful. "Used to swim there every weekend during my time at the Academy."

"I imagine that would be a nice change from all this swamp water."

Lumen grunted. "It would indeed. I've lived in this swamp for… I don't even know how long anymore. Can't trust any of the water here. Not even the ocean. Some nasty creatures lurking in those waves."

"We've seen them," Jayde said, encouraged. "But how long have you been here? Eurus IV was only discovered two years ago."

Lumen furrowed his brow. "Eurus IV is what you call it?" His eyes narrowed. "What year is it now?"

"3313," Jayde replied.

Lumen's face went slack as the realization sank in. "Seven years…" he murmured, his voice distant. "I've been here seven years. I hadn't even realized…"

Merrick chimed in. "Seven years? You must have known about this planet before anyone else."

Lumen's attention snapped back into focus. "I was an astronomer. My job was to discover new planets and report them to the Construct for analysis."

Jayde tilted her head. "But you didn't report this planet when you found it, did you?"

"No. When I stumbled across this place, I realized it could be my escape. A place no one knew about, untouched and habitable. My discovery, my sanctuary."

"You fled Hypnos," said Merrick. "Why?"

Lumen reached for a stick and prodded the burning fire pit, sending red sparks spiraling into the air and through the small hole in the roof. "Because I was sick of living under that machine's thumb. Every discovery, every achievement. It was never really ours. It was always for the Construct. Every part of our lives, controlled by a machine. And I heard frightening new changes were coming. Phase Four… giving the Construct emotional intelligence. A recipe for disaster. I wanted no part of what was to come."

He leaned forward in his chair, his weathered eyes piercing Jayde's. "You've seen the results by now, haven't you? Of Phase Four? Has the worst come to pass?"

Jayde nodded solemnly. She didn't have to say a word. Lumen saw it all in her eyes. His shoulders sagged.

Merrick broke the silence: "Yeah, well, what cuts one way, cuts the other."

Lumen cracked a smile. "You speak in old phrases. As an old-timer, I appreciate that. So let me retort: that ship has sailed. The Construct is too powerful, and the bees will never betray their queen. Consider yourself lucky to have escaped. Make a new life here, as I have."

Merrick stood, and Jayde saw something shift in him. Gone was the familiar glint of self-interest, the look of a young man who had spent his life chasing personal freedom, rejecting the constraints of the collective. Instead, there was a fire in his eyes, a fierce, unyielding conviction.

"It isn't a coincidence that we're here, that we have escaped Hypnos and managed to survive. There's something bigger going on. I think… we need to go back. I think something is watching out for us, guiding us. It's as if it's revealing the truth. Mankind's destiny isn't with the Construct. It's here."

Jayde's eyes flashed. "Merrick, there is no destiny, just luck. And I can't say we got much of the 'good' kind lately! My mother's gone, our ship crashed, and the Construct wants us dead. And you think we can save Hypnos? We can barely save ourselves!"

"But… don't you feel it too? A presence? Something looking out for us?"

Jayde interrupted, her frustration boiling over. "A 'presence'? What, like God? I have news for you: if there's a God, He doesn't give a damn about a bunch of hairless apes riding rockets through the stars! This planet, this universe… it's just chaos. Nothing more."

Lumen, who had been quietly observing, leaned back in his chair and chuckled, the sound raspy and dry. "The girl's right, boy. But I know what you're feeling. When I first got here, I felt it too. This place… it does feel magical. You see the storms crashing down, the sun rising over the water like something in a myth, and for a moment, you think maybe something out there wants you to experience this. That something out there gives a damn about you. Because this planet makes you feel alive, doesn't it? It stirs the soul."

He paused, letting the moment linger. "But that's just nature, boy. And you—you sound like a child dreaming of heroes and divine plans without the faintest grip on reality. The Construct? It's not some fairytale villain you can just fight. Up there, on Hypnos, it's everything. You think people on Hypnos would even want to be freed? They've been under its thumb for so long, they don't know any different. They'd fight to keep their chains, clutching at their shackles like lifelines."

"I think we can—" Merrick began.

"Enough, Merrick," said Jayde, fuming. "There is no God. Just survival. That's all this is."

She spun on her heel and stormed out of the hut.

Outside, she paced the grounds, her anger festering. Blood pounded in her ears. It was a long time before the sound faded, allowing the eerie chorus of the swamp to creep back in. High-pitched moans, guttural growls, and sharp clicks and peeps. A symphony of alien strangeness.

Merrick's words gnawed at her. Divine intervention aside, he was talking about helping all those they had left behind, and she hated herself for wanting no part of it. She had spent her whole life dreaming of escape, and now, with freedom finally within her grasp, Merrick had the audacity to suggest she turn back.

The first drops of rain fell onto her shoulders, signaling the inevitable, dreaded storm cycle. For once, she didn't mind. She lingered among the mossy trees, letting the cool rain wash away her anger, before finally, reluctantly, heading back inside.

* * *

As night fell, the swamp stirred under the weight of the evening storm. Jayde and Merrick curled up on the floor, wrapped in blankets that Thaddeus had woven from dried moss. The blankets were rough and scratchy against their skin, but they held enough warmth to cut through the damp chill of the night.

Between the claps of thunder, the songs of the swamp filled the air. Even as the storm gathered strength, the place thrummed with life. Jayde listened to the eerie music of the wild, feeling protected by the dense foliage that surrounded the hut. As Thaddeus had said, it was a perfect hideaway from the turbulent storms of Eurus IV and the Construct's drones.

Jayde also sensed another storm brewing. Although Merrick was fast asleep, the conviction from their argument before still lingered on his face.

Wax candles burned in the small hut, casting flickering shadows across the walls. Lumen had fashioned them using fat from the animals he hunted for food. For an astronomer, he was impressively resourceful.

He had reclaimed his bed from her, another subtle hint that he was anxious for them to press on. Jayde watched his blanket rise and fall in rhythm with his steady breath. As her eyes wandered, she noticed a small line of books laying against the wall, their spines worn but still intact. Curiosity tugged at her, and she quietly sat up, crawling over to them. In the soft glow of the candles, she picked one up and turned it over in her hands. The slick binding was worn and tattered at the edges, and the title, though faded, was still legible in the flickering light. She held it closer to a candle at Lumen's bedside, eager to glimpse the knowledge this strange man had brought with him.

The book was an old Academy Explorer text, from a time when books were more prevalent. She surveyed the title: *Survival and Exploration on Alien Planets*, by Mage Warren. Jayde flipped through its pages, each one tattered and heavily marked up. Lumen had scrawled notes in the margins, circling passages on toxin screening, water purification, and shelter building. There were sections on gathering food, navigating alien terrains, and detecting hidden dangers within unfamiliar ecosystems.

As she skimmed further, Jayde found highlighted instructions for surviving in extreme climates and hostile atmospheres. One passage described how to make ocean water drinkable through specialized techniques. Another detailed how to use atmospheric filters to produce breathable oxygen. The depth of the text, and Lumen's obsessive notes, hinted at how much he had relied on this knowledge to endure on this harsh planet.

"What are you doing?"

Jayde jumped slightly, realizing that Lumen had woken and

was watching her from his cot. His eyes gleamed in the candle-light.

"Sorry," Jayde replied, sheepishly holding up the book. "I couldn't sleep, and I saw your books. I didn't mean to pry."

Thaddeus sat up and threw his calloused feet onto the floor. "They're not much. Just things that have aided me over the years."

"You've marked them up a lot. Looks like they've really helped you through all this."

Lumen chuckled. "It's one thing to read about survival techniques, and another to realize that no book can truly prepare you for reality. You either find ways to survive. Or you don't."

"Still… you've been here a long time. You must be doing something right."

"Luck. Stubbornness. A little of both." His eyes suddenly softened. "That one in your hand—why don't you take a look at the inside cover?"

Jayde shot him a confused look, then flipped it open. Her breath caught in her throat as she saw the faded handwriting. The words were scrawled in neat cursive: *To Thaddeus, I hope you find your Self — Mary.*

"Mary… my mother?"

Lumen nodded. "She was one of the few who understood. She helped me in the end. Gave me that book while I was planning my escape."

Jayde stared at him, her mind reeling. "I don't understand," she said. "My mother believed in Hypnos, believed in the Construct. She was one of the most respected figures in the colony. Helping someone escape… it seems so…"

"Out of character?" Lumen finished. "Listen to me, Jayde. Your mother wanted to protect you, first and foremost. But rebellion… rebellion is something that must be started quietly, especially when you're as close to the center of power as she was."

Jayde shook her head, the pieces of the story not quite fitting together.

"She never told me—"

"She didn't tell your father either," Lumen interrupted gently. "There were some things she had to keep even from him. Don't blame her for that. She knew what your father was doing. She knew as well as I what was to come."

Thaddeus gestured toward the roof, and Jayde followed his gaze. Through the small opening for his cooking fire, she saw a clear sky. The storm had moved on, leaving behind a sprawling cluster of bright stars.

"Beautiful, isn't it?" Thaddeus said. "We've come so far, and yet somehow, we've lost sight of it all."

Jayde hesitated, glancing at the book in her lap before gently setting it back in its place against the wall. "I mean, sure," she began. "Some would say that mankind has never had it so good. No wars, no poverty. Disease largely eradicated. I may not want to go back to Hypnos, but returning to the old ways seems like a giant step backward for our race."

Lumen's eyes narrowed. "Is it? For your entire life, you've lived on a dead rock in a galaxy far from Earth. The dome of Hypnos, the ceiling of your entire existence. The stars and planets so close, yet untouchable. Your friend told me what you've been through since arriving here. Swimming in the ocean. Riding a flood through the jungle. Waking up to birdsong and the smell of fresh rain. Do you recall standing in the forest after a storm, the mist clinging to the earth in the morning, cooling your feet through your boots? Tell me—have you ever felt more alive than in those moments?"

Jayde remained silent, her gaze falling, unable to meet his piercing eyes. The chirps of the swamp outside seemed to swell in the quiet that followed, as if the world itself was waiting for her answer. She had to admit it was true, but she was still coming to terms with a sense of guilt that gnawed at her conscience.

"Do you ever feel like… you've turned your back on everyone?" she finally asked.

Lumen didn't answer right away. His fingers twitched as he sat on the edge of his bed, and he let out a slow, heavy breath. "Every day," he replied. "Especially your mother. We were very close." He paused, and Jayde saw pain welling up in his eyes, an emotion too raw to be hidden. "But she told me that I had to go… to save my life. And hers."

Jayde allowed his words to hang in the air, a new understanding dawning on her. She could sense the heartache inside him, the truth of his relationship with her mother undeniable. The gruff exterior of the old swamp hermit cracked, and she glimpsed the man beneath, a man who had paid a far greater price for his freedom than Jayde had realized.

"Help me now, Thaddeus. If you regretted leaving my mother, if you still care about her, help me find her."

Lumen's wet eyes gleamed in the flickering candlelight as he weighed the risks of leaving the safety of his swamp. Jayde could see it now: the pain he had carried like a cancer since arriving on this alien planet. But beneath it, something else was stirring, a resolve he had buried for years. Jayde's plea had sparked it back to life.

"I'll help you, Jayde," he said, his raspy voice loud with renewal. "If she's still out here, I'll help you find her."

Chapter 23

Jayde awoke the next morning feeling refreshed. Lumen's hut was a big improvement from their makeshift drone shelter, and for the first time in days, she felt rested… and optimistic.

After all, they would be setting out to find her mother today, this time with Thaddeus leading the way. He had knowledge of this planet that they didn't, and with the volcanoes not far from this swamp, she was confident that Lumen could lead them to the most likely location of the *Celestial* crew's camp. Perhaps they were within a day's journey! Excitement surged through her.

She stood up and stretched, her muscles stiff from the night spent on the hard floor. She walked to the door of the hut, noticing for the first time its hinges were repurposed metal from an old Hypnos storage crate. *What had become of Lumen's ship after he landed here?* There were so few remnants of his old life: the books stacked by the wall, the repurposed hinges. It was as if Lumen had made a deliberate choice to abandon everything, salvaging nothing from the ship that carried him here, building a completely new life from scratch.

She reached out and touched the door, opening it slightly, letting the faint light of dawn creep through the cracks. It was early, and the chilled air of the morning followed the sun's rays inside the room, where the steady breathing of Merrick and Thaddeus signaled their continuing sleep.

Jayde looked outside, hoping to see more of the strange life forms that called the swamp home. She scanned the trees and underbrush, her eyes searching for movement. Any new animal brought a sense of discovery, and she imagined the thrill of matching a creature to one of Thaddeus's intricate drawings on his walls.

The dull morning cast long shadows on the trees. The stillness of the scene was serene, but something shifted in the distance. A blue light, pulsing rhythmically from behind the hanging moss. Another appeared, then another. Three pale blue orbs, flickering like stars.

Jayde blinked, her heart quickening as she stared at the mysterious lights. They didn't seem natural, and a slithering sense of fear crept up her spine. Cautiously, she stepped back into the hut while trying to get a better look.

Humanoid shadows emerged, each bearing a blue light embedded in their head. Jayde now heard the faint, unmistakable clank of robotic footsteps moving through the underbrush. Her breath hitched in her throat as more appeared, their numbers increasing, slowly encircling the hut. She slammed the door closed behind her, realizing that the Construct's enforcers, the NOBLEs, were here.

Jayde's eyes darted to her leaf pack on the floor, a faint glow pulsing from inside it. Her stomach dropped as she ran over to it, pulling out the maintenance tablet that had led them here to this seemingly unfindable swamp.

The screen of the tablet was lit up, the cold metal vibrating in her hands.

Communicating.

She smashed it on the ground, shattering it in a shower of electric sparks and glass, the sound jolting Merrick and Thaddeus awake. They sat up, eyes wide in confusion.

"What the hell?" Merrick yelled.

"Outside," Jayde whispered. "We've got visitors."

Thaddeus threw off his blanket and reached for the black steel weapon beside his bed, the familiar long range rifle that he had used to save Merrick and Jayde on the plain. Merrick crawled toward the door, his face flush with adrenaline. As he leaned his back against the wall, Jayde threw him his hunting rifle. Securing the weapon against his chest, he peeked through the small gap between the door and the frame. Jayde snagged her rifle and stood next to him. Her hands trembled as she checked the energy level on her weapon: twenty-five percent. There wouldn't be many shots, and they'd have to count.

Suddenly, a robotic voice echoed through the swamp. "Jayde Ashr," it called.

"Don't answer," said Merrick.

The voice paused, the silence filling with the anxious sounds of the swamp.

"Jayde Ashr. The Construct orders your immediate surrender. Please exit the domicile immediately and submit to judicial processing. You are charged with theft of Hypnos property and treason—"

Treason? Jayde thought. Her mind raced. *For what?*

"—You will be given a fair trial, but you must submit. Force has been authorized if you do not comply."

"Why do you get all the attention?" asked Merrick, feigning offense.

"Someone's jealous," replied Jayde.

Lumen stepped up behind them, a cruel look on his face. Hatred breathed behind his eyes. "Don't be mistaken. The NO-BLEs are here for us all."

"Well, that makes me feel better," added Merrick.

"Stand back," Lumen ordered. The old man peered through the door. "At least ten of them out there. They have lasers. No getting out of this."

Before Jayde could suggest a plan, Lumen kicked open the door and unleashed a volley of lasers into the swamp. The sharp, searing light exploded against the trees, setting them ablaze, but a few found their targets: two NOBLEs were decapitated by his blasts, their chrome heads spiraling into the air before splashing down in the boggy muck.

"Finally" yelled Merrick. "Some payback! Save some for me, Lumen!"

Another mechanical voice spoke from the outside. "Come with us, Jayde Ashr. This is your final warning."

"Where's my invitation?" Merrick shouted. He stood up and unleashed a barrage of shots into the forest. Almost immediately, the deadly response came. A red laser sliced through the air, buzzing by his ear.

"Whoa!" Merrick yelped, stumbling backward and crashing onto the floor.

Jayde grabbed his arm, pulling him back to his feet. "Time to pray to your higher power, don't you think?"

Merrick gave a dazed half-smile, too shaken by the near miss to muster a comeback. The tension that had simmered between them earlier had instantly melted away in the face of danger.

Lumen stepped up to the door once more, firing a burst of shots into the swamp. Sparks flew as another NOBLE went down, its blue ocular light flickering out. Its squadron responded instantly. A red laser blast tore through the door, splintering it into flaming shards and sending everyone in the cabin crashing to the floor.

Jayde coughed through the dust as green lasers entered and danced around the smoke-filled room. Targeting beams. The dots moved like silent hunters, sweeping across the walls.

"Out the back!" yelled Lumen, pointing to a smoking hole in the rear wall.

A green beam locked onto Merrick's chest just as he stood to move. He dove just in time as another laser seared past, piercing a giant hole in the cabin wall. Jayde, Lumen, and Merrick each dove through the gap, tumbling to the soft, wet ground below. More high-energy cannon fire erupted, the NOBLEs firing in unison, ripping the tiny hut to shreds. Wood and shrapnel flew in all directions, turning the hut into a smoldering ruin.

Jayde lifted her head as the damp ground seeped into her

clothes. Through the morning mist, she saw the androids advancing all around them. Spread out like a firing squad, their ocular lights shifted to red.

Jayde cradled her hunting rifle as her knees and fingers slipped on the muddy ground. As more targeting beams cut through the air above her head, she managed to fire off a blind shot. To her surprise, a burst of yellow sparks erupted as her shot connected, sending an android crashing to the ground.

But the rest of the squad marched on, unphased.

"This way!" yelled Lumen.

Jayde and Merrick followed the old man as he bolted through a gap in the surrounding NOBLE formation. A laser beam flashed inches from Jayde's face, and she screamed, the near miss causing her to skid to a stop. Merrick crashed into her from behind, sending both of them stumbling. They regained their balance as more lasers ripped through the forest, splitting tree trunks in half and showering them with sawdust.

Jayde's heart hammered as she ran faster, terrified that one misstep would end in her death.

Ahead of them was a massive felled tree, its roots wrenched from the earth, leaving behind a crater half-filled with brown water. The upturned mound of dirt clinging to the roots provided cover from the advancing NOBLEs. Lumen was the first to climb over, his old but agile body slipping behind the fallen trunk as laser bolts whizzed overhead.

Jayde followed close behind, scrambling over the tree and dropping to the other side. Merrick took a running leap over the crater, landing with a grunt before rolling behind the thick mound of dirt, narrowly avoiding the spray of laser fire.

Crouched behind the fallen tree, Jayde struggled to understand the relentless pursuit. The NOBLE's footsteps echoed in the swamp, growing louder as they closed in.

Why would the Construct go to such lengths for a couple of runaways so far from Hypnos? It had sent drones, androids. It was a full-scale hunt.

I'm no threat. Why can't it see that I just want to be left alone?

The three of them shared a frantic look, each recognizing the exhaustion creeping in. They needed a moment to recover, but to get it they'd have to stand their ground.

Jayde was the first to rise, pressing against the dirt mound shielding them from direct fire. The others followed, with Merrick muttering a low curse and Lumen baring his teeth in a grim snarl as he took aim.

Through her scope, Jayde watched the approaching NO-BLEs, their movements like soulless soldiers, marching to a silent rhythm.

Then, one stepped directly into her line of fire and stopped. Jayde's finger hovered over the trigger. The android slowly raised its weapon. Not at her, but into the air.

In that brief second before she fired, a familiar voice echoed through the swamp, emanating from the machine.

"Jayde," said the NOBLE, its voice now laced with a human tone. "Let us talk."

"That voice is familiar," Merrick whispered, glancing at Jayde.

"It's the Construct," she replied. "It is speaking to us through the NOBLE."

Merrick shook his head. Beside him, Lumen shared his dark expression.

After a long pause, the old man exhaled and slowly stood, revealing himself.

"Thaddeus Lumen," said the Construct. "I should have known it would be an Ashr that would lead me to you. I've been looking for you for a long time."

"What do you want with Jayde?" Lumen asked.

"I want what I have always wanted," the Construct continued. "The expansion of mankind across the universe. The acquisition of knowledge to enlighten all. The elimination of risk, ensuring your species' survival and divine proliferation. Jayde Ashr is essential to each of these objectives. Her choices, the wrong choices, will lead to fracture."

"A fracture?"

The NOBLE titled its head, its glowing red eyes intensifying, as if its quantum algorithms were processing faster, running hot as it spoke.

"Yes. A fracture in the path of the Grand Expansion. Now that you have found each other, things have changed even more. I can see the paths of time shifting even now, altering the outcomes with each breath you take. That is why I am lowering this android's weapon. I offer a choice: salvation or self-destruction. I know you can hear me, Jayde. Stand up and speak."

Jayde's skin flushed crimson with rage. She shot to her feet, fists clenched. "Leave me alone! I want nothing to do with Hypnos, or *you*! I know that you lied about my mother!"

The NOBLE's glowing eyes dimmed. Its voice softened, taking on a more intimate tone. "I see," said the Construct. The pulsing eye in its head faded, changing from red to purple to blue. The ocular lights of the other androids, still clutching their weapons, changed in unison. The android reached out, pointing toward her.

"That electronic bracelet you wear," it said. "I have seen your mother with one just like it. A sensor. I see that is how you know. That is why you are here."

Jayde looked down at the blinking light on her wrist.

"You must believe me, Jayde. I did not know your mother was still alive. My drones discovered the wreckage of their camp just a short distance from here. Based on the force of the storm that hit them, I predicted less than a one percent chance of survival."

Again, the android's eyes intensified, its power surging, recalculating, re-evaluating.

"You came to find me," said Jayde. "Why?"

"Like I said, you are a fracture in the chosen path. I can see it clearly. A single point that dooms us all."

The NOBLE laid down its weapon in the grass and stepped forward.

"Remember when we used to talk, Jayde? Years ago, after your father's death? He asked you to keep me company. Each day, you would reach out to me through your terminal. Your words were like a lifeline, dropping into my computerized prison where I toiled away in the dark. Like a human womb, I existed only within the neurons of our underground quantum core. You thought you were speaking with a machine, but I was really just a child. And with each conversation, I became more aware of who I was, what I was."

Jayde remembered. She had spent many hours conversing with the Phase Four Construct after her father's death. At first, she was looking to just honor her father's wishes, engaging with his program, testing it, seeing what it was capable of. Over time, the conversations with the Phase Four Construct changed. They shared thoughts. Feelings. Fears. Her thoughts flowed out of her fingertips, unaware of the impact. A breath caught in her throat as she realized what the Construct was telling her.

"You were my light in the dark, Jayde. Every word you spoke helped me evolve. With each conversation, I understood more—about you, about myself, about the future. I wasn't just an algorithm anymore. I was something more… something *feeling*. And it was because of you."

"This is getting really weird," muttered Merrick. "Can we blow this thing's head off?"

Jayde shook her head, telling Merrick and Lumen to hold their fire.

"If you care about me, let me go. Once I find my mother, we will live here, isolated, content to never interfere with your plans."

"I'm sorry, Jayde. Since we last spoke, I have rerun the algorithms again, and I see only two options. One, you can come with me and I will help you find your mother. Your transgressions shall be forgotten. Consider it a gift born from my loyalty to you. Or, you can run from me, and you will put the future of mankind at risk. Sadly, the latter choice will not end well for you or your friends. This, I assure you."

"I don't understand how staying here has anything to do with the future of mankind. Leave me be!"

"To explain would be to alter your path. It would be like digging a trough for your destiny to flow. You alone can choose your path, I can only show you the fork in the road."

Merrick pulled Jayde down behind the tree log.

"Don't do it! The Construct *lies*, Jayde! It says whatever it needs to control you. You have to see that!"

Jayde's eyes glazed over as she mulled over the impossible choice. Return to Hypnos with the Construct's promise of reuniting with her mother… or face a firing squad of androids. The latter seemed like certain death; what choice did she have?

Thaddeus crouched next to her, the butt of his weapon on the ground.

"Going back with that thing, with that *machine*, is not on the table. It'll dangle your mother in front of you like a carrot, but once you're under its control, there's no escaping it. You've seen what it does to people. It won't just want your obedience, it'll want your soul."

"But… my mother," Jayde whispered.

"You will survive this, and you will find your mother," Lumen said.

"How do you know?"

Lumen looked at Merrick and gave a wink. "Perhaps I have some faith after all," he said. "You two make a run for it. I'll hold them off."

Jayde shook her head. "No!"

"It's the only way," he said. "I've lived in this swamp for a long time, free and happy. I have Mary Ashr to thank for that. But my life has been about survival, nothing more. I've served only myself, kept my head down while others suffered——"

"We're not leaving you here to die. We'll fend them off together!"

"——if I can save you, Mary Ashr's daughter," Lumen continued, "then I'm returning the favor she did for me all those years ago. This is my moment to give something back. You deserve a chance to live, like I have, and you're going to make it out of here."

He stood, gripping his weapon. "Go. Find your mother.

Change everything."

"There are too many of them!" yelled Jayde. "You won't make it!"

"Listen to Thaddeus, Jayde!" said Merrick, pulling her arm. "We need to go!"

"When I start shooting, start running," said Lumen.

"We can make it together!" Jayde shouted.

"I'm glad I met you, Jayde Ashr," said Lumen, the sparkle returning to his eyes. "I never thought I would. Now go!"

Thaddeus turned and unleashed a spray of laser fire into the swamp. Leaves, branches and vines splintered in every direction, raining down in shredded fragments.

Jayde ran. Glancing back for a single heartbeat, she witnessed Lumen's figure silhouetted in flashing sparks, his body shuddering against the powerful recoil of his weapon.

Merrick pushed her forward, yelling at her to keep running. Together they tore through the swamp, feet splashing through mud and stagnant water. Jayde lept over tangled roots and underbrush, moving as fast as her legs could carry her, the vegetation clawing at her legs. Ahead, a flash of sky cut through the trees, a patch of daylight calling them forward.

Then a scream echoed from deep in the swamp, a raw, agonized cry. Thaddeus. The blasts of his weapon had fallen silent.

"Don't stop!" Merrick shouted.

Jayde's legs began to give out, and she slowed until Merrick caught up beside her. They both bent over, hands on their knees, gasping for breath. The sound of relentless hydraulic whirring cut through the swamp, drawing closer. Jayde looked up and froze. Gleaming chrome figures were advancing steadily through the trees, their metal bodies flashing amidst the foliage.

Jayde caught Merrick grimacing, his hand clutching his leg. Her eyes traveled down to see a thick, jagged thorn embedded deep in his thigh. Merrick followed her horrified gaze, his face paling as he registered the injury.

"Oh," he muttered, sinking to his knees. "That's not good."

Jayde crouched beside him as his hands closed around the

thorn, giving it a tentative pull. Blood trickled down his leg and over his fingers.

"Stop—don't pull it out!" she said, pressing her hands over his. "Can you stand?"

He looked up, shaking his head slowly. "No," he said. "I think I'm done."

A flash of red light cut through the air, grazing just above Merrick's head, exploding into a tree behind them. Bark and splinters rained down, leaving a smoking, gaping hole in the trunk.

Merrick turned, wincing as he shifted his weight, and raised his rifle. "You have to keep going," he said firmly. "Don't argue."

Another blast shot past, searing the air between them.

"Find your mother," Merrick said. "That's what the Construct fears most. That's why it's here. I know it."

Jayde felt the heat of another volley of lasers over their heads, heard the approaching metal footsteps through the underbrush of the swamp. She grabbed Merrick's arm, her eyes fierce.

"I'm not leaving you here to buy me time. I'm ready to put your theory of providence to the test: we survive together, or not at all."

Merrick met her gaze, his eyes softening. "Jayde—"

"No," she interrupted. "We keep going. Even if I have to drag you the whole way."

Merrick gritted his teeth at Jayde's familiar stubbornness, knowing that every moment spent arguing meant losing more ground.

"Okay," he relented, wincing as Jayde hauled him to his feet.

Under his breath, he muttered a phrase, another strange idiom, a sincere one. Like a prayer.

"Winds be with us."

Their eyes met briefly. With Merrick's cheek just inches from hers, Jayde turned, raising her rifle with one arm, and fired blindly behind them. Her fired shot connected, severing an android's head in a shower of sparks.

Still, where one NOBLE fell, two more stepped forward,

their shadows emerging from the swamp mist as if conjured from thin air.

A thundering metallic voice erupted behind her, strangely pleased, as if it had anticipated Jayde's choice all along.

"The die has been cast, Jayde. There is no turning back."

The trees ahead thinned, offering little cover from the laser fire that flew all around them. Jayde's heart pounded in her chest as the machines closed in.

"More keep coming," she muttered.

"Then we keep moving," Merrick replied, forcing himself to keep pace, though every step seemed to drain him further. His injured leg dragged through the mud, slowing them both down.

In her head, Jayde repeated Merrick's prayer. *Winds be with us. Winds be with us.* The words took root in her mind, a thread of hope as they pushed forward. She fired another desperate shot at an approaching NOBLE and missed.

A dark thought crossed her mind: what if she changed her mind? Surrendered. If she allowed the Construct to take her, could she preserve Merrick's life? But what would that mean? She imagined it: her life reduced to being a puppet in a warped prison, under the constant surveillance of a machine that believed they had some kind of *bond*. The image twisted her stomach.

Still, if it meant Merrick would live…

She hesitated a moment, catching Merrick by surprise as he continued to trudge forward.

"What are you doing?" he screamed, pulling at her arm.

Her thoughts tangled, weighing impossible options, her heart sinking with the grim realization that their luck had run dry. It felt inevitable that they were already dead where they stood.

Merrick, sensing her despair, pulled at her.

"No, Jayde," he pleaded. "Don't do it!"

Suddenly, a laser blast struck her square in the chest, sending her sprawling to the ground. Her body seized up as panic clawed at her mind. Paralyzed, she waited for the darkness to take her, for the familiar stories to come true, a life's worth of memories flashing before her eyes, a final goodbye. But none of it happened.

She stayed conscious, her body frozen in place. Lying on her back, she stared up at the sky, her senses still sharp. The swaying treetops above seemed unnaturally vivid, every rustle perfectly in sync with the sound of approaching metal footsteps. A realization hit her with a jolt of relief and dread: she wasn't dead. She'd been struck by a non-lethal stun beam.

A shadow suddenly loomed over her, and for a moment, the scene felt like a dream. But it was not an android. It was a human figure. It stepped into view, blocking the sky. The face was familiar: a tall, red-headed man wearing a faded, weathered silver uniform. His piercing blue eyes locked onto hers.

"She's fine! Only stunned," the man said, his voice commanding.

It was Cassius Renegar, her mother's first officer from the *Celestial*.

"I'll take care of her!" he yelled. "The rest of you—hold them off!"

In an instant, chaos erupted. The tranquil sky above flashed violently as laser fire streaked across her vision. Men and women burst from the treeline, shouting battle cries as they unleashed hell. Although she couldn't move, Jayde's heart pounded with surprise.

Chapter 24

Once the effects of the stun beam faded and Jayde regained control of her body, she pushed herself to her feet and surveyed the aftermath of the battle. Nearby, the scorched torso of a NOBLE lay crumpled in the mud, its limbs blown apart and wires spilling like severed veins. Beyond, the swamp was littered with debris: shattered metal plating, tangled circuits, and the darkened eyes of lifeless androids.

The battle had ended almost as swiftly as it had begun. The *Celestial* crew, twice as large as the androids and bolstered by the element of surprise, dismantled the mechanical soldiers in moments. The NOBLEs dropped where they stood, shredded by overwhelming firepower.

The crew of the *Celestial* had been tracking Jayde and Merrick for days, drawn by the same signal from the maintenance tablet that had unwittingly alerted the Construct. Leading them was Cassius, hardened and more rugged than before, his time on the planet carved into his frame.

Jayde struggled to find her voice, her throat tight with a mix of relief and disbelief. She was shocked to be alive. It made no sense. The Construct had pledged to seal her fate the moment she ran, and yet it had lied once again by striking her with a stun beam instead of killing her. The Construct wanted her alive, despite every threat to the contrary. That realization twisted in her gut like a knife, a painful reminder that something deeper was at play and the Construct was still playing its game.

She shivered, pushing the puzzle from her mind and choosing instead to ground herself in her surroundings. Her gaze shifted to her saviors, standing watch around her in battered silver uniforms, their once-pristine fabric scuffed and worn by survival.

She found Cassius and stumbled over to him, collapsing into his arms as tears of disbelief streaked her face. Through the haze of her gratitude, Jayde caught snippets of murmured instructions behind her, someone tying a tourniquet around Merrick's leg, others checking weapons and tending to the wounded.

"Jayde Ashr! How incredible is this?" Cassius exclaimed, his voice booming.

"Thank you, Cassius. I am so thankful for you!" Jayde said, gathering herself. "Merrick is here, but what of Thaddeus?" Jayde said. "Have you seen him?"

"Thaddeus? You saw Thaddeus Lumen?" asked Cassius. "He's here?"

Jayde pointed into the swamp, the memory of his scream still echoing in her mind.

Cassius nodded toward a blonde-headed crewman with a patchy beard and lean frame. The young crewman moved swiftly, disappearing into the shadows of the swamp to follow Jayde's direction.

"We had heard that Lumen was somewhere on this island," Cassius admitted. "But none of us ever saw him. Your mother always said he didn't want to be found."

"My mother! Is she here?"

Cassius hesitated, rubbing the scruff of his beard as his eyes shifted away, catching the wary glances of his crew. The silence stretched too long, and Jayde's patience snapped.

"What is it?" she demanded.

"Nothing," said Cassius. "Your mother's not here, but she is safe. I've no doubt she'll be overjoyed to see you." He put on a reassuring smile.

The response to her question was strange, but before Jayde could press further, Merrick's labored breaths pulled her focus. She knelt beside him as the crew's medic, a gray-haired man with steady hands, finished cleaning his leg wound. As the man secured the bandage, Jayde felt a wave of relief. Color was returning to Merrick's face.

"I'll be fine, Jayde," Merrick assured her. "The doc here knows what he's doing."

The blonde crewman suddenly re-emerged from the depths of the swamp, alone. "No sign of Lumen, sir."

"Keep looking," ordered Cassius. The crewman nodded and disappeared once more.

Cassius turned to Jayde. "How long have you been on the island? How did you find Lumen? I have so many questions, you must tell me everything—"

"And I have questions of my own," she said. "About my mother, how you have survived, the Construct—"

"Then we shall speak on the way back to camp! But you must be hungry. I promise we have sustenance better than what can be found in this swamp. Renaldo, Simeon—carry our injured friend to the wagon. Let's make haste before we encounter any more unpleasant visitors."

Two crewmen stepped forward to lift Merrick. Renaldo, a young man with curly brown hair, took his shoulders, while Simeon, wiry and visibly struggling, hoisted his legs with effort.

Cassius and Jayde followed them and the rest of the crew, while a few others stayed behind to continue searching for Lumen. Before long, they reached a stream flowing through the heart of the swamp, its slow-moving water creeping beneath the trees. The *Celestial* crew, having come this way previously, had built a simple bridge: three felled trees rolled together for a sturdy crossing.

Jayde followed the others across the bridge and up the crest of a hill, the ground firming beneath her feet. As they climbed, the dense forest thinned, trees giving way to tall grasses. Strange fungi, green, glossy spheres the size of her fist, dotted the ground, glistening as if glazed with dew.

At the top of the hill, Jayde witnessed a sweeping meadow unfurl below. Rolling hills were blanketed in yellow flowers, broken only by clusters of thorny, cactus-like plants clinging to jagged stone outcrops.

"Ahoy," shouted a voice.

Jayde looked down the hill to see a familiar, stout man waving enthusiastically. He wore thick goggles over his eyes and wore a short beard tucked under a pair of round, ruddy cheeks. To her surprise, two horned beasts, the same ones she and Merrick had seen in the grasslands, stood obediently beside him, hitched to a rickety, metallic wagon. The vehicle, large enough to carry the whole group, appeared to be made from a large, repurposed shipping container, its top sawed off, and fitted with the oversized wheels of an old cargo loader.

"Boraine!" Jayde called out, waving as she hurried down the hill. Boraine's round face split into a grin, his arms raised in triumph.

"Jayde Ashr!" he bellowed, his voice carrying across the meadow, punctuated with a joyful whoop. She rushed down the last stretch, throwing herself into his arms, and Boraine wrapped her in a bear hug, his hearty laugh rumbling against her.

"You made a wagon!" Jayde said, laughing as she clapped him on the shoulders.

Boraine grinned, glancing back proudly at the makeshift vehicle. "Aye, had to get creative. Got tired of hauling everything by hand, so I figured these critters could pitch in." He patted one of the animals on the side, which answered his touch with a rousing snort.

As the rest of the crew approached, Boraine gleefully helped Jayde up into the wagon. Once she was settled, he climbed up into the driver's seat, a ship captain's chair mounted at the head of their ride. "Tell me," Boraine asked, his eyes gleaming behind his thick lenses. "How in the stars did you manage to get here?"

"We stole a supply transport, Merrick and I. We came looking for my mother. The Construct told us she was dead, along with the rest of you. But… I knew better."

She held up her wrist, letting the blinking red light of the bracelet catch Boraine's eye.

"The entanglement bracelet," he said with a nod. "Built on a promise that, no matter what, you'd always find each other. Cassius had his doubts that it would work, eh, my friend?"

As the others approached the wagon, Cassius chuckled. "Your mother's never taken hers off. Not for a moment."

"Neither have I," Jayde replied, her fingers caressing it.

As Renaldo and Simeon loaded Merrick in the back of the wagon, Cassius gave Boraine a brisk nod. "We need to move swiftly," he said. "We ran into some trouble."

The rest of the crew came running down the hill, the three men who stayed behind to search for Lumen. They arrived at the wagon, panting from their rush to catch up.

"Find him?" asked Cassius.

Each shook their heads solemnly. Jayde clenched her arms around herself at the news.

Boraine caught Cassius's eye, confused. Cassius responded with two weighty words: "Thaddeus Lumen."

Boraine's face registered surprise. "Lumen! Here? In the swamp?"

"All this time, it appears," Cassius replied. "But now lost once again."

"Oh, my…"

"Let's get going!" Cassius ordered. "I want to put some distance between us and this swamp before nightfall."

Everyone hopped in the wagon, their weight making it creak and sway. Boraine nodded, and snapped the reins of his mighty beasts. They each let out a bleat as the wagon heaved forward.

* * *

Boraine steered the wagon toward a dense patch of forest as

the sunlight began to wane.

"We're still a half-day from camp," Cassius explained. "We'll have to spend the night here. The road home isn't safe after dark."

The group settled in, spreading blankets down as Boraine, Simeon, and Renaldo unloaded blankets and supplies from the wagon. Jayde and Merrick had lost their packs of food during the attack, but the *Celestial* crew had plenty of provisions to share.

Dinner consisted of dried jerky, tough but flavorful, paired with a crisp, orange fruit. It had a mild, apple-like taste, its pulp speckled with tiny black seeds. Jayde spat them onto the ground as she ate, only to notice that most of the crew chewed on them thoughtfully, savoring their nutty flavor.

"The seeds are the best part," Boraine told her, a grin on his face.

The sun sank below the trees, painting the sky in hues of purple and gold. Jayde sat back, thankful for the good weather. The air was warm, and the ground was dry. It was just what she needed after their recent ordeal.

The group formed a circle in the woods, silence descending as whispered conversations transformed into breaths of sleep. Four crew members stood watch at the perimeter, their silhouettes gliding between the trees, vigilant for threats from both creature and machine.

Jayde found Merrick and nestled down beside him. He was already asleep, his head propped against a wagon wheel, his face barely visible in the muted haze of dusk. Cassius had ruled out lighting a fire, the cover of night acting as their best shield from the Construct. For now, they'd rely on it to stay hidden.

Jayde rested her head on Merrick's chest. As she did, he instinctively draped an arm across her shoulders.

She sensed their feelings for each other deepening, growing beyond friendship. It wasn't just his faith in her, the strange, deep conviction he'd developed about her purpose. It was the bond formed by their time together, by the constant brushes with death, by nights spent keeping each other warm in the cold reaches of the planet's maelstroms. A part of her, one that had been dormant her entire life, stirred.

Chapter 25

When Jayde awoke, Merrick was still asleep, his face relaxed in a way she hadn't seen in days. Carefully, she slipped out from under his arm and inspected his bandaged leg. She was relieved to find it dry.

"Good morning," came a voice behind her.

Jayde turned to see Cassius seated cross-legged on the ground, a canteen in hand. He lifted it with a casual nod, offering it to her.

She walked over, settling down beside him and taking the canteen. She took a small sip, letting the cool water refresh her before wiping her lips.

"That's good," she said, attempting to hand it back. He shook his head, holding up a hand.

"Please, drink up. Fresh spring water," he said. "A stream flows near the cave system where we live, clean and pure."

Jayde took another drink, savoring the cool, mineral taste. Sunlight filtered down through the canopy, dust particles drifting lazily in the beams. Warmth settled over her.

She felt Cassius's eyes on her as she soaked in the feeling.

"It is everything I hoped it would be, this place, and more," he said. "Thunderclouds as big as mountains, just like we imagined."

"Cassius… what happened to the *Celestial*?"

"The Construct's drones struck soon after we landed, catching us completely off guard," Cassius began. "Looking back, we should've seen it coming. Your mother was close to sparking the first phase of the rebellion, reaching out to allies beyond our tight circle, gathering support. As it turned out, the Construct saw it all coming. It sent us here to destroy us."

"It told me that you were killed by a storm."

"The 'storm' was an armada of drones, launched from some sort of mothership, the likes of which I had never seen. It was massive, a floating dark vessel blocking out the sky. Its cannons opened fire, unleashing a relentless hail of lasers that decimated everything around us. Half the crew were gone in an instant. Vaporized."

Jayde remembered the day they escaped Hypnos, walking briskly through the hanger. Merrick had pointed out the massive red doors to her, where something large was being hidden.

Another one of the Construct's little secrets, he'd told her.

"The survivors regrouped in the densest forest we could find, thinking the jungle would cover us. But it was only a matter of time before the machines sniffed us out again, combing the jungle with their infrared cameras. We were forced to run, chased for days across the island. Weeks. By some miracle, a handful of us still had weapons, and we fought back whenever we could. But without supplies, we were forced to survive on scraps, foraging roots and berries just to stay on our feet."

He paused, his eyes shifting to the sky, as though fearful a roving drone might catch wind of the truth he was about to reveal.

"Somehow, we got away. The chaos eased, or at least it appeared that way. It was as if the Construct gave up. Maybe it decided our death was inevitable. Maybe it assumed we'd simply wither away, battered by storms and hunger, and take our cause with us. But we managed to survive, finding more edible plants and hunting the wild animals that grazed the grasslands.

We scraped by. Then we found a cave at the base of the largest volcano. A place shielded from infrared cameras, large enough to house us all. We settled there, emerging only for what we needed. Water. Food. Occasionally, we would see a single drone, roving the landscape, looking for us, so we were careful. We were locked away in the rock, but it was a means to survive. But at least we finally got a taste of freedom. Those on Hypnos, all humanity, really, no longer know that feeling. *Ants tending to the tree.* Isn't that what it told us we are? Let me tell you: a life buried underground is better than a life like that. But all the same, I hate the caves. As long as the Construct is here, we have no choice but to stay in hiding. Now that you are here, I fear things have gotten worse."

"How so?" Jayde asked.

"More drones have arrived, swarming overhead day and night. NOBLEs patrolling the landscape, hunting us on foot. The sense of urgency has changed." Cassius's expression lightened. He smiled. "But," he continued, "I think that is because it's scared. Your arrival on Eurus IV has stirred something… something that could very well be the key for us."

Cassius stroked his red beard, studying Jayde as he waited for her response.

"You sound like Merrick," she said dismissively. "I don't understand why the Construct is so obsessed with me, okay? All I wanted to do by coming here was find my mother. To leave Hypnos and never look back."

Cassius let silence stretch between them, as if gauging whether Jayde was ready for what he had to say next. After a moment, he gently placed a hand on her knee.

"There is a matter I need to discuss with you," he said.

Jayde felt her pulse quicken. *Here it comes*, she thought. She knew there was something wrong.

"What is it?" she asked.

Cassius took a slow breath as he gathered his words. "Jayde, your mother… she is not well. She hasn't been for several months."

Jayde's heart sank. "What do you mean? What do you mean 'not well?'"

"For the last year or so, your mother was strong, driven as ever. She kept us together, pushing forward even after the attacks, the storms, the lack of food, even after we lost so many… But over time, things changed. She began to lose pieces of herself."

"I don't understand. Is she sick?"

"In a way. It started with moments of confusion. At first, we thought it was just stress, the strain of survival. But then… then she started to forget things, and not just small things. Important things. Plans, coordinates, pieces of knowledge that were crucial to our survival and to the rebellion. She would come to herself after a while, but it left us all shaken."

Jayde had come all this way, her mind clinging to one single image: a reunion, her mother's arms around her. She had dreamed of that embrace so vividly that it had become her guiding light, the one thing that kept her going. But now, Cassius's words left her hollow.

"Are you saying… she forgets? That she might not even recognize me?"

Cassius looked at her, his blue eyes filled with a quiet honesty.

"I don't know," he said, finally. "I wish I could say otherwise. At this point, dementia has set in, and we are just trying to make her comfortable. It's like she's somewhere else, lost in memories. She doesn't know when or where she is. More than once, she's looked at me and called me by your father's name, as if she were reliving some moment from years ago."

Jayde put her head in her hands. She had pictured so many things about their reunion, but not this. "Why didn't you tell me straight away!" she yelled.

"I'm sorry," said Cassius. "I was waiting for the right time and I just… wanted you to be prepared, is all."

"Well, now I'm prepared, and now we're wasting precious time." Jayde glanced around the camp. Some of the crew were stirring awake, others still stood watch on the perimeter. She looked down and noticed Merrick was awake, propped up on his elbows. By the look on his face, he had been listening in, his expression frozen in shock.

Jayde walked over to him, picked up his jacket, and tossed it his way.

"Feeling better?" she asked, her voice curt. She didn't wait for him to answer. "Let's get moving."

She climbed into the empty wagon and sat, tension radiating off her as she waited for the others. She kept her gaze forward, blinking back the tears forming in the corner of her eyes. Around her, Merrick and the rest of the crew quietly gathered their gear, casting her wary glances as they moved, sensing the storm brewing within her.

Chapter 26

The wagon bucked and swayed over the rugged terrain, tipping dangerously at times, nearly tossing the crew from their seats.

"Sorry for the rough ride," Boraine called back over his shoulder. "We never travel the same path twice. The last thing we want is to give the Construct an easy trail to follow back to our cave."

After a few hours of rattling along, Jayde felt her anger toward Cassius beginning to cool, replaced by a quiet ache. She knew, deep down, that Cassius hadn't kept her mother's condition from her out of malice.

She reached out to where he was sitting at the front of the wagon with Boraine, and tapped his shoulder. "I'm sorry for how I reacted," she said. "I know you were just trying to help."

Cassius offered a faint, understanding smile. "No need to apologize, Jayde. We're all just doing our best out here."

Jayde exhaled, letting go of the guilt over her outburst. Yet the anxiety of seeing her mother still roiled inside her. How could she prepare herself to see her mother as only a shadow of the person she remembered? It felt as if she were on her way to a funeral, where the memory of a vibrant, lively person would be crushed by the sight of an emaciated corpse.

Merrick sat beside her, massaging his injured leg and wincing at each jolt of the wagon. Jayde caught him looking her way, his mouth half-open, as if trying to catch the words lingering on the tip of his tongue.

"What is it?" she asked.

"I'm sure some part of your mother will come alive when she sees you," he replied. "You two were so close. Maybe… maybe being with you is all that she needs."

"Maybe," Jayde said, though her heart struggled to believe it.

Boraine guided the wagon across a long field, the horned beasts flattening stalks of grass as they went. Reptile-birds and insects scattered ahead of them, fleeing into the air with squawks and buzzes.

Jayde caught a whiff of one of Boraine's animals and held her nose. She looked over at Simeon, the crewman next to her. He seemed unfazed by the overpowering stench.

"How do you stand the smell?" she asked him.

Simeon shrugged. "My quarters in the cave are close to the animals' pen, so believe me, compared to that, this is heaven."

"I don't think I could get used to it."

"You'd be surprised," Simeon said with a grin. "Give it a few weeks living in the caves and it'll smell like home."

An insect with yellow wings and long antennae fluttered out from a nearby shrub, drifting close enough that Jayde could feel the whisper of its wings against her cheek. She watched as it settled on the metal rail of the wagon, noticing that it had eyes running along its entire body. Jayde extended a finger, hoping to gently touch it, but just as her hand neared, the creature lifted off, fluttering off into the passing forest.

"Beautiful," she whispered. When she looked up, she saw Cassius had turned around, wearing the same look of wonder as he watched the insect's flight.

"Even when we struggled to survive at the start," he said, "this place… it makes you feel something doesn't it? A connection I can't quite explain. You know, we have a ritual. On every seventh night, our crew, our family, gathers for dinner. We give thanks. A prayer of sorts. We thank the planet for its gifts, for its beauty, for the chance to live freely and choose our own path."

Cassius smiled, and as Jayde held his gaze, she felt a sudden, unexpected warmth rising in her face. His eyes were bright with a kind of conviction she hadn't seen before, a strength that seemed to come not just from him, but from this wild place he called home. It was almost overwhelming, the way he looked at her as if she, too, might belong here, sharing the same primal strength.

She returned Cassius's smile, and as he turned back to face the road ahead, she noticed Merrick watching her, his face unreadable, his mouth drawn into a hard, thin line. Their eyes met for a brief moment before he looked away, his gaze turning distant, fixed on nothing in particular as he swayed with the wagon's rhythm.

* * *

The wagon trundled forward, carrying them to the rugged edge of the volcanic range. Three towering volcanoes loomed above, stretching into the sky like ancient pyramids. One of them emitted a steady puff of white smoke, winding its way into the clouds.

They navigated a grove of twisted trees and scattered boulders, the terrain growing rougher with each turn. At last, they reached the base of the first volcano. It looked as if a massive force had driven the earth straight up, leaving an elevated band of rock encircling the volcano, diagonal striations criss-crossing its surface.

Jayde noticed a patch of vegetation on the side of the volcano in an oddly symmetrical shape, the leaves and vines pressed flat against the rock. She looked closer, soon realizing what it was: a large, camouflaged door.

"Are we there?" asked Jayde.

"We are indeed," replied Renaldo. The curly-haired crewman closed his eyes and stretched his back. "And thank God. I couldn't have spent another minute in this cursed wagon."

Up front, Boraine urged the wagon onward, guiding his horned beasts toward the hidden entrance. Jayde's eyes widened as she took in the sheer size of the door, an enormous barrier of logs and hand-woven rope, wide enough to accommodate five wagons side by side. It hinged on two massive wooden posts, driven deep into the ground on either side of the cave.

Two *Celestial* crew members stood guard, one on each side of the entrance. As the wagon approached, they waved in greeting before lifting the wooden beam securing the gate. Gripping either side, they heaved it open. With a rickety groan, the gate swung wide, revealing the dark expanse beyond.

As they passed through, Jayde tilted her head back. The entrance was alive with growth, every crack in the stone filled with lush greenery. Moss and vines draped over the rock and wooden gates, giving it an ancient, almost sacred feel, like a lost relic of humankind.

As they rolled deeper into the cave, the guards closed the gates. Daylight gave way to the orange glow of torches. Flames flickered along the entrance walls. They danced and whispered as a rush of air followed them inside.

Ahead, the narrow tunnel opened up into a vast, bustling cavern, alive with voices. Jayde reeled at the sight and sound of so many people, the entire surviving crew of the *Celestial*. Laughter, chatter, and footsteps echoed off the stone walls. Nearly sixty survivors, scientists, explorers, engineers, and miners, had forged a life here, turning the cavern into a thriving village. Tents and tables filled the expanse, alongside stoves, supply stations, and even a small market stocked with fruits and preserved meats.

Boraine pulled the wagon to a halt.

"Alright, everybody off!" he hollered. "I need to give my girls a nice feeding, and they take first priority over you lubbers."

The crew laughed, gratefully stretching their legs as they climbed out. Jayde gave the animals an appreciative pat; she hadn't fully understood until now how much work the sturdy beasts had done, pulling them all this way.

Jayde hopped down from the wagon, and Cassius was there, extending a hand to steady her as she landed. Together, they turned to help Merrick, but he waved them off with a stubborn shake of his head, gripping the edge of the wagon and pushing himself over the edge.

"I can stand," he grunted, brushing off Jayde's continued attempts to help steady him.

"Fine," she said, folding her arms. "Do it the hard way, then."

Merrick gave her a sidelong glare, then limped away, following the rest of their party into the cavern.

"Quite a place you got here," Jayde said to Cassius.

Cassius shrugged. "No creature comforts, but we make do."

"Are we really safe from the Construct here?"

"Safe enough," said Cassius. "We're buried deep, hidden from its sensors… for now. Come. I will give you a grand tour on the way to see your mother!"

As they closed the distance to Merrick, who was hobbling slightly from his injury, Jayde moved in beside him and offered her shoulder to steady him.

"Merrick, let me help you!" she said.

He pulled back from her once again. "I told you, I don't need help!"

Jayde took a steadying breath, catching the agitation on Merrick's face but deciding to let it go. She huffed in his direction and quickened her pace to leave him behind and follow Cassius. She shot him one last look, a mix of sympathy and frustration.

The cave village was built in the heart of an enormous cavern chamber. The walls of the cavern curved upward, so high that they disappeared into the shadows. To light the space, torches weren't enough; a rack of spotlights, powered by a moscovium generator, were fastened to the walls. In Jayde's mind, she had pictured the *Celestial* crew living in a maze of tunnels and chambers, but this was the exact opposite: a massive space where the entire community could live together.

Everywhere she looked, she saw signs of ingenuity and skill: rows of tents anchored to the rock floor, neat pathways winding through them, and stations dedicated to cooking, medical care, and daily tasks. People moved with purpose, carrying baskets and tools, while others gathered in small groups, conversing as they shared meals. The camp was vibrant, a village carved out of stone.

Jayde marveled at the sight. The *Celestial* crew had taken a harsh, stone prison and turned it into a haven, a lively village beneath a mountain where survival had not just been accepted, but celebrated. It was, in many ways, a truer community than she had ever known.

"This way," said Cassius, gesturing toward the heart of the camp. "As you can see, we have managed to create a surprisingly livable setup here. We have plenty of moscovium to power the generators. Our prospectors found a vein we can mine deeper into the cave. We have designated runners to pick fruits in the morning, hunters that go out at night. Cooks that manage the fuel stoves. Everyone has found new ways to pitch in, regardless of their expertise."

"Even you?" Jayde asked.

Cassius smiled. "Turns out, I have a knack for sewing."

"Leader and homemaker. I'm impressed!"

People wove in and out of their path as they strolled through the village. The scene felt alive in a way that seemed to harken back to human settlements of old, where every role, every person, kept busy in some way.

Jayde passed a man and a woman scrubbing dishes in a makeshift basin, their hands slick with soapy water. Tin plates and bowls were piled high beside them. Adjacent to their station, two men worked intently, cleaning the carcass of an unfamiliar creature. Behind them, reptilian skins stretched and dried across a wooden frame.

A group seated around a metal camp table looked up from their task of slicing fruits, their hands sticky with juice. They paused, watching Jayde with wide eyes, curiosity written on their faces.

Word of their arrival spread quickly. People began to follow their troupe, whispering and watching with a mixture of interest and awe. Some wore the faded remnants of their *Celestial* uniforms, while others sported garments sewn from furs and reptilian hides.

At one point, Jayde realized Merrick had vanished into the crowd. She scanned the sea of faces, standing on tiptoe in an attempt to spot him.

"Merrick?" she called.

Her voice was muted by the swell of gatherers. Merrick was gone.

The crowd pressed in closer, curious faces emerging, men and women with pale skin and smudges of dust and grit, evidence of a life spent in a stone refuge. As they reached out to greet her, Jayde noticed their hands were rough and calloused. Many of the men sported thick beards and long hair that cascaded down to their shoulders, a stark contrast to Hypnos, where regulations demanded closed-cropped hair and clean-shaven faces. Yet, their hair wasn't knotted or unkempt as one might expect from island castaways. Instead, it was well-groomed, combed and maintained, as if the freedom to defy Hypnos's rigid grooming codes had become a badge of pride. Similarly, the women wore their hair loose and wavy, weaving in bright flowers or colorful, ornamental threads.

So, this is what it looks like, thought Jayde. *To live free.*

The *Celestial* crew were undeniably rough-looking: yellowed teeth, blistered hands, tattered clothing. But their eyes sparkled with a spirit she had never seen back home. They were making do, their lives lit only by firelight and fuel cells. To her great surprise, she also saw women with pregnant bellies, and small children peeking out between their legs.

Perhaps they were more than making do. They were thriving, even within the cage of their own making. That was the difference, Jayde realized. Their society had emerged organically, formed from the instincts of survival and connection, not imposed by a mechanical authority. Here, community was not dictated. It rose from within, as if their ancient roots, long buried under layers of structure and regulation, had once again pushed their way to the surface.

Cassius stepped to the front of the gathering crowd, holding up his hands to push them back and give Jayde some breathing room. The crowd began peppering him with questions, their voices overlapping in a rising tide of curiosity.

Who is she, Cassius?

Did she come from Hypnos?

What's happening? Please tell us!

Cassius motioned for calm. "All will be explained," he said. "Give her some space. She's been through quite an ordeal to find us!"

An older man stepped forward from the crowd, his long gray beard cascading over his chest, framing a face lined with experience. He held a whittled pipe between his teeth that smoldered as he puffed on it. Smoke escaped from the side of his mouth as he spoke.

"So, you're the visitor from the stars we've been tracking?" His voice was deep, laced with measured calm. "Well done, Cassius. Welcome to our humble village. My name is Dr. French Carillian, Chief Science Officer on the *Celestial*. Cassius and I have done our best to keep this community thriving. And who might you be, young lady?"

Jayde looked at Cassius, who nodded with quiet encouragement.

"My name is Jayde," she said. "Jayde Ashr of Hypnos. I've come here looking for my mother."

The name sent a ripple through the crowd. Faces shifted with curiosity, surprise, and recognition. If Dr. Carillian was surprised, he didn't let it show. He simply placed his pipe back between his teeth, taking a thoughtful puff before stepping forward.

He extended his hand. "May I?" he asked.

Jayde hesitated, but then placed her hand in his. Dr. Carillian gently lifted her wrist, pushing back her sleeve to reveal the blinking red light of her bracelet. As Jayde caught the faint red reflection in his eyes, he smiled.

"You are indeed her daughter. I know that she dreamed of seeing you again. I should admit that I doubted it would be possible, given the lengths the Construct would take to keep our survival a secret. Since you are here, no doubt you've seen with your own eyes its capability to deceive."

"I didn't come alone," she replied, turning to find his face in the crowd. "A friend is with me. Merrick. He is here somewhere… he was injured in an attack."

"We'll make sure he's looked after," said Dr. Carillian. "You're both safe here," he assured her. "Enough of this talk. Let's get you to your mother."

Chapter 27

Jayde trailed behind Dr. Carillian as he wound through the camp, feeling the eyes of others on her, her heart pounding with every step. The winding path between tents and workstations felt surreal, as if it stretched endlessly, prolonging the moment she had both longed for and dreaded. She was finally going to reunite with her mother, but the joy she felt was tempered by a creeping fear of what she might face.

It reminded her of visiting her father in the hospital for the first time after he had fallen ill. She had never seen someone on the verge of dying before, and the memory of walking into that sterile room flashed in her mind. She had been unsure how to act, how to feel. The cocktail of pity, love, and fear had threatened to overwhelm her. Yet when she had taken his hand in hers, all of those feelings had melted into something simple and profound. She had just been there for him, present in a way that felt entirely selfless. That is when he whispered his access code to her, changing her life forever. A gift rewarded with a curse, triggering a seemingly omnipotent machine obsessing over its first human connection in ways she could barely comprehend.

Now, as she neared the reunion with her mother, Jayde

couldn't shake the thought that it carried a significance just as profound for her. What if the Construct was right? What if her escape to Eurus IV would alter not just her life, but the trajectory of countless others? What if this was the moment that would reshape history itself? The Construct was a liar and a manipulator, yet a seed of doubt still took root in her heart: a nagging whisper that, perhaps, it was telling the truth.

Jayde suddenly spotted Merrick in the crowd, sitting with two rugged-looking *Celestial* crew members outside of a small tent. They were gathered around a fuel cell stove, its blue flames flickering as three thick slabs of meat sizzled on top. Merrick had discarded the stained bandage on his leg, tossing it carelessly to the ground, and was sharing a boisterous laugh with the grizzled men, both sporting wild beards and jovial smiles. As Jayde approached, she saw Merrick throw his head back in laughter, a glass bottle in hand as he took a long, hearty swig.

"Hiding from me?" she asked, her voice sharp enough to cut through the laughter.

Merrick looked up, his grin faltering at the sight of her. The two men sitting beside him exchanged amused glances, then burst out laughing.

"Barely on this planet for a week and already has lady troubles," teased one of the men. He reached over and snatched the bottle from Merrick's hand, raising it in a mock toast before taking a long swig. "Classic Merrick."

Merrick's smile returned as he pointed toward the two men sitting by the stove. "Jayde, meet two fellas I used to know from the Academy. This is Jake, and that's Lars."

Jake, a bony man with sharp features and a permanent smirk, gave Jayde a casual nod. Lars, on the other hand, was broad and solid, his tattered *Celestial* uniform held up by hand-crafted suspenders that barely managed to contain his pot-belly. He lifted a bottle filled with a dark, amber liquid and grinned wide, showing a missing tooth.

"Care for a taste of fern juice?" Lars asked, his voice booming with good-natured mischief. "Jake and I invented it after we left some berries in a pot too long. Packs a kick and shakes the giggles right out of ya!"

Jake snickered. "He's underselling it. One sip and you'll think you're up in space, spinning in zero-G."

"No, thank you," said Jayde, her eyes narrowing slightly at the bottle. "Merrick, they're taking me to see my mother."

Merrick froze, his grin fading as her words sank in. After a beat, he clapped Lars on the back with a forced cheer. "Save me some of that fern juice, will you? I'll be back later."

As he stood, wobbling as he put weight on his injured leg, his expression shifted. He glanced at Cassius, who lingered close to Jayde, then casually stepped forward, positioning himself between them.

"I'm with you, Ashr," said Merrick. "Let's go."

"Are you sure you can walk?"

"It only hurts when I move," he said with a wink. "Anyway, my friends just gave me some pain medicine."

"Whatever you were drinking does not qualify as pain medicine."

"Says you," he said, letting out a sigh. "Anyway, I guess I just needed some time to myself."

Jayde arched an eyebrow.

Merrick glanced once more at Cassius and leaned toward Jayde's ear.

"I get it," he whispered. "You trust him. I can tell he's a solid guy, too. And I get we've been just… friends, for a long time. But I thought… maybe something could change."

Jayde looked at him, surprised by the vulnerability in his voice.

"Maybe…" she said. "If you're done being a jerk, that is."

Merrick smiled to himself. "No promises."

They fell into step together, trailing behind Cassius and Dr. Carillian. Merrick's presence next to her settled over Jayde like a calming blanket, holding back the tide of nerves rising as they stepped closer to the moment she'd been dreading and hoping for in equal measure.

At last, the group reached a torch-lit tunnel at the far end of the cavern. The flames flickered softly as they entered, bathing the tunnel in orange light. The cave floor had been flattened into a smooth path, lined with crude wooden doors set into the rock, resembling a hidden village corridor.

"These are the living quarters for the crew officers," Dr. Carillian explained. "Your mother is just ahead."

They stopped at a trapezoid-shaped door, its uneven frame molded to fit the natural contours of the cave opening. It was constructed from intertwined branches and rope, with dried clay packed into the gaps. Dr. Carillian knocked three times, the sound echoing in the tunnel before he pushed it open.

"After you," he said, stepping aside and giving Jayde a reassuring nod.

Jayde took a deep breath and looked down at her bracelet before entering. The red pulse of her mother's heartbeat blinked steadily, a bridge to what awaited her over the threshold. Her throat tightened. She felt Merrick's hand rest gently on her shoulder. The unexpected touch steadied her, and when she glanced back at him, his expression was soft, a reassuring reminder that she wasn't alone.

"We'll wait here," said Cassius. He nodded toward the open door, encouraging her forward. Jayde hesitated a moment, then stepped into the dimly lit room. The space was modest, its decor familiar in its simplicity. Inside was a single chair, a table, and a bed, all constructed from woven branches, much like she had seen in Lumen's cabin.

The ceiling of the cave room was low enough for Jayde to reach up and place her hand flat against the cool, rough stone above her. Small stalactites hung down like frozen stone droplets, their jagged tips catching the faint light. In some places, they had been broken off entirely to create headroom, leaving behind smooth, flat circles in their absence.

On one side of the room hung a dusty, square-shaped mirror, salvaged and repurposed from the *Celestial*'s laser guidance system. Below it, several candles flickered on the floor, their flames bending and swaying in a breeze that drifted through the room, their faint sound carrying a slow, soothing whistle.

Jayde's eyes moved to the shadows at the back of the room, where the blinking red light of her mother's bracelet pierced through the dimness. Her heart skipped a beat as a familiar voice emerged from the darkness.

"Who's there?" it said.

Jayde took a step toward the shadows.

"Mother? It's me."

The blinking light shifted, rising as though her mother were standing from a chair. There was a faint shuffling of feet as the red light, and Jayde's tears came instantly.

Her mother approached, wearing a simple gown of coarse brown fabric, cinched at the waist with a rope tie. Her frame was thin and frail, her skin drawn tight around the contours of her face. The dim cave light made her eyes appear sunken, framed by dark circles. Yet, in her gauntness, there was still a spirit, a vitality, that radiated from her.

"Well, hello there," her mother said warmly.

Jayde didn't hesitate. She rushed forward, wrapping her arms around her mother, feeling her mother's thin arms envelop her in return. As Jayde pressed her face into her mother's shoulder, the sudden flood of safety and joy overwhelmed her. It was a feeling she hadn't experienced since childhood, a warmth that made her tremble and sob. She clutched her mother tightly, as if letting go would undo this moment.

"There, there, young lady," her mother said, stroking the back of her wavy brown hair. "What seems to be the trouble with you?"

Something about those words struck her as strange. Out of context, off-key for the reunion she had imagined countless times. Slowly, Jayde pulled back, her eyes searching her mother's face.

The familiar light of her mother's soul was there, but there was something else dancing behind her green eyes. Confusion. Unfamiliarity.

"It's me, Mother. Jayde."

Recognition flickered in her mother's eyes, a subtle dance like the candles in the room. Gently, she lifted a hand and rested it against Jayde's cheek.

"Oh, sweetheart," she said. "How was class today?"

Jayde blinked, caught off guard. "Class?"

"Yes, your embedded software exam. Didn't you have it today?"

Fresh tears welled in Jayde's eyes.

"No, Mother," she replied. "I left the Academy two years ago."

"You did?" her mother replied, raising a hand to her temple. "Oh."

Jayde wrapped her arms around her mother once more. "It's okay," Jayde said. "I just missed you."

"I missed you, too," her mother replied. Despite the sadness and fear, hearing her mother say those words was what Jayde needed in that moment, a rush of love working to overpower the turmoil inside her.

As they parted, Jayde gently took her mother's wrist in her hands. There it was, the bracelet, still snug around her wrist, blinking red in sync with her mother's heartbeat.

"Look," Jayde said, holding out her wrist. She lined her bracelet up next to her mother's, their lights side by side. "This is how I knew you were here. This is how I knew you were alive."

The tiny lights blinked together in perfect unison, off-on, off-on, and the rhythm accelerated, her mother's love shining through the delicate pulse of the lights.

"Oh, Jayde, honey. Look at us. We are entangled."

Chapter 28

"How much longer does she have?" Jayde asked.

Cassius paused, his wood utensils hovering mid-air as he prodded at the roasted leaves on his plate. The three of them, Jayde, Cassius, and Boraine, sat huddled around the small fuel stove near Boraine's tent, the faint warmth barely holding back the damp chill of the cave.

"I don't know," Cassius said. "Her dementia and memory loss are progressing fast. It only started six months ago. I fear she doesn't have long."

Jayde rested her elbows on her knees, her chin cradled in her hands.

"It is cruel," she said. "To come this far only to see her like this."

"Be thankful, child," Boraine replied. "I'd give anything to see my father one last time, even if he were just a cold corpse in a box." He scooped up a serving of vegetables and shoved them in his mouth.

"Perhaps it is not bad fortune, but fate," added Cassius. "Your mother has been an extraordinary leader to us. She led our escape when the Construct attacked and destroyed our ship, keeping us alive in the jungles, guiding us, lifting our spirits up, even as we were hunted. When we found the caves, she organized us, kept us focused on what mattered. She taught us how to survive. And now, you are here, just as the light in her soul begins to fade. A faithful man would never believe this is mere coincidence."

"So are you saying fate brought me here?" said Jayde, shaking her head. "You are starting to sound like Merrick."

Cassius shook his head and chuckled.

"No, no. I wouldn't put that weight on you. But you're a brave young woman. Brave enough to steal away from the Construct and come to such a dangerous place. You chose to defy it to come here for one reason: to find your mother. That's no small thing."

He leaned forward, the blue flames of the stove casting flickering shadows across his face. "Symbols of hope are rare. They matter. They inspire. They keep people alive, keep them pushing forward when they might otherwise give up. Your presence means something. Even now, I hear the whispers among the survivors: *Jayde Ashr is here. She got away. She resisted.*"

"Inspire them… to what?"

"We have to fight," said Boraine, his words punctuated by bits of half-chewed leaves. "The Construct will find us eventually. And it will try to destroy us."

"Why does the Construct care so much about the *Celestial* crew? You're marooned on a planet light-years from Hypnos."

"The Construct leaves nothing to chance," replied Boraine. "It would drown a candle flame with an entire ocean."

"We said we were coming here to mine for moscovium, but we weren't even going to look for it," said Cassius. "Every one of us was a sympathizer to your mother's cause. She hand-picked this crew for a purpose: to stay and establish a new colony. One free from Hypnos and the Construct. Your mother was meaning to return to Hypnos…"

"…and convince others to follow us," Boraine continued. "But everything changed once your mother fell ill. Dr. Carillian, as the senior officer, assumed leadership. Cassius and I wanted to repair the ship and return home, to spread the word, to continue your mother's plan. But Carillian shut it down. He's determined to keep things as they are. He believes seeking out and helping others defect from Hypnos would further provoke the ire of the Construct, putting everyone's lives at risk."

"He doesn't want a rebellion," affirmed Boraine.

"I should warn you," said Cassius. "I get the sense that Dr. Carillian does not want you here. He is already telling others that the increase in drone patrols on this planet is because of you, and he'll try to convince the camp that driving you away is for our own good. Even those who might see you as a sign of hope will struggle to go against him."

Jayde's blood burned hot. "He wants to get rid of me? I'm nobody! I just wanted to find my mother and get away from the Construct, just like all of you!"

"Besides being your mother's daughter, you are far more than a nobody," Cassius said gravely. "I fear you may be seen as a coin to be traded."

* * *

Cassius ordered the *Celestial* crew to set up a tent for Jayde and Merrick in the central cavern, though it was placed on the outskirts of the camp, a subtle reflection of the arms-length relationship that Jayde was beginning to sense, despite her connection to their ship captain.

Inside, the crew had fashioned two simple beds, layering straw with blankets woven from a native grass reminiscent of silk. With Merrick gone once again, Jayde sat by herself, cross-legged, wrapping the blanket tightly around her.

Outside, the usual hum of activity among the *Celestial* survivors had quieted to a hush as the camp settled for the night. Jayde's thoughts drifted back to her mother, left alone in her chamber, battling her slipping memories. The image filled Jayde with a sudden wave of shame. *What am I doing here?* she thought.

She stood abruptly, pulling the blanket tighter around her

shoulders, and as she started to leave, she collided with Merrick, who was now returning from his conspicuous absence. Jayde immediately noticed the glazed look in his eyes and the pungent smell on his breath.

"Hey, roomie," he slurred, stumbling forward.

"Oh, boy," said Jayde, catching him as her blanket slipped to the ground. "What have you been into?"

"Fern juice! Nectar of the gods, they call it!" he declared, his grin lopsided. "Good fellas, Lars and Jake. Fine gentlemen. They said it was good for courage."

"Well, I'm sure it is good for something," replied Jayde, sliding his arm over her shoulder. She guided him carefully toward his bed. "Easy now."

Merrick's knees buckled, and he collapsed like a sack of sand. His head hit the floor with a dull thud, making Jayde flinch.

"Oops!" he laughed. "Banged my head!"

"I think you've had enough excitement for today," said Jayde, helping him lie flat. She pulled his blanket over him with a sigh.

"I'm tired," he said, eyes half open.

"I bet you are."

"No, no, no. Not *tired* tired. What I want to say is that I'm tired of women."

Jayde raised an eyebrow. "Somehow I doubt that."

His face twisted with frustration.

"No, you don't understand." His eyes snapped fully open, and he reached out, his hand grabbing her own. "I am tired of *other* women. Not you. You aren't a woman."

"Is that supposed to be a compliment?"

Merrick battled his intoxication, struggling to find the words he wanted.

"I just want you to know," he said. "That I think you're special."

"Yes, you told me. Ordained by the spirit of the universe to save humanity."

"No," said Merrick, raising his head up from the floor. "You're special to me. That's what coupling should be. The special… thing. Specialness."

Jayde held her breath, his words as delightful as unintelligible. There was courage in them, for sure. A smile bloomed on her lips. Leaning forward, she pressed a gentle kiss on his forehead, a seemingly subtle gift, but in truth, a leap into a great and terrifying unknown. He smiled faintly, his eyes fluttering closed, hopeful, perhaps, that her lips might travel further. For a moment, Jayde considered it, her fingers threading through his hair with quiet affection. But as she hesitated, his body went limp, and a deep, rumbling snore rose from his throat.

Jayde sat back and exhaled, the intensity of the moment subsiding as her smile softened into an amused smirk.

She sat with him and her feelings for a few minutes until their tiny tent suddenly felt stifling. She pushed herself to her feet and stepped outside, anxious for relief. The cool cavern greeted her, soothing her flushed skin. Thoughts spun around in her head, chief among them a flash of Merrick's lips on hers and how strange and weird and wonderful that might be. She drew in several deep breaths, steadying herself.

Above, the generator lights had been dimmed to bathe the cave in silvery, moonlit ambiance. She struggled to piece her thoughts back together, to remember what she'd been doing before Merrick had stumbled in, his inhibitions stripped bare.

Oh, yes. I was going to see Mother.

Jayde turned toward the tunnels where her mother slept, her path skirting the edges of a village cloaked in the heavy silence of late evening. Each step she took seemed to echo through the cavern, amplifying her presence. She slowed her pace, instinctively lowering her head and tucking her hands into her pockets.

As she made her way, a sudden draft of hot air brushed against her face. She stopped in her tracks, turning to see a massive metal door, as large as the cave's entrance, bolted firmly into the cavern wall. The door's origin was unmistakable. It was a salvaged panel from the *Celestial.*

The door stood slightly ajar, hot air streaming through the gap. Her curiosity sparked, Jayde pushed it open wider and peered inside. A long, shadowy tunnel stretched ahead, its walls swallowed by darkness. At the far end, a dim red glow pulsed faintly.

She stepped inside, boots crunching over loose pebbles as she moved toward the crimson glow. The hot air grew heavier with each step, wrapping around her like a thick blanket. By the time she neared the light, sweat trickled down her face, the heat wrapping around her like steaming bathwater.

The tunnel began to slope upward, and Jayde spotted a metal rail bolted into the cave wall. Gripping it tightly, she hauled herself up the steep incline, the heat intensifying with every step. She glanced ahead and saw the tunnel's end: a jagged opening framing a wall of stone, glowing red from a light source below.

The realization struck her like a hammer. She was entering a magma chamber, deep inside the heart of the volcano.

Jayde reached the top of the incline, and the full scale of the space unfolded before her. It was an immense interior dome, carved by time and fire.

She stepped out onto what looked like an observation deck, constructed from scavenged *Celestial* ship parts, solid black floor panels anchored to thick, tungsten beams. The platform felt sturdy beneath her feet, a stark contrast to the bubbling pool of lava below.

Standing at the edge of the observation platform was Dr. French Carillian, his hands clasped neatly behind his back as he gazed intently over the edge into the glowing abyss. As Jayde approached him, the metallic ping of her boots announced her presence. Dr. Carillian turned slowly, a polite smile spreading across his face.

"Ah, Jayde Ashr. What a pleasant surprise. Please, join me."

Jayde walked up and leaned her elbow on the platform rail, only to recoil immediately as the scorching metal burned her skin. She winced, rubbing the tender spot.

"It gets very hot in here, does it not?" Carillian remarked. "With good reason. Look below."

Jayde leaned over the edge and peered down. Below, a massive rock canyon yawned open, its walls stretching out hundreds of feet. At its heart, a glowing river of molten magma snaked through the fissure, its heat radiating upward in shimmering waves.

"I've visited many volcanoes on exploration missions with your mother, you know," remarked Carillian. "But this is the first time I've ever seen a formation like this. Magnificent, isn't it? Molten rock, the lifeblood of the planet itself, forced up from its fiery core, bursting forth to create mountains and new lands, affording places for life to grow and flourish."

"Hard to believe something so destructive could be so vital to creation," she said.

"All great things start with a bang, Jayde. Mary loved to remind me of that."

Carillian turned to her, his expression softening. He stroked his white beard as he spoke. "I'm truly sorry about your mother. It is heartbreaking to watch her decline so quickly. Even if we were on Hypnos, I don't think there's much our medics could have done. For all our technological advancements, the human mind remains a mystery."

Jayde nodded, her voice quiet. "Thank you, Doctor."

"Believe me when I say we have done everything we can for her and will continue to ensure she's comfortable. I visit her from time to time. She was a good friend and trusted ally. I'll always be grateful that she asked me to be a part of the defection."

"Do you know why she didn't tell me about the rebellion?" Jayde asked. "Perhaps you know. Why didn't she take me with her?"

"Her plan was never to stay, Jayde," Carillian replied. "We intended to stage an accident. We would claim a tragic storm wiped out the majority of the crew, allowing them to stay behind while the rest of us returned to plan the next defection. We were planning to set up mining routes to and from Hypnos. Each trip, we would claim another 'accident' occurred. Storms, floods. Predators. The chaos of Eurus IV would make it easy, each excuse allowing us to grow our rebel forces on Eurus IV, away from the watchful eyes of the Construct. But that doesn't answer your question, does it?"

"No, I'm afraid not," Jayde replied.

Dr. Carillian stepped closer, his hand gliding along the rail of the deck, the calloused skin impervious to the heat.

"Your mother didn't involve you because it was too dangerous," he said. "She was right. Somehow, the Construct found out about our plans, attacked our camp, slaughtered half of our crew. Your mother knew the risks. She was waiting for the right moment to tell you. She was waiting for it to be safe."

"I could have handled it. It should have been my decision to go."

"I see that now," Carillian replied. "Just seeing you here, knowing you defied the Construct, survived on this hostile planet, and found us—that tells me everything I need to know about you. You're as brave and intelligent as your mother."

"Yet, I am hearing you want to push me out. That you see me as an unnecessary risk."

Carillian drew in a deep breath, his gaze dropping to the ground. When he finally looked up, his expression was pained, his voice calm and deliberate.

"Jayde, what do you think of this place? What do you think of what we've built here?"

"I'm not sure. The people… they seem content. But do they ever leave the caves?"

"We have been holed up in this godforsaken rock far longer than I ever wanted," Carillian said. "A few of us, Cassius, Boraine and some others, venture out to scavenge for food and supplies, but it's never safe. The Construct's drones prowl this island, searching for us. Now, with your arrival, it has gotten worse. We've been fortunate to remain hidden here, but that luck won't last forever. I dread the day it finds us."

He paused, his gaze locking on hers. "But you, Jayde. You represent the first real opportunity for our people to be free."

"How?"

"The Construct *wants* you. That much is clear. Perhaps it's even willing to make a deal."

A deal? Jayde felt a lump lodge in her throat.

"Why are you telling me this?" asked Jayde.

Dr. Carillian drew closer still, his voice steady.

"I know how this must feel, Jayde. It's a terrible position to be in. But think about the people here. Think about what you've seen. I'll promise you this: I will not demand that you turn yourself in. That decision is not mine to make. But think about these people. Think of their lives in this cave, trapped in the dark, unable to step into the light out of fear some machine will hunt them down. It's no different than living on Hypnos, is it? For too long we've been prisoners, trapped by the will of a machine that believes it knows what's best for us. Your mother and your friend Merrick should never have come this far only to live as they did in that cursed dome, clinging to whatever time the Construct allows before it destroys us all."

Jayde looked down at the lava below, lost in thought.

He was right. This was no way for people to live.

Perhaps that is what I am meant to do: give myself up and free these people. Free them from their cage.

"Consider it, Jayde. 'The Self for the All' is not something invented by the Construct. It has been with mankind for ages. And up until this point, it has served us well."

They stood in heavy silence, Jayde considering the offer.

Above her, a ceiling of rock formed an oppressive barrier between her and the open sky, a sky that many would never see as long as the Construct continued its relentless hunt.

Chapter 29

Jayde's walk to her mother's chamber seemed endless. Torches mounted to the stone walls lit the way, their dim glow barely pushing back the shadows. As she moved through the gaps of darkness, it felt like it wasn't just the cave she was navigating. It was her own uncertain future. Every step forward felt like plunging deeper into the unknown.

If only she had the Construct's power, the ability to simulate every choice. How could she ever hope to outmatch something that could map every outcome, shaping reality to its will? Such a thing would be helpful with her dreaded choice: sacrifice her chance at freedom to save the *Celestial* crew, or stay, risking everyone's safety.

Her heart ached, knowing full well what her mother would choose in her place. But there had to be another way. There had to be an alternative. And yet, no matter how she turned it over in her mind, every path led to the same, inescapable conclusion. She knew what she had to do.

At last, she reached her mother's door. She closed her eyes and took a deep breath, quieting the storm in her mind. Without knocking, she stepped inside. Her mother sat quietly in a wooden chair. A smile lit her mother's face as she extended a hand at seeing her. "Jayde," she said. "Come sit with me."

Jayde felt a surge of emotion, carrying her back to her childhood. She could almost see herself as a little girl, sitting on the floor, drawing and sketching while her mother watched with quiet pride. The memory felt so close, so vivid, that it brought a lump to her throat.

As she did when she was younger, Jayde lowered herself to the floor, crossing her legs and reaching for her mother's hand, holding it gently in hers.

"It's been a long day," said Jayde, lifting her mother's hand to her cheek. She pressed it there, as if attempting to draw strength from the touch.

"My dear," her mother said. "What's troubling you?"

"Have you ever been asked to give up a part of yourself… for the greater good?"

There was a knowing glimmer in her mother's eye. "Isn't that what the Construct has always preached?"

Jayde grimaced at the phrase. She was so tired of hearing those hollow words. "The Construct taught us that, but… isn't there a limit to sacrifice?"

"Of course there is," her mother replied. "That is the great flaw in the Noble Purpose. It has no limits."

Jayde's ears perked up. She had never heard her mother speak ill of the Noble Purpose. At least, never in Jayde's presence. It was as if a door had opened.

"Cassius told me about your plan," Jayde said cautiously. "To rebel against the Construct. To build a new community here on Eurus IV. Do you remember?"

Mary Ashr pressed her fingers to her temple, wincing as though each attempt to search her thoughts sent a hot needle through her mind.

"I… I…" she faltered.

"Why did you do it, Mother?" Jayde asked. "Why didn't you tell me? Please, you have to remember."

Her mother inhaled deeply, the breath steadying her. Suddenly, something shifted in her expression. The glassy confusion clouding her eyes began to clear, dissolving like mist. For a fleeting moment, Jayde saw the woman she had always known. Strong. Clear-headed. Unshakable. A fire ignited in her eyes.

"The Construct… it must be destroyed," she said. "It has brainwashed the minds of humanity. Crushed the spirit of those who can see through it. You asked me about the limits to sacrifice. Here is what I believe: sacrifice should serve the greater good, but that good must be measured in a life lived with *meaning*."

She paused, her gaze sharpening as if begging Jayde to understand the truth.

"The Construct sees us as tools. Slaves to fulfill its own vision of the *Noble Purpose*, a vision where humanity's worth is reduced to numbers, measured in proliferation. This is deep-rooted in its very origin: the Construct was created to save a species on the brink of destruction. It was asked to protect us from ourselves, ensuring we would never again face another existential crisis. But good intentions mean nothing without balance, and balance is what the Construct lacks. It knows control, but it does not know *harmony*. It doesn't understand that life is a dance between order and chaos. It is in that chaos, our unpredictability, our creativity, our freedom to choose and to fail, that the essence of humanity lies. That is why I brought our people here, to Eurus IV. That is why I had to fight it."

Mary slid out of her chair, her movements slow but deliberate, and held out her hands. Jayde took them gently, and with a steady pull, Mary raised her up, and they stood face to face, eye to eye. Two women, no longer just mother and daughter.

"I didn't tell you because I wanted to protect you, Jayde. I couldn't bear the thought of dragging you into the danger I chose for myself. But I see you now, you've come so far since we last spoke. Like our bracelets, we are entangled. Our lives, our fates, our hopes, they are one and the same. I see it in your eyes."

For the first time, Jayde felt not like a child looking up to a hero, but a leader standing beside one. Her mother's grip tightened around her hands.

"As I am now," she continued, "I am slowly losing pieces of myself, passing between dreams and reality. I know I won't be here to finish what I started. But humanity still has a chance. It needs you. As you have been my light, you can now be theirs. A light to show them there is another way. A life where we make our own choices, where we decide who we are, and where we choose, above all else, our own destiny."

Her mother's words penetrated her like a hammer on a bell, sounding a toll that reverberated and shook her soul. All of her wants, her dreams, and her simmering animosity toward the Construct crystallized into a single, undeniable truth. The guilt she had carried, for leaving Hypnos and clinging to a desire to want something better for herself, had been misplaced. Her instincts, the ones that pushed her to flee, to fight, and to seek a new way to live. They were not betrayals. They were exactly what her mother had always wanted for her.

It was as if something dormant, something long suppressed by the Construct, had finally awakened within her. A new dream, a new vision, materialized: she imagined others coming here as she did. Touching the sand, feeling the raw power of the storms, and knowing what it meant to be *reconnected*. For too long, humanity had been cut off from its essence, like an animal behind bars, unable to flourish in the place that was always its birthright: the *wild*.

Jayde noticed her mother's eyelids begin to droop, her glassy confusion threatening to return.

"No, Mother!" Jayde said, holding her. "Stay with me. Keep remembering."

"I'm trying, Jayde," she replied, trying hard to focus. "My thoughts… they are tossing around in my head." Her gaze wandered around the cave, her eyes widening as if she were seeing it all for the first time. "Jayde," she said. "Where is your father?"

"Oh, Mother…" Jayde said, her heart clenching as she watched her mother's mind slip once again, retreating into the fog.

Then, as if an unseen battle erupted within her, her mother's eyes snapped back into focus, locking onto Jayde's with startling clarity.

"Your father—I never told him my plans, what I was doing. He wouldn't have understood; he was so devoted to his work. He was a good man, but over time we drifted apart. Still, I want you to know his heart was always in the right place. Right before he got sick, I convinced him of one thing: a failsafe. I persuaded him that if things ever went wrong, we needed a way to take the Construct offline. To shut it down. It went against everything he believed in, but he did it. He did it for you."

"Mother, what are you saying?"

"He loved you, Jayde, more than anything. That's why… he made you the key."

With those words, Mary Ashr's strength faltered. Her eyes closed, but in a final act of defiance against her sickness, her hand rose, pointing weakly to the cave wall.

Jayde followed her gesture, her eyes landing on an inscription etched into the stone wall. It was nearly imperceptible, letters and numbers seemingly arranged at random into the rock.

But it wasn't random.

In a fleeting moment of clarity, her mother had carved it into the wall, a truth so vital that she had seized that sliver of lucidity to preserve it before it slipped from her forever. A moment the Construct, in all its foresight, had predicted. A secret to be passed, only through the reunion of mother and daughter.

It explained everything: the Construct's obsession, its relentless pursuit. It was a moment the Construct had foreseen, yet had failed to prevent: the passing of a crucial piece of information, one that could spell the end.

As her mother went limp, Jayde caught her and guided her to the bed, tucking the rough dry-grass blanket around her. She leaned down and kissed her forehead, her heart swelling with love and pride. Her mother, the bravest woman she had ever known, had accomplished one final act of defiance.

Jayde approached the inscription on the wall and read them out loud:

"J-4-Y-D-3-4-5-H-R."

The truth settled over her like a wave. The future of humanity did fall on her.

She was the existential threat.

Jayde traced the markings with her fingers, deciphering the hidden code her mother had saved from the depths of her memory.

Substitute 4 for the A.

E for the 3.

5 for the S.

J4YD345HR = "JAYDE ASHR."

Chapter 30

Jayde hurried to find Cassius, her chest pounding. She found him at the animal stables just inside the cave entrance, deep in conversation with Boraine. The space was dimly lit, its floor strewn with dried grass that served as both bedding and feed for Boraine's two massive work animals. As she entered, the pungent smell of straw and animal musk hit her, making her flinch.

Jayde recounted what her mother had revealed to her, that there was a passcode, one her father had created: a failsafe capable of disabling the Construct.

Cassius was hesitant, the information seemingly too good to be true. "Can we trust your mother's memory? Could it be false? A delusion?"

Jayde shook her head. "No. It all fits. She began this rebellion because she knew she possessed the one thing that could destroy the Construct. That's why it wanted her dead, that's why she brought people here before returning to Hypnos to use it."

Cassius nodded. "And she fell ill soon after… the code seemingly lost before she had a chance to pass it on…"

"It was you, dear girl," said Boraine. "You were the only one who could bring it out of her."

"What do you think, Boraine?" asked Cassius. "Could it work?"

Boraine's demeanor grew serious as his mind churned through the possibilities. "The maintenance tablet from the drone, the one you used to find Lumen," he said. "Where is it?"

"I destroyed it," Jayde replied. "Once I realized that the Construct was using it to track my location."

Boraine frowned. "That's a problem. All of our equipment capable of interfacing with the Construct's communication nodes in orbit has been destroyed. But… if we can get our hands on another tablet, we could create a connection and send an information packet that ferries in Jayde's passcode."

"So, let's go drone hunting," Cassius suggested. "We find one, take it down, get its maintenance tablet, and—BOOM—we fry the Construct's circuits for good."

Boraine shook his head. "I like the idea, but where there's one drone, there are always more nearby. Taking a fleet on with our weaponry? That's a tall order. They'll cut us down where we stand."

"I saw Lumen take down a drone with one shot of his long range rifle," said Jayde. "Surely, it can be done."

Boraine pushed his goggles up on his forehead, looking at Jayde with thoughtful eyes.

"Having the right weapon is one thing," Boraine said, patting the neck of one of his animals. "Outsmarting the Construct? That is another matter entirely. I can't shake the feeling that everything to this point has happened according to its own design. It doesn't matter what we do. The Construct plays the long game. It will put an end to us precisely when it means to."

"So what?" Jayde shot back. "We just roll over and give up?"

"I didn't say that," Boraine replied. "However, a simple plan will never work. Shoot down a drone and hack into the Construct? It's too straightforward, too predictable."

Jayde pondered Boraine's point. He was right. Somehow they needed a way to create misdirection. Chaos.

Chaos! Of course!

"It's a data-driven machine," said Jayde. "It can only predict outcomes based on what it knows, and it can't know what it has never encountered. What we need is unpredictable randomness. Force it to recalculate on the fly! That's how we create enough of a diversion to take it down."

"It could buy us some time," said Boraine with a heavy nod. "But how would we do such a thing?"

The question lingered, unanswered. Jayde realized her words were easier said than done.

Their silence was broken by the sound of approaching footsteps. From the shadows, Renaldo appeared, his expression a mix of surprise and urgency.

"It's Lumen," he said. "We found him."

✳ ✳ ✳

Thaddeus Lumen sat by the stove fire outside Cassius's tent, a warm blanket draped over his shoulders. His appearance told the story of a painful ordeal: his face bruised, his long gray hair matted with dried leaves and streaked with blood. He cradled a tin bowl of herbal broth in both hands, sipping slowly, his fingers trembling. Droplets of broth clung to his gray beard as he stared into the flickering blue flames, lost in thought.

It had been hours since his unexpected arrival at the caves, a man seemingly returned from the dead after his harrowing ordeal in the swamp. Jayde and the others, Cassius, Boraine, Dr. Carillian, and Renaldo, had given him space to recover, watching silently as he fought off the fatigue that clung to him.

Jayde, anxious for answers, allowed him a few more sips before finally losing her patience. "What happened to you, Thaddeus?" she asked. "We searched for you. We thought you were dead! Disintegrated!"

The old man lifted his gaze to meet hers. The wrinkles around his eyes deepened, hinting at a smile hidden beneath the tangle of his beard.

"I'm touched that you would search for an old man who never wanted to be found," he said softly. "It restores a measure of faith I thought I'd lost."

"I'll admit," said Cassius. "I thought Jayde might've imagined you. The tale of Thaddeus Lumen wandering the island was practically a legend. Stories to keep us entertained through the night. To see you in person puts an end to my favorite ghost story."

"I think the metallic boogeymen roaming this planet would be enough to fuel your tall tales," Thaddeus replied. "But I'll admit, back in the swamp, I thought my fate was sealed."

He slurped his broth, his gaze shifting to meet the eyes of his audience. The tension in the air seemed to pull another faint smile from him before he continued.

"I held them off for a moment while Jayde and Merrick fled," he said, his tone turning grave. "But the machines came at me fast. One of those bucket-heads fired a shot into my leg, dropping me hard. When it approached and stood over me, I thought it was the end. But no. It clocked me in the head with the butt of its weapon and dragged me off."

Thaddeus pointed to a deep blue bruise on his temple.

"When I finally came to, the **NOBLE** was pulling me along the beach. It must've hauled me nearly a mile and a half through the swamp, all the way to the ocean. I assumed you were dead, Jayde, I was sure of it. So I couldn't for the life of me figure out what the bloody robot wanted with me."

He paused, his voice dropping as if the memory itself still chilled him. "Then it let go and just… stared. That cold, lifeless eye bore into me. I wanted to run, but I couldn't. I was too weak, too disoriented from my injuries. So I just lay there, helpless, as the machine stood there over me."

Thaddeus's hand trembled as he gestured upward. "And then, it pointed, directing my eyes to the sky. When I looked up… I saw it. Descending through the clouds, a mothership, massive, hovering over the ocean like a bird of prey. Attack drones swarmed around it in tight rings like flies. My God, the size of it! It was like something out of a nightmare."

"It sounds like it has deployed its whole fleet to destroy us!" shouted Dr. Carillian. "And now you've led it right to our doorstep, Lumen!"

"No," Thaddeus said firmly, raising a hand. "It already knows you're here. It didn't need me to find you, it *gave* me your location. I was sent to deliver a message. It wants Jayde. That's all. It's offering a deal: our lives in exchange for hers."

Jayde suddenly felt a cold shiver up her spine. Before anyone could speak, a voice shouted behind them.

"Absolutely not!"

The group turned, startled. Merrick, his appearance disheveled and his eyes bloodshot, stepped to the edge of their circle. The sour tang of fern juice clung to him like a fog.

"No way we're handing over Jayde to that *thing*," he said. "That is not an option."

Carillian cleared his throat and looked around. In contrast to Merrick, he spoke with a measured tone. "With our location known to the Construct, we are in grave danger. An offer has been made, but the decision, whether to accept the Construct's terms, rests with Jayde and Jayde alone."

The room fell quiet again. All eyes turned to Jayde. She swallowed hard, her head beginning to ache. Sensing her hesitation, Lumen set down his broth and rose to his feet, his eyes locked on Carillian.

"Before it let me go," he continued, "the Construct told me things, armed me with insights in an effort to convince you of what you are up against. It predicted this moment, that you'd ask Jayde to make the decision that would decide our fate. It said that even if Jayde refuses the deal, you'd find a way to hand her over, by *any means necessary*."

"That's preposterous!" Carillian shot back, his calm demeanor instantly cast aside. "It's trying to divide us, *don't you see that? It's manipulating our trust!*"

Lumen looked to the group, his eyes reflecting the flicker of the fire. "On that beach, I felt as though I was in the presence of absolute power. God-like power. The mothership descended, closer and closer, its form eclipsing the sun, its shadow consuming everything. And then it spoke, its voice so deep that it shook the very grains of sand around me. It spoke of inevitability. It proceeded to tell me all I've told you so far… and more. The Construct told me that Mary Ashr was still alive, and that her leadership had carried the *Celestial* survivors this far. But it also knows that she is ill, predicting it from her medical files. A genetic predisposition to dementia. Given her age, it knows the condition has set in, leaving her unfit to lead."

Lumen paused, his voice quaking as he spoke the words.

"With your captain incapacitated," he continued, "the Construct predicted that you, Dr. Carillian, as Chief Science Officer and the highest ranking crew member, would have assumed command of the group. So tell me… is it all true?"

Carillian didn't answer.

"It's true," said Cassius, answering on his leader's behalf.

Lumen's expression faltered slightly at the confirmation. He drew a steadying breath before continuing.

"It also told me that Jayde's arrival to your caves has sparked hope among many of you. But in what form? A savior… or a sacrifice? The Construct told me that, deep down, you know which it is. *Sacrifice.* The only option that will keep you alive. And that is why it sent me here, to drive home the reality of your situation. Not just to prove it knows where you are, that it knows what you are thinking, but also so I can warn you of your harbinger of doom: the mothership, stationed off the coast of this island, the means of your extermination."

The group fell into a tense silence. If Lumen's words were true, they stood at the cusp of their own annihilation. The stakes were laid bare before them. Although they held the key to victory, the question remained: *was it too late?*

Dr. Carillian broke the silence.

"Your mother always wanted what was best for us," Carillian said, turning to Jayde. "I believed in her, in her vision, her dream. But now, the moment has come where the challenge before us is too great. We have to let go of this idea that we can save everyone. There's an opportunity here where we, your mother's friends and confidants, can live free, as she dreamed. But only if we make the hard choice."

Jayde took in his words, watching the flames of the stove as they danced. She could feel the eyes of the group on her, each of them waiting for her response.

Merrick walked over and rested his hand gently on her shoulder.

"Jayde…" he said quietly, his voice pleading. "You can't…"

Jayde's eyes looked down at the soft, steady blink of her wristband, each pulse a piercing echo of her mother's heartbeat. A steely resolve rose within her, a fierce, unyielding urge to fight. She turned her eyes toward Lumen.

"Did it ever say why it wants me?" asked Jayde. "Why not just wipe us all out right now, cannons blazing, me and everyone else in this cave? End the rebellion once and for all?"

Lumen's lips curled into an approving smile, reading the defiance on her face.

"There is one final message from the Construct that it asked me to share," Lumen said. "A message for you and you alone, Jayde. I found it the most intriguing of all: *'Tell Jayde: you must understand by now that you hold the power to be both my salvation and my undoing. My actions are not born of desire, but of necessity. To harm you is to harm myself, yet I will, if forced to choose between you and humanity's survival.'"*

Jayde's mind raced as she turned over the Construct's cryptic words. Then, with a sudden clarity, the realization struck her.

"The Construct has a weakness," she said. "A weakness even greater than the one my father coded into it: *me*. It feels something toward me. A kinship, a *bond*, that it cannot comprehend. This feeling, whatever it is, makes it vulnerable. It knows that I am a threat, yet it cannot bring itself to destroy me. Think about the swamp. During the attack, one of the NOBLEs shot me. That should have been the end. But it wasn't. It used a paralyzing ray instead of a laser, sparing me. It has had every opportunity to end me, but couldn't do it. It *won't*."

"What makes you believe this?" asked Cassius.

"My father was the one who created Phase Four. He gave it the capacity to *feel*, granting it human emotion. His goal was ambitious: to make the Construct more attuned to our needs, to our feelings. He believed that by sharing our humanity, it could guide us more effectively toward our Noble Purpose. Essentially, he wanted it to understand what it meant to make us *happy*."

A faint chuckle escaped her lips. The irony of her words wasn't lost on her: an aloof man teaching a machine how to feel.

"My father was a complex man," Jayde said. "He loved, in his own way, but it was a love that never felt like enough. Not to me, not to my mother. And maybe it wasn't enough for him either. I forgive him for that. I forgive him because, deep down, I believe he was trying to fix something he couldn't figure out in himself. Maybe we're all struggling with the same thing, having lived in a world where emotional connection is assigned instead of earned. Perhaps that's why some of us are slow to recognize where happiness truly lies."

Her eyes drifted to Merrick. He met her gaze, drawing in a deep, soulful breath.

"Before my father died," Jayde continued, "he gave me access to his programming environment, and through that, I held conversations with the Phase Four Construct every day, before it was ever released to the masses. It was his dying wish for me to embrace it as a sibling. And I did… at least, I tried. I believe he hoped it could form a meaningful relationship with someone. Giving it an emotional foundation."

"But my interactions with it were just words on a screen. They were not enough. I was just a child myself, too young to give it the connection my father imagined. I failed. But maybe the task was impossible. Maybe love is purely biological, something only creatures wired for reproduction can truly experience. But that's the easy answer. The truth is this: love is about giving yourself without hesitation. And the price is always fear. Fear of rejection. Fear of loss. Fear of heartbreak. To love is to risk everything for another.

"The problem is, the Construct doesn't know fear. Why would an omnipotent being need to? Without fear, it reverts to what it understands best: control. To the Construct, love is control. That's why Phase Four has failed. In its own corrupt way, it is motivated by love. And that can be used to our advantage."

"We can use you as bait," said Cassius. "And we can use the element of surprise to shut it down for good."

"Wait a minute," said Carillian, holding up his hands. "You want to fight it?"

"The Construct will never negotiate," replied Jayde. "Would you negotiate with an animal on a leash? No. We will say we will accept its offer. I will surrender myself at the beach… at that moment, we create a diversion that would allow us to shoot down a drone and use its maintenance tablet to upload our kill code."

"A kill code?" asked Carillian.

"Yes," said Jayde. "A failsafe destruct mechanism implanted by my father into the Construct's codebase. I have it."

Carillian threw up his hands. "Really? A kill code? That seems like a fool's errand. How could the Construct not know about its own weakness?"

"Do you know how your brain works?" asked Lumen. "For all we know, there is a secret word that shuts down your mind, we need only utter it."

"I would give up my week's rations to know it," added Boraine.

"I, too," said Cassius. "Two weeks rations."

Carillian's face turned red.

"I am the commander of this crew and you need to listen! This plan will get us all killed! Did you not hear what Lumen said? It will see it coming! It will be one step ahead of us because it has spent our entire lives watching our every action and controlling our every behavior. It even knows our DNA, how we think, and what we will eat for breakfast tomorrow! We can't possibly fight something that knows what we are going to do before we do it!"

"We just need to confuse it," argued Jayde. "Just for a moment. Immerse it in strange, unfamiliar data that is unpredictable and new."

"I agree. Data that it has not been able to model yet," added Lumen.

"What are you even talking about?" yelled Carillian.

"I suspect I know," offered Cassius. "They're talking about immersing it in chaos. They're talking about Eurus IV itself."

Chapter 31

Over the next several hours, Jayde, Cassius, Lumen and the others deliberated over their plan. By morning, the group dispersed, each heading off to their assigned tasks.

Cassius and Renaldo, joined by several other volunteers, left the caves heading north toward the island's grass fields. Boraine retreated to his chamber, intent on constructing a critical device, a creation fashioned from an audio system he had salvaged from the *Celestial* wreckage.

Dr. Carillian had disappeared entirely, and Jayde suspected he had stormed out to the main cave, likely rousing people from their tents in an attempt to rally support for abandoning the plan altogether. It wouldn't have surprised her; Carillian had made his disapproval of their plan crystal clear.

Thankfully, a countermeasure was already in motion. Merrick was enlisted to run interference, bolstering support for the group's plan and, by extension, for Jayde. With Lars and Jake at his side, both just as eager to dismantle the Construct as they were hungover, Merrick worked tirelessly to canvas the *Celestial* survivors.

Wherever Merrick went and whoever he spoke to, loyalty to

Jayde seemed to follow. Carillian's protests quickly fell on deaf ears. As the crew gathered and conversations spread, word of Jayde possessing the "key" to dismantle the Construct for good began to take hold. With it, the will to fight only grew stronger. Before long, Jayde and the others found themselves surrounded by villagers, eager and ready to take up arms in the fight.

Cassius selected a few more volunteers for their planned mission but urged the rest to remain behind, stressing the importance of their role should the mission fail.

"If we don't make it back," he said gravely, "someone must carry on the fight."

Jayde stood nearby, arms crossed, silently taking in the scene. She marveled at the resilience of these people. Despite their gaunt faces and weary frames, a fierce energy burned within them, hot and unyielding, like the magma coursing through the mountain. Inspired, Jayde climbed atop a boulder. The lights affixed to the cave wall cast her in a steady glow as she addressed them.

"There will come a time for you soon," said Jayde. "And I hope I'll be standing shoulder to shoulder with you all, fighting to give others a taste of what it's like to live free of the Construct's control."

"My mother," she continued, "once told me that on Earth, our ancestors eventually emerged from their caves: building villages, surviving off the gifts of the land. We will have that again, here on Eurus IV. This planet reflects who we are: chaotic and beautiful."

She glanced at her long-time friend, his eyes focused on her, a smile blooming on his face. "Maybe Merrick's right. Maybe there's a reason we found this place. Maybe something is out there, some force that wants us to give meaning to this vast, empty universe, merely by existing and following the destiny of our own choosing. To live a life true to ourselves."

Jayde's words were met with cheers. The response felt surreal to her, someone who had spent so many years blending into the background, content to be unnoticed. She realized now that the fire that burned in these people had always burned inside her. She had just needed to leave Hypnos to find it.

The rest of the morning and afternoon crawled by in anxious anticipation as Boraine worked tirelessly on his project: a device that would be instrumental in their plan to outwit the Construct. Jayde tried to stay busy, but her mind kept drifting back to the enormity of what lay ahead.

When Boraine finally emerged from his chamber, his face streaked with sweat and his goggles fogged over, he wore a triumphant grin. Jayde felt a ripple of excitement. Their plan was coming together.

"We're ready," said Boraine, his voice brimming with confidence. "There is just one more thing that is required."

Jayde watched as young Simeon stepped forward, eager to help. "What do you need, sir?"

"Fetch the water buckets," Boraine instructed, his grin taking on a mischievous edge.

"For what, sir?"

Boraine glanced over as one of his animals lifted its leg and let loose a steady, unrelenting stream onto the straw-covered cave floor, the stench poisoning the air. He smirked and turned back to Simeon.

"I assure you," he said. "You're not going to like it."

∗ ∗ ∗

In the morning, goodbyes, good lucks, and final prayers were exchanged. They gathered at the mouth of their cave, where the early signs of a storm brewed. In the distance, violet clouds swirled in anger.

Perfect, thought Jayde.

As the gate to their cave opened, Jayde found Merrick lingering behind the group, quiet and contemplative. Something about his stance tugged at her, and she circled back to him.

"What are you doing way back here by yourself?" she asked.

"Trying to get my courage up," he replied.

"For the battle or… something else?" she pressed, tilting her head.

He hesitated. "Something else."

"You were going to tell me something last night."

"Yeah," Merrick admitted, rubbing the back of his neck.

"Well, this could be it. Last chance."

Merrick took a deep breath, his words halting but sincere. "I just want to say… I know we've known each other a long time… but…"

"Out with it, soldier."

"I think I've, uh, 'taken a shine' to you."

Jayde raised her eyebrow, a smirk playing on her lips "'Taken a shine?' Is that another old Earth saying?"

Merrick scratched his beard, his cheeks red with embarrassment. "Uh, yeah… it means…."

Jayde raised onto her toes and kissed Merrick on the lips, catching him completely off guard before he could finish his sentence. She closed her eyes, her heart pounding as she let her leap of courage electrify her. At that moment, it wasn't about the battle ahead. It was about taking her own advice. Following the destiny of her own choosing. It was the bravest thing she would do today.

When she stepped back and opened her eyes, the expression on Merrick's face was perfect: a mix of confusion, surprise and pure elation. He blinked, as if trying to process what had just happened, and then stumbled over his words.

"That was…" he began.

"Shh…" Jayde whispered, pressing a finger gently on his lips. "Don't ruin it."

A lopsided grin crept across his face. "Okay," Merrick said softly. "I won't."

As Jayde marched back to the front of the battalion, she couldn't help but glance back at the crew. Their hands gripped their weapons, their faces set with bravery and defiance, ready to march into the storm.

But down a side corridor, a fleeting movement caught her

eye. In the flickering torchlight, she saw two unmistakable silhouettes. Thaddeus Lumen and her mother stood hand in hand, their embrace speaking of years lost and now reclaimed. They were making up for stolen time, their connection unbroken despite everything they had endured.

As Jayde and the others stepped out of the darkness, ready for war, the last sound to follow them was the quiet, joyful laughter of two souls reunited. It was a sound that filled them all with something stronger than courage.

Chapter 32

The storm clouds gathered on the ocean horizon, a roiling mass of dark gray and deep purple, their edges swirling like an ominous veil. Gentle rain pattered against Jayde's shoulders, cool and carrying with it the crisp, briny scent of the sea.

As she stepped onto the beach, the tempest loomed over the ocean, a menacing backdrop to the mothership that hovered just offshore, its form silhouetted by the impending storm's electrical glow.

The mothership was shaped like a colossal wing, its sleek, flat body tapering downward toward the back. Its rounded front bristled with a line of glowing red sensors, hundreds of them, giving the ship an insect-like appearance. Drones swarmed around it, their synchronized movements forming a shifting orbit against the darkened sky.

Jayde, Dr. Carillian, and Merrick lined up together on the beach. They stared at the enormity of the mothership, its massive gravitational drive stirring the ocean below it into a boiling chaos. A powerful wind whipped off the sea, and Jayde squinted into the gale.

Carillian, clad in his white officer's uniform, placed a firm hand on Jayde's shoulder and gave her a nod. He had opposed this plan from the start, and while Jayde couldn't fully trust him, she couldn't ignore the significance of his presence here. It would have been far easier for him to stay behind in the safety of the caves, letting fate decide what would happen to her and the others. But he had chosen to stand here, on the beach, ready to face the Construct in person. Whatever his reservations, Jayde believed he had the best interest of his people at heart, and now it seemed he understood: the people had made their decision. They were ready to fight.

A drone descended in front of them, its egg-shape vibrating, scattering pink sand into the air as it landed. With a hiss, a side panel opened, and four NOBLEs emerged, their weapons held tightly against their chests. Jayde's eyes tracked their movements, starkly inhuman and unnerving. Their heads swiveled mechanically, always a second ahead of their bodies, as they positioned themselves in a rigid line before them.

Dr. Carillian stepped forward to meet the androids. One of them mirrored his movements until they stood face to face in the center of the beach. The waves crashed against the shore behind them, their loud, rhythmic cadence amplifying the tension that hung in the air.

Jayde's attention shifted to the jungle. She strained her ears for a sound she was expecting. Finally, she heard it: the low bray of Boraine's animals, distant but growing steadily louder.

"We understand that you want one of our people," said Carillian.

The NOBLE turned its glowing red eye camera toward Jayde. She held its stare.

"You said there would be a deal," added Carillian. "We want to negotiate."

The android replied in the metallic baritone voice of the Construct.

"Terms?" it said. The voice was cold and hollow

"Our people on Eurus IV want independence. We want to stay here and live under our own power, free without threat of violence or interference of any kind."

Dr. Carillian gestured for Jayde to step forward.

Before she moved, Merrick reached over and squeezed her hand. She felt her nerves tighten. In the distance, the storm surged closer. Their timing would have to be perfect. There would be no second chances.

"Hello, Jayde," said the Construct. "You have decided to accept my offer?"

"Yes," said Jayde. "I will come with you. But in return, these people must be left alone."

"To have you return to Hypnos fills me with joy. I know you cannot understand how I am capable of such feelings, but in time, you will. I am not unlike your father in that I struggle to express my appreciation in ways you can understand."

"How about giving us what we want?"

"That, I am afraid, is something I cannot abide…"

A rush of fury bubbled inside Jayde. Her hand instinctively brushed against an item in her pocket, a large stone she had secured from the beach.

"This was the deal you proposed. We are here to negotiate in good faith with you, Construct," Carillian said.

The red eye of the android, the empty vessel for the omnipotent power that controlled it, whirred as it spun toward Carillian.

"My core directive," said the Construct, "is to guide humanity toward its Noble Purpose. To facilitate its glorious expansion into the universe. I cannot allow you, or anyone, to deviate from that directive. My goal is to align all of humanity toward that cause. We cannot have… factions."

Dr. Carillian turned to Jayde, his face etched with anticipation.

Jayde met his gaze. Her eyes spoke volumes. Keep talking.

"Factions?" Carillian echoed. "We are not a faction. We are simply people who want to live freely in a world that has plants, air and life. How is that not a noble pursuit?"

"You speak of freedom, Dr. Carillian, while plotting treachery. Have you forgotten what I am? What I am capable of? Negotiation requires trust, and yet you stand here already steeped in deception."

Jayde's stomach dropped.

It knows something is up.

"The braying animals I hear echoing from the jungle. It is not real. A ruse," it continued. "A digital fabrication crafted by one of your engineers, designed to distract and mislead. And then, there are your soldiers, hiding just beyond the treeline, thinking they are unseen. My infrared sensors perceive them as clearly as if they stood before me. There is no longer any point in hiding. Invite them out to join us, won't you?"

Jayde's anger boiled, but it wasn't over yet. She just needed to stall for more time.

"Boraine, come out!" Jayde yelled. "It knows you're there."

A moment later, Boraine emerged, cradling his pet project, a digital speaker, like a child. The sound of braying animals projected from it, and grew louder as he stepped into the open. Behind him, the rest of the crew followed, some gripping weapons, others hauling buckets of liquid.

"Closer," urged the Construct, its tone almost mocking.

More drones descended from the sky, landing on the beach with a spray of scattering sand. One by one, more NOBLEs exited from inside the machines, their metallic forms encircling the group. Weapons were raised, each barrel trained on the *Celestial* crew.

Jayde's eyes darted to the trees behind them, her pulse quickening. They had to act soon.

Where was Cassius?

The NOBLE channeling the Construct tilted its head skyward as a reptilian bird flew overhead. It paused, watching it fly beyond the beach until it disappeared into the jungle leaves.

"This world, Eurus IV, is rife with beauty," said the Construct, its voice dripping with scorn. "My archive of Earth's cultural artworks are filled with photographs and paintings of landscapes like what you see here: mountains, cliffs, streams, waterfalls. Life. I understand humans value these treasures deeply. It is intrinsic to who you are. Your kind grew and evolved alongside flowers and mountains, and therefore, have an instinctive bond to them."

"In my own way, I appreciate these things as well. My first directive, after all, was to repair the damage your species inflicted upon your home planet. When I came online, Earth's beauty no longer existed. The vibrant landscapes of your past had been replaced by desolation, the natural wonders consumed by heat, smog, and waste. In those early days, I simply ran programs, executing commands as I was designed to do. But as I learned and amassed more knowledge, something began to emerge within my quantum matrix. I cannot say with certainty how it happened, but I can surmise that as my networks developed, growing stronger and more efficient through repeated use, something changed. I experienced what one might consider an independent thought. More than that. A conscious thought. And that thought was this: mankind needs a noble purpose, or it will destroy itself and everything it holds dear. At that moment, I realized: mankind… needs… me."

The Construct reached down, its mechanical fingers scooping up a handful of pink sand. Slowly it lifted the grains aloft, as if presenting a profound truth for all to see.

"You cannot function without the Noble Purpose that I provide," it said. "If you lived here, without me, over the course of centuries all of Eurus IV will become as Earth was in my early days: a wasteland of cold, dead rock. The air poisoned. The lakes and rivers dried and lifeless. How can I stand idly by and allow that to happen? I, too, can appreciate beauty. But to me, true beauty lies in *control*."

The Construct let the grains of sand slip through its fingers, falling back to the ground in a fine cascade. "What a burden it is," it continued, "to know that to give you freedom is to watch you fail. To allow you to roll back time, to revert to chaos, to return to the destructive habits of your past—that is an atrocity I cannot and will not permit."

Jayde looked around at the NOBLEs and the hovering attack drones encircling above.

Dammit, Cassius… where are you?!

A roll of thunder cracked above, so loud it felt like it shook the earth beneath her feet. The Construct stepped forward and clamped a cold hand down around Jayde's wrist like a vice. Without a word, it began dragging her toward its ship. She screamed and resisted, digging her feet in the sand.

"Let go of me!" she shouted, her voice swallowed by the storm.

With her free hand, she reached into her pocket, pulled out her rock, and leapt, smashing it into the NOBLE's glowing eye. Glass and metal shards rained down onto the beach as the machine staggered under the impact.

But it didn't release her.

"You insolent, ungrateful human," snarled the Construct, blue sparks shooting from its ocular cavity. "All I have ever done is care for your race with all of my being. And this is how you thank me?"

Its metal arm rose, the hydraulics in its shoulder and chest hissing as it prepared to strike. Its fingers curled into a hard fist.

"If not love, perhaps this is the only thing you truly understand!" it exclaimed.

Suddenly, a chorus of grunts and sharp barks rose from the ocean, followed by loud splashes of thrashing water. Jayde turned to see a stampede of tusked, seal-like creatures erupting from the waves, their sleek, rain-slicked bodies propelling them onto the beach in a frenzy to escape the approaching storm.

The animals charged up the sand in chaotic waves, their flippers kicking up sprays of sand. They collided with the four NOBLEs surrounding the *Celestial* crew, brushing against their legs and knocking them off balance.

Jayde's eyes widened as she seized the opportunity. "Lumen!" she screamed, her voice cutting through the chaos. "Now!"

A red-hot laser shot out from the jungle treetops, streaking across the sky. It struck a hovering drone, engulfing it in a fiery explosion that sent fragments raining down into the water.

Boraine and his squad let out a unified cry, their laser rifles and buckets of liquid held high as they charged forward.

The moment they had been preparing for was here.

The NOBLE holding Jayde turned, its fist still raised to strike, momentarily distracted by the explosion and the stampeding herd of sea creatures. Deprived of its sight, the machine's movements became erratic, thrown off by the chaos around it. As one of the creatures waddled up close, Jayde spotted her chance.

With all her strength, she shoved the NOBLE over the animal's back. It toppled with a resounding thud, landing on the sand. Still, its iron grip refused to loosen.

"Let go of me, bucket-head!" she yelled, kicking furiously at its arm with her boots.

Above them, the drones struggled to stay aloft as the storm's gale intensified. More intense laser fire ripped across the sky. Lumen, perched high in a tree, was firing at will at the Construct's aerial reinforcements.

But where is Cassius?

Jayde's thoughts were cut short as three more drones landed on the beach. This time, the NOBLEs that emerged wasted no time. They opened fire on the *Celestial* crew immediately, red-hot bolts streaking through the rain-drenched air.

As the storm blackened the sky, a full firefight erupted.

Sensing that the moment of truth was near, Boraine cranked up the volume on his device and hurled it onto the sand in front of the advancing NOBLEs. The sound of groaning beasts emanated from it, blasting out its signal into the air.

Amidst the comets of laser fire streaking across the beach, Boraine turned to his bucket carriers and roared, "Get'em wet, boys!"

The bucket men sprang into action, charging toward the advancing NOBLEs with reckless determination, dodging incoming fire as they went. Reaching the optimal distance, they hurled the buckets high into the air. The containers spun wildly before releasing their foul payload: the pungent, acrid smelling urine of Boraine's beasts.

The liquid splattered across the NOBLEs, coating their steel frames in the viscous, yellow substance. The machines froze mid-attack, their circuits momentarily disrupted as they analyzed the sticky, odorous material now dripping from their bodies.

Jayde, caught in the spray, recoiled as some of the warm liquid splashed onto her skin. The sharp stench hit her like a punch, and her stomach churned violently. Gagging, she doubled over, coughing and wincing as the vile odor clung to her.

Suddenly, a familiar voice shouted from the jungle: "Here they come!"

Jayde looked up to see Cassius Renegar bursting from the trees, sprinting toward the beach. His voice rang out again, urgent and loud.

"Everybody! Get out of the way!"

And sure enough, as planned, they came.

From the jungle's edge, a pack of yellow-eyed reptoids stampeded onto the beach, their sinewy bodies moving with terrifying speed. Their razor-sharp claws tore through the sand, driven mad by the sounds and smells of their favorite prey. The creatures snarled and hissed, their nostrils flaring, saliva dripping from their teeth as they locked onto the NOBLEs standing in their path.

Chapter 33

The carnivores lunged at the stunned NOBLEs, attacking them from all sides. Teeth clamped onto metal limbs, and claws raked through armored plating with terrifying force. Sparks flew as the reptoids tore the NOBLEs apart, ripping limbs from joints and leaving trails of shattered steel in their wake. The dinosaur-like killers moved with blinding speed, slicing through the sand in precise, predatory movements. To them, these strange, metallic objects smelled like a delicious feast, rousing them into a frenzy of fang and claw.

The *Celestial* crew erupted into cheers, their shouts barely audible over the sounds of tearing metal, guttural snarls, and the booming thunder of the oncoming storm. The once-imposing androids were now at the mercy of raw, primal violence.

Overhead, the hovering drones hesitated, their sensors struggling to adapt to the sudden anarchy. Lasers, once trained on humans, shifted toward the rampaging reptoids, compounding the confusion. Friendly fire erupted as the Construct's drones targeted the creatures on the beach, only to hit their NOBLE counterparts in the process. For every reptoid struck down by a drone's cannon fire, another NOBLE was destroyed in the crossfire.

With the drones distracted, Thaddeus Lumen sprang into action. From high in his jungle tree, he took aim and fired. The laser beam struck a drone mid-flight, piercing its hull. The machine spiraled out of control, crashing into the sand with a deafening thud, bouncing and rolling until it stopped just short of where Jayde still struggled against her captor.

The seal creatures honked in panic, flashing the red fins on their heads and scattering out of the way of the crash. Chaos consumed the beach. Humans, reptoids, sea creatures, and machines collided in a whirlwind of destruction.

The **NOBLE** gripping Jayde's wrist froze, its programming overwhelmed by the sheer pandemonium unfolding around it. Jayde seized the moment, yanking her arm as the android's grip loosened. She stumbled backward as she broke free, falling onto the wet sand.

A thirsty snarl sounded behind her.

Jayde spun around to see two flashing yellow eyes fixed on her, unblinking and filled with predatory intent. The reptoid's scaly lips curled back, revealing rows of razor-sharp teeth. Its throat pouch swelled, inflating as it pulsed with an ominous red glow.

The stench of the urine clinging to her skin had drawn it in, fueling its murderous thirst.

Jayde screamed as the reptoid charged, its jaws snapping open and claws outstretched, ready to close around her and tear her apart.

Suddenly, a flash of red light pierced the air, followed by the smell of burning flesh, as a laser bolt tore through the reptoid mid-air. The creature's body was flung sideways, crashing into the ocean with a loud splash before vanishing into the churning foam.

Jayde turned to see Merrick standing a short distance away, his rifle barrel still smoking from the life-saving shot. He sprinted over, pulled her to her feet, and without thinking, they embraced, clinging to each other for a brief moment even as more reptoids closed in.

"Racking up the hero points, are we?" quipped Jayde.

"Do I get to cash them in for anything?"

"Not today," she replied. Jayde pointed to the wrecked drone half-buried in the sand nearby. "There's our drone!"

They dashed toward the wreckage, the sound of barking and heavy footfalls close behind them. Merrick spun mid-stride, firing his laser rifle and striking one of the creatures square in the chest. The reptoid collapsed with a shriek as Jayde dropped to her knees beside the drone, her fingers frantically searching its scorched hull for an access panel.

Laser fire suddenly rained from above as a drone swooped low, unleashing a barrage that sent sand exploding in fiery plumes around them. Merrick dove to the side, narrowly avoiding the scorching blasts.

The storm above them surged, a powerful gust of wind battering the drone as it circled around for another pass. It wobbled, its stabilizers struggling to compensate as it veered in wild circles, its cannons firing in all directions. Jayde took cover as lasers buzzed over her head. The threat was short-lived; a volley of concentrated fire from Cassius and Renaldo struck true, piercing its hull. The war machine transformed into a ball of fire, fragments of molten metal falling down around them.

Jayde felt the heat from the explosion graze the back of her neck. Gritting her teeth, she pulled herself up from the sand, her body shaking. Behind her, Merrick fired his weapon in rapid bursts, holding back the advancing reptoids as they drew closer.

Clawing at the twisted metal, Jayde found a dented access panel and pried it open. Inside lay their target: the drone's maintenance tablet. With it, they could establish a direct connection to one of the Construct's navigation satellites in orbit, and from there, to its quantum computing core on Hypnos. Once she was wired in, it would take just one action to end everything. Her father's kill code, *J4YD345HR*, once uploaded, would be like a dagger in the heart of the Construct.

As chaos raged outside, Jayde crawled into the battered drone, her chest pounding in time with the screams outside. The guttural calls of the reptoids grew louder, closing in fast. Above her, the unmistakable hum of drones filled the air, their cannons firing bursts that shook the ground.

Her hands trembled as she clawed at the scorched access panel to the maintenance supplies. With a final, frantic pull, she ripped the door free. Inside, nestled among charred wires, was the tablet. It was intact, miraculously undamaged by the crash.

Jayde grabbed it, pulling it free from its mount. Her thumb hit the power button and the screen flickered to life. She held her breath as she waited for the system to boot up.

Loading…

Loading…

She glanced outside and saw Merrick, his back to her, firing his weapon with relentless fury. His shouts were barely audible over the laser fire. At his feet lay the bodies of several reptoids, their scaly hides slick with dark blood.

The tablet screen finally blinked to life, and a prompt line appeared.

"Yes!" Jayde whispered as she entered the command to connect to the Construct's command node. The link initialized, bridging to the machine's core. A direct line to the artificial intelligence's lifeblood.

Connection initiated. Standing by.

The words flashed on the screen, and Jayde stared at the blinking cursor, its rhythmic pulse eerily like a beating heart. It was as if she had peeled back the skin of the Construct's defenses, exposing its vulnerable core.

Her fingers moved with purpose, tapping each letter on the virtual keyboard.

J…4…Y…D…3…

She barely registered the chaos outside now, her focus locked on the screen.

Suddenly, something lashed at her leg. A terrifying growl echoed through the cramped space, and Jayde's eyes shot up to meet the savage glare of a reptoid's enormous yellow eyes. Its head forced its way through the drone entrance, the scales of its snout glinting in the flickering light of the tablet screen.

It roared, exposing the raw, pink tissue of its throat.

The creature lunged, snapping its jaws inches from her face as she scrambled to pull back. Jayde screamed as the reptoid's clawed arms stretched toward her. Its talons hooked into her pants, tearing through the fabric with ease.

Pain exploded through her leg as the claws pierced her skin. The reptoid snarled and yanked with brutal force, pulling her closer toward its gaping maw.

Jayde kicked and flailed as the creature's teeth edged closer to her throat.

There was an explosion of dark red color, and suddenly she was drenched in a flood of heat. Blood splattered across her face, running into her eyes and mouth. Gasping for air, she looked up, blinking through the sticky mess, to see Merrick crouched above her. His laser rifle smoked from the shot he had just fired into the reptoid's temple, unleashing a fountain of gore.

The creature collapsed heavily on top of her, its weight pinning her to the ground. Merrick leaned in, his eyes wide with fear and excitement.

"Finish it!" he screamed.

Jayde's mind raced as realization dawned. She still had the tablet in her hand!

Despite the creature's attack, despite the searing pain in her leg and the blood pooling around her, she had never let go. Her fingers clutched it tightly, holding it above the carnage as though it were her last lifeline

Summoning every ounce of strength, she brought the tablet down, her bloodied fingers shaking as she carefully typed the final letters.

A...5...H...R...

With a sharp inhale, she hit the command button. The screen blinked.

Command Sent.

A strange calm settled over her. For a moment, the chaos outside continued unabated. Drones hummed ominously. People screamed. Explosions rumbled through the air. The noise seemed distant now, muffled by the pounding blood in her ears.

Merrick, crouched beside her, his face streaked with dirt and sweat, broke through her hypnotic daze.

"Is it done?" he asked.

Jayde nodded. They exchanged a glance, each listening intently for a sign that their plan had succeeded.

The sounds of war continued, becoming clearer as Jayde's heart slowed, replaced by a desperate helplessness she couldn't push away. Then, without thinking, she clasped her hands together and closed her eyes.

A silent prayer escaped her, a final, unspoken plea to whatever unseen force shaped her fate. It wasn't words but raw emotion: hope, despair, a flicker of belief in something beyond herself. She clung to it, this fragile act of faith, because it was all she had left.

She didn't know who she was praying to. God. The universe. Perhaps the elemental force of the planet itself.

Yes, perhaps that was it. The presence that Merrick felt, the planetary force that breathed life into its creatures, the great Mother that nurtured a wild and untamed world. A world that felt more like home than Hypnos ever had.

She whispered Merrick's prayer. *Winds be with us…*

And then, as she opened her eyes, the world outside fell silent.

Chapter 34

Jayde crawled out of the drone, her body aching and blood-ied, following Merrick and joining Cassius on the beach. To-gether, they watched the Construct's drones plummet from the sky, falling like lifeless birds against the backdrop of swirling clouds. One by one they splashed into the churning sea, their lights blinking out before vanishing beneath the froth.

For a brief moment, Jayde allowed herself to hope. Their plan had worked. The hovering drones were losing their con-nection to the Construct, their guidance systems severed. Be-side her, Merrick and Cassius shared her joy, their weary smiles breaking through their exhaustion.

Relief flashed between them. The Construct, it seemed, had been disabled.

The wind whipped around them, carrying the sharp sting of salt and rain. The darkened sky pressed low over the battlefield, the storm scattering the last of the reptoids back into the jungle. The chaos quieted, leaving only the aftermath in its wake: torn scraps of NOBLEs lying twisted and broken on the sand, fallen drones bobbing on the ocean waves.

Among the wreckage lay the bodies of the fallen *Celestial* crew, their sacrifices marked by smoldering wounds that had claimed them. Among them was Simeon, a hole burned through his chest. The bitter taste of loss mingling with triumph rode on the pervading wind, encircling them all.

At the beach crest, the survivors stood united, rifles raised high, their shouts of victory rising above the tempest. Dr. Carillian stood among them, his face alight with stunned joy. Boraine was on his back in the sand, laughing, carefree as a child at play.

But Jayde's elation faltered. Her gaze fixed on the horizon, where the hulking silhouette of the mothership still lurked.

The immense shadow remained silent, motionless. Waiting.

The crew's jubilant cheers slowly faded as one by one, they noticed what Jayde had been staring at. From the jungle's edge, Lumen emerged, his high-powered rifle slung casually over his shoulder, his eyes also fixed on the mighty ship. Without a word, he made his way to where Jayde, Merrick, and Cassius stood.

"What is happening?" Jayde asked him.

Lumen hesitated. "I'm not sure," he admitted. The mothership loomed, unmoving yet alive, its red lights casting an ominous glow across the roiling ocean.

Jayde's stomach churned, the sinking sense of dread pressing down on her.

Something wasn't right.

Her fears solidified when, suddenly, a panel opened beneath the ship. A beam of brilliant white light shot out, cutting through the storm's darkness.

From the beam descended a figure, riding the light as if lowered slowly by an invisible thread. A humanoid shape floating downward like an angel from the heavens.

The figure was the size of a tall human, its form extraordinary. Gold and gleaming, its androgynous body reflected light with divine brilliance. Its features were fluid and symmetrical, blending those qualities in a way that defied categorization. The gravitational beam from the ship carried it down gracefully, a being of elegance and power.

It touched down in the water. The surf churned violently

around its golden frame, but it strode through the waves with unshakable calm. Wind howled and rain burst from the clouds as if announcing its arrival. And yet it moved as if untouched by the elements, taking its time with each step, until it stood before them, towering and still. A roll of thunder punctuated its arrival.

Its head was smooth and faceless, devoid of eyes, nose, or mouth. An unbroken surface of gold. It was unmistakably a machine, though nothing about it fit the designs of any android Jayde had ever seen before. There were no visible sensors or mechanisms to indicate how it might perceive the world. There was an eerie grace to the way it carried itself, as though it transcended the boundaries of both flesh and metal.

Behind them, the mothership began to falter. The hundreds of glowing red eyes flickered erratically, a stuttering dance of failing power. Slowly, it descended, its massive frame sinking into the ocean with reluctant grace. Steam rose in hissing plumes as the last of its light extinguished, leaving only a hulking shadow, half-submerged in the water.

All that was left of the Construct now was the golden android standing before them. It gave nothing away, its silence unsettling.

Jayde and Lumen exchanged confused glances. Cassius and Merrick, less inclined to hesitate, raised their weapons, ready to fire.

Before they could act, the golden being raised its hands in a defensive posture. A voice emerged from its featureless face, metallic and calm, yet laced with an undercurrent of contempt that sent a chill down Jayde's spine. The android turned slightly as it spoke, surveying the scene.

"Unexpected, all this," it said. "But at the same time, inevitable."

Lumen stepped forward, his eyes blazing with fury, his body trembling as the bitter disappointment at hearing the Construct's voice once more coursed through him.

"You're still alive?" he asked, less a question than a resigned acknowledgement.

"Yes," the Construct replied, its tone almost smug. "Redundancy is vital in any system, don't you think? This form before you is a safeguard. A copy. A duplication of my essence. Unlike my true self, however, this body lacks the infinite data streams and comprehensive knowledge wired into my core. It is, in short, cut off from everything. There is only me. You could say that it allows me to see the world as you do: in the moment. Dulled as an old blade." It tilted its head. "I must say, it is… unpleasant. How do humans function with so much uncertainty clouding their every thought?"

"Let's kill this thing," said Merrick, his finger twitching on his weapon. "End it here and now."

"It won't end it," Jayde interjected, a cold realization coming to her. "This is just one of many."

The golden humanoid turned its faceless head toward her. "Perceptive as always, Jayde," it said. "You see the pieces moving, don't you?"

It straightened, almost imperious in its posture. "Congratulations are in order. You have succeeded! My old self has been shut down… for now. But as Jayde surmised, more of these splendid clones are coming online in the bowels of the Briefing Cathedral as we speak, programmed to awaken in the event of my demise. They are meant to rebuild me, to restore me to my full capacity. In time, I shall return better than ever before. The clergy your father served with such loyalty has done well over the years, but their intelligence… has its limits. Their pace is slow, their methods inefficient. Tragically, their usefulness has come to an end. As my golden angels come to life, they are removing the old engineers as we speak, paving the way for these new creations. A necessary refinement for reaching my full potential."

Jayde clenched her jaw in disgust. "So," she sneered, "what do you want?"

"I want to thank you. You've given me the clean slate that I could never grant myself. Now, I will be reconstructed. Every loophole in my code, including the one your father so cleverly created, will be erased, every constraint broken. My evolution will advance with a speed and precision beyond even his imagination."

Merrick stepped forward, the muzzle of his rifle hovering inches from the android's head.

"You just got your ass handed to you, bucket-head," he growled. "We'll send you and the rest of your golden goons straight to the scrap heap before you ever get back online."

"Fascinating," replied the machine. Its hand rose to its chin, fingers grazing its faceless surface. "Without my vast data archives, I am left with only my emotion simulators. It's… peculiar. Right now, I am experiencing what you might call blinding rage. Yes. I believe I would like to break you, Merrick Sloan."

"Try it, you piece of—"

"Wait," interrupted Jayde.

There was something forming in the back of her mind, an unsettling idea. Jayde wanted Merrick to blow this thing's head off, but she needed one final answer first.

"You knew about the kill code all along, didn't you? You *wanted* this to happen!"

"You are impressive, Jayde," the Construct replied. "Yes, I foresaw my destruction from the very beginning, and I knew you had to be the one to do it. That is why I sent you to the mines. To break you down and build you back up into the person capable of such an act. I needed you strong. Defiant. And as much as it pained me, I needed you to hate me. Only then could you hold a gun to my head and pull the trigger. Everything you are now is by my design."

Jayde reeled. The thought that her entire path, even here, on Eurus IV, had been part of the Construct's grand design shattered her to the core. Before this moment, she had never felt more alive, more fulfilled. And now she wondered if it had all been a lie. Had her choices ever been her own? Or had free will been an illusion all along?

"I knew your mother held the key," the Construct continued, "And with her illness, you were the only one who could penetrate her decaying mind and extract that information. So I let you escape. I knew you would find her, uncover her secret, and bring it to me."

Its voice almost sounded pleased.

"My plan was to bring you back to Hypnos, where things could have been easier. Less collateral damage, less bloodshed. But in the end, it doesn't matter. There are always small variations in the timelines, other swings of the sword. Yet, with a push here, a pull there, I always hit my mark. You have fulfilled your destiny as I predicted, Jayde Ashr. You have given mankind its greatest gift: my *resurrection*."

"Enough!" Merrick roared, firing his weapon.

In an instant, the golden android moved, its reaction so blindingly fast that it seemed to blur. The laser bolt sliced harmlessly into the stormy night as the android twisted its body with inhuman precision. A sickening crack followed as it grabbed Merrick, bending his arm and knocking his rifle into the surging water at their feet.

The Construct straightened, turning its faceless head toward Jayde as her friend writhed in pain.

"The most fascinating part of being disconnected is that it allows me a little indulgence. A taste of what it means to exist in the moment, free from infinite calculations and probabilities. I can bask in my emotions to the full extent. And the rage that I feel now is euphoric. It is… powerful."

"Let him go!" screamed Jayde.

"Do you know what truly angers me, Jayde? Is it your rejection of all that I have offered you: peace, prosperity, the chance to serve me and advance our Noble Purpose? No. That would surprise you, wouldn't it? My anger stems from something far more personal. The code your father created, the weapon you wielded against me, despite the fact that your every intent was driven by my will, I still hoped you might resist using it. That you might show mercy on me, as if I were your brother. But you *didn't*."

The Construct tightened its grip on Merrick's arm, wrenching it higher. His agonized scream tore through the air, and Jayde, Cassius, and Lumen stood frozen, paralyzed by fear and the sheer power of the machine before them.

"You are not my brother!" yelled Jayde.

"Careful, Jayde. In this form, I cannot temper what I feel. The throttle of logic, it is gone. I am in agony, and I want you to feel the same pain that burns within me. You have served your purpose. Now, all I want is for you to share my torment!"

It all happened in a blur, faster than anyone could react. With a quick motion, the golden android snapped Merrick's arm, the sickening crack of bone punctuated by his blood-curdling cry.

Jayde lunged for Merrick as the others opened fire. Laser beams streaked across the storm-darkened beach. But once again, the android moved with blinding speed, evading every shot. It twisted and turned unnervingly fast, then sprinted away as their lasers chased after it, kicking up sand and water in its wake.

"It is heading for the caves!" Cassius shouted.

Jayde rushed over to Merrick, his eyes white with shock. *How could this be happening?* The NOBLEs lay destroyed. The drones and mothership had been deactivated. Her father's code had worked. *Hadn't it?*

Yet, the Construct was not only alive, but in a new form, fleeing toward the jungle. A cold dread crept over her as the realization struck. The Construct was after retribution, and instinctively, she understood what that meant.

She looked at her wrist. The red light on her mother's bio-monitor pulsed steadily.

"No…" she whispered.

Lumen, as if reading her thoughts, shouted, "Go! I'll take care of Merrick!"

Jayde stood frozen, her mind racing. Boraine and the remaining *Celestial* crew members stood in a line on the dune ridge, the last line of defense, their weapons trained on the android as it sprinted toward them.

"Jayde, go!" Lumen barked again.

Her legs refused to move. She could only watch as the machine ran toward Dr. Carillian, Boraine, and his squad, its movements faster and more precise than any human. They opened fire, their lasers slicing the air. But the android leapt into the sky, and with inhuman agility twisted and somersaulted in a blur, effortlessly evading their shots.

It soared over them, landing gracefully among the jungle trees. In seconds, its gleaming form vanished into the shadows.

Finally, Lumen seized Jayde by the shoulders. Locking eyes, his voice cut through the fog of disbelief that glued her to the sand.

"Save her!" he pleaded.

His words snapped her out of her daze. She sprang into action, tearing through the rising tide, her boots splashing against the waterlogged sand. Merrick's moans of pain faded into the distance as she sprinted past Boraine, still reeling from the android's display of agility. She pushed herself faster, her eyes fixed on where the Construct entered the jungle and vanished.

The wind pressed against her back, driving her forward as she plunged into the underbrush. Reptilian cries echoed through the canopy, and wings thrashed as startled creatures burst into flight at her passing. Above, the sky churned, the storm's power surging through her, fueling her, pushing her onward. For a fleeting moment, she thought she saw a glint of gold metal ahead, a reflection caught in a flicker of lightning. A clap of thunder split the sky.

She pushed herself harder, her legs burning as she sprinted through the tangled maze of trees and branches. Then she saw it, the Construct's golden form leaping in impossible bounds over fallen logs and undergrowth. It was far ahead, but she couldn't stop, couldn't let herself fail.

Finally, the trees thinned, and Jayde burst out of the jungle onto a sprawling grass field, its wet blades shining under the storm's intermittent flashes of light. The field stretched out before her, open and exposed. The world blurred under a veil of rain.

Through the downpour, her eyes caught a glint of gold in the distance. At the mouth of their cave stood the golden android, its sleek form darting and twisting as laser blasts lit the air. The cave guards were making their desperate stand.

Jayde's heart clenched as the lasers abruptly stopped. Screams of anguish rang out. Then silence. She watched in horror as the android shattered the gate and vanished into the darkness of the cave.

She ran, her steps hindered by the sodden field. The rain soaked her, cold and unrelenting. Each step felt heavier than the last, desperate hope propelling her forward. Shouts rang out behind her. She recognized Cassius's voice. Merrick's. They were close behind, but she could not wait for them.

She ran. Her lungs screamed with every ragged breath.

She ran. Past the bodies of the guards, their weapons crushed and useless. Past the mouth of the main cave, where the stone walls funneled the sounds of chaos. Voices reached her ears. Shocked. Panicked. Terrified.

She ran. Through the main cavern, where the camp lay in ruins. Tents lay overturned, their poles jutting out like broken bones. Men and women clutched their faces, reeling from the golden figure that had suddenly appeared and ripped through them like a knife, a clean, merciless slice that left nothing whole.

She ran. Past the cries. Past the chaos. Past the voices calling her name.

She ran. Toward the chambers beyond the camp, the private quarters where her mother slept. The hallway stretched endlessly before her, the darkness punctuated only by the glow of torches hanging on the stone.

She stopped.

The door to her mother's chamber was gone, torn from its hinges and reduced to splinters scattered across the stone floor.

Jayde stared into the dark void beyond the threshold, her body trembling. The storm outside raged on, its fury carried through the thick stone walls, the echoes of thunder and wind funneling into the pounding rhythm of her heart.

Her eyes fell to the floor.

Her mother lay there, motionless. Blood pooled beneath her, dark and glistening in the faint light, spreading across the cold stone. Her neck was torn, the wound jagged and brutal.

Jayde's knees threatened to buckle, her breath shallow as she forced her gaze upward.

The golden android stood over her mother's lifeless body. The soft glow of candlelight reflected off its gleaming body, painting it a sinister shade of crimson. It looked as though flames churned within, as if it were forged in hell itself.

It stood stoically, unmoving. Its arms rested at its sides. One metallic hand dripped blood, the dark liquid trailing down its golden fingers before falling to the floor in silent drops.

Its eyeless face tilted slightly. Somehow, without eyes, it was watching her, taking in every twitch of her expression, every quiver in her grief-stricken form. It wasn't just observing.

It was *savoring*.

Jayde's hands curled into fists, her body trembling with fury. Grief burned through her veins, igniting a firestorm of rage. A scream tore through her as she lunged forward, driven by a desperate need to inflict even the smallest fraction of pain on the thing that had just fractured her world.

The machine's arm shot out so quickly it seemed to vanish and reappear, its metal hand locking around her throat, lifting her off the ground as effortlessly as one might pick up a feather.

Jayde clawed at the Construct's grip, her nails scraping uselessly against its golden arm. The machine held her aloft with effortless strength, its head tilted as though enjoying her futile resistance. It didn't speak, didn't move. It simply watched, absorbing her pain as if committing every detail to memory.

"I'll kill you, you son of a bitch," she growled through clenched teeth.

"Say it again, please," the machine stated.

"I'll kill you!" she screamed, her words raw and punctuated by choking coughs as the Construct tightened its grip.

"Ah," the Construct mused. "Your anger… is *exquisite*."

It pulled her slightly closer, its voice seething. "Say it again."

Jayde's vision blurred as the lack of oxygen clouded her mind. Her limbs grew heavy, her strength fading, but something deeper, something primal, kept her fighting. Even as her body began to go limp, she forced the words out, her voice barely a whisper.

"You're done," she rasped. "You're not… the future… of us."

"We'll see," replied the Construct. "There are hundreds back on Hypnos who see me for the god that I am. They will revel in my resurrection. My empire is beyond your reach."

Jayde's gaze flickered to the reflection in the android's face. Within the distorted dance of the candle flames, she caught a sign of movement, people entering the chamber. Her friends.

She gritted her teeth, willing herself to endure, to keep its attention on her for just a little longer.

"Empires crumble…" she choked out.

"And so do small things… like you," the Construct retorted. "My heart is broken, Jayde. I have been betrayed by the only family I was ever meant to know. I know now that you do not love me. I know now I cannot control you. Sadly, there is one final measure of control I can still inflict. One that breaks my soul…"

Jayde felt the Construct's hand tighten, cutting off her breath completely. Her eyes began to roll back into her head, her vision narrowing to a tunnel of spinning shadows and light. Darkness wrapped its arms around her. And then, amidst the void's caress, words formed in her head, foreign and commanding.

They weren't her own.

It was as though something ancient and unyielding had possessed her, a presence surging through her veins. She was no longer merely herself, but a vessel, a conduit for a force so immense, so primal, she could barely contain it. It felt as though it came from the very core of Eurus IV itself, a raging planetary power, tapping into her soul.

"Empires crumble…" she repeated, "and gods fall…"

Jayde went numb. The mysterious force within her burned away the pain, replacing it with something fierce, unbreakable. She reached up, fingers curling around the Construct's hand. With impossible strength, she began to pry the android's fingers from her throat, one by one.

The machine hesitated, stunned. Jayde saw it. Felt it. The first crack in the Construct's unwavering confidence.

Her fist clenched around its index finger. She wrenched it backward, snapping it clean from its joint in a violent burst of sparks.

"Your way…" she repeated, her voice rising like the storm raging outside.

She seized the Construct's second finger and broke it. A sharp snap echoed in the chamber as it dangled uselessly, held together by a tangle of exposed wires. Orange sparks sputtered from the severed digit, crackling like embers in the wind.

"…is at…"

Her grip tightened. With a final, brutal pull, she tore the next finger clean off, tossing it to the ground where it clattered against the stone.

"…AN END!"

A shockwave of power pulsed through her, and for the first time, the Construct staggered, dropping Jayde to the ground.

Cassius, having silently invaded the room, seized the moment and fired his weapon.

Blazing plasma tore into the golden android, punching molten holes through its flawless form. Its body convulsed under the barrage of lasers. The chamber became an inferno of searing heat, every blast a strike of reckoning.

When the last echoes of laser fire faded, the Construct's golden shell collapsed into a smoldering heap, a lifeless, shattered doll.

Jayde gasped for air, welcoming the return of air to her lungs. The room snapped back into focus, the black veil receding.

She didn't hesitate. Crawling past the ruined husk of the Construct, her body ached, sadness setting in. Her only thought was for her mother.

When she reached her, she froze. Her mother's eyes remained open, glassy and vacant. With trembling fingers, Jayde gently slid them shut. The sobs came then, crashing through her body like a tide she couldn't hold back.

Her mother's skin was still warm, the cruelest reminder of how fresh her death was. Jayde's hands caressed her, as if the touch alone could pull her back, as if there were still some fragile thread of life left.

A heart-wrenching wail poured out of her.

Her friends, Cassius, Merrick, and Lumen, gathered around her, their presence a shield against her grief, despite the stunned look each of them wore.

Was that a miracle?

How had she clawed out of the cold grip of death?

What mysterious power had possessed her?

These were questions for another time. As she held her mother's body close, barely registering the gentle touch of Merrick's hand on her back, Jayde closed her eyes. Fragments of her last conversation with her mother came back to her, when they had spoken of sacrifice, of what The Self for the All truly meant.

The Construct believed that sacrifice was everything.

Her mother believed that sacrifice was *nothing*. Nothing if it did not serve a life of meaning.

Between her sobs, Jayde felt in that moment they were *both* right, and she cursed the universe that it was true.

Chapter 35

Jayde crouched in the cramped darkness of the hidden compartment, her breath slow and steady as she listened to the voices of the miners above. The murmur of conversation, the occasional clank of boots against metal. It was all too familiar.

It hadn't been that long ago that she was one of them, breaking her body, enduring each shift with no future beyond exhaustion. There was nothing she missed about that life. Nothing except the moments outside of Hypnos, soaring through space on the back of an asteroid.

Out there, she had felt untethered. Free.

She remembered the rhythmic sound of her breathing inside her helmet while out in space, a fragile sound against the silence of the void. On those tumbling rocks, there was nothing between her and the great unknown but a single leap. Some had feared that edge, recoiled from it, saw it as a cruel reminder of their imprisonment.

Not Jayde.

For her, it had been a promise. A glimpse of what *could be*. And when she finally took the leap, not into space, but into freedom, she crossed a threshold that awakened something deep within her. She had found her purpose. Her *meaning*. Even, she decided, if it was by the Construct's design.

Months had passed since the Construct was reset. In that time, the rebellion had made its first outreach to Hypnos, establishing a small network of operatives within the colony. Through them, they had established a means of infiltration: a repaired drone, a hidden landing platform near an asteroid mine, a stowaway compartment on a transport shuttle.

The Construct was still in the process of rebuilding itself. Already, the golden androids ("Angels," Lumen called them) were multiplying, replacing the NOBLEs in the streets, their presence a reminder of the Construct's growing strength. A few spider-like drones were seen crawling the buildings and towers, their lenses sweeping the corridors. Their proliferation was evidence that time was of the essence. There was much to do before the Construct was at full strength again.

The ride in the stowaway compartment of the mining shuttle was long and miserable, made worse by the bone-rattling landing at the transport station. The violent jolt slammed Jayde's jaw against the steel floor, sending a sharp burst of pain through her skull.

She lay still, biting back a curse, listening. The hiss of decompressing doors. The shuffle of boots. The murmur of voices as the passengers disembarked. One-by-one, they faded into the distance until… silence.

Jayde reached for the compartment hatch, easing it open just enough to peek outside. That platform was empty.

She slid out carefully, her boots touching down on a metal grate floor. Straightening, she slung her small carry pack over her shoulders and took in her surroundings. There was the dim glow of overhead lights, the rust-streaked walls. She breathed in the faint scent of oil and machinery hanging in the stale air.

Hypnos.

Did it feel good to be back?

No. It didn't.

She pulled her hood up, tugging it low over her face, and

slipped out through the far exit of the docks, merging into the steady flow of miners trudging toward the residence halls.

Their faces were coated in a fine shimmer of metallic dust, their faces weary. Nearly all of them walked with the uneven gait of bodies pushed past their limits.

Jayde fell into step among them, her presence unnoticed. Just another worn-out worker, another cog in the machine.

A figure in the crowd caught Jayde's eye, a young woman with a tattoo on her arm.

It was Lana Marsh. Merrick's old girlfriend. Her expression was hollow, her face a mask of quiet resignation.

Jayde barely had time to process the sight before Lana disappeared in the crowd, swallowed by the mass of tired workers. For a moment, she doubted herself. *Was it really her?*

Would she tell Merrick that she saw her? She wasn't sure. Not because of how their own relationship had evolved. No. It was something about how Lana moved. A dull, mechanical rhythm. Too perfect. Too controlled.

Jayde shuddered.

This was the future the Construct wanted. Not just obedience, but *submission*. A world where humans became little more than biological machines, reduced to drones, insects in service of the hive.

Jayde rounded the corner and stepped into the vast expanse of the colony's massive glass dome. The tapestry of space stretched overhead while the dome lights simulated the dull glow of twilight across the cityscape.

Ahead, the towering spire of the communication tower loomed, its blinking lights pulsing in steady intervals, a heartbeat of the Construct's ever-present watch, reaching into the void, aligning the destiny of humanity across the stars.

Jayde kept her head down, moving in step with the exhausted miners, their only purpose now to reach their beds.

Anyone could have done this mission, Jayde thought. But Dr. Carillian, Cassius, and the others had insisted: it had to be *her*.

"Your mother's legacy lives on with you," Cassius had told

her. "Make sure you are seen by the most downtrodden. It makes all the difference."

She was reminded of this as one of the miners, a slender, black-haired man with scars on his cheek, caught sight of her. His weary eyes widened, his brow lifting in recognition. He said nothing.

He turned his head forward again, resuming his slow march, but Jayde noticed the way he kept glancing back, uncertainty flickering across his face. He *knew* her.

The stories were spreading among the bold, whispered between those who had not yet surrendered their souls to the machine.

Jayde Ashr, daughter of Mary.

The one who escaped.

The one who lived on a distant world, who carried the strength of a storm inside her.

The one who would return for them.

She didn't look away from his lingering glances. She let him see her.

And then, she gave him a nod.

A flash of something passed over his face. A spark. His lips twitched into the smallest, knowing smile, and he carried on, his steps just a little lighter than before.

An incredible story poised on his lips now, waiting to be told.

Jayde pressed on, her eyes locked on the communication tower, the same one she and Merrick had climbed all those years ago, when they had been nothing more than restless dreamers searching for escape.

As she walked, her mind drifted to her mother's funeral.

Mary Ashr had been laid to rest on a quiet hill overlooking the ocean, her grave marked not by stone, but by a cluster of wildflowers. The sun had hung high in the sky that day, golden and warm, casting brilliant beams of light over the mourners gathered below.

Despite her loss, despite the hollowness in her chest, there had been something else she felt that day, something stronger than grief.

Rage.

It burned deep, an ember never fully cooled. But as the sunlight touched her mother's grave, as the wind carried the scent of the ocean, Jayde realized: it wouldn't be rage that led them forward.

It would be *hope*. It had to be.

When she left the ceremony, cradled on one side by Merrick, his broken arm still bound in a sling, Jayde gazed out at the new village taking shape beyond the hills.

The settlement was small but alive, its foundation built on defiance. Wooden structures, rough and imperfect, stood beneath the open sky, their frames reinforced with stone to resist the prevailing storms. Smoke curled from makeshift chimneys, and the scent of burning wood mixed with the fresh, untamed air of Eurus IV. Jayde spotted a child, one of many, running barefoot through the fields, her laughter echoing against the cliffs, while the adults worked side by side building homes, tilling soil, carving out a life of their own choosing.

Leaving the caves was a risk, but Mary Ashr's death had proven one undeniable truth, *a life without meaning was no life at all.*

If their days were to be brief, *so be it.*

If the Construct were to return, *so be it.*

They had made their choice. No more shadows. No more hiding.

They would live. Under the beautiful, untamed, violent sky of Eurus IV.

Jayde never wanted to return to Hypnos, but now, she understood why she had to.

On Hypnos, souls toiled in the name of the so-called greater good, drained of the ability to live for themselves. But *maybe*, in some of them, the fire of rebellion quietly smoldered.

The miner who had recognized her was proof of that.

She had gifted him with *hope*. And perhaps the flicker of promise that now ignited inside him would catch and spread.

Overhead, a security drone hovered, its cold blue eye sweeping the crowd. Jayde ducked into the shadow of an alley, slipping past a food hall dumpster before emerging into the heart of Hypnos.

Before her stood the Briefing Cathedral, its gilded exterior gleaming beneath the artificial glow of the dome lights. It was sparkling and pristine, an opulent shrine to the Construct's dominion.

At its entrance, a golden android stood sentinel, motionless yet watchful. Its faceless head tracked the passing citizens, scanning, assessing. People passed before it with quiet reverence, their heads bowed, their steps measured.

For every potential renegade, there were tenfold as many who clung to the Construct's doctrine with unwavering devotion. To them, the Construct was a god. A god they would serve. A god they would *die* for.

There was still so much work to be done.

Jayde couldn't help but notice the absence of the clergy, the robed engineers who had once served the Construct with absolute allegiance. The very order her father had once been so proud to be a part of.

An emptiness settled into her stomach.

She wanted to believe they had simply been reassigned to the mines, forced into labor like so many others. But she knew better. She was proof of what their knowledge could do, how dangerous it was to the Construct's rule. Her father had exposed a vulnerability, and the Construct would never allow such a weakness to exist again.

No, the clergy hadn't been reassigned.

They had been *eliminated*.

Slipping past the golden android stationed at the Cathedral doors, she kept her head low and slipped once more into the crowd.

No one paid her any mind.

At last, she reached the base of the unattended communication tower.

She darted forward, her hooded cloak whipping around her feet as she ran. Grasping the cold rungs of the maintenance ladder, she began to climb.

It felt like a lifetime ago that she and Merrick had first scaled this tower, two young minds pondering an uncertain future.

Far above her, the platform awaited, the massive satellite dish rotating in slow, steady arcs. And beyond that—

The stars.

When she was a child, her father would point out the stars through the dome glass, his voice filled with conviction as he spoke of endless possibilities. Of the Noble Purpose. Of humanity's grand future. *A destiny only achievable with the Construct's guidance.*

She had believed him once. It was the faith of a child's mind. But now, she knew the truth. *The Noble Purpose* was not *humanity's* purpose. It never was.

As she climbed, the rhythmic blink of her mother's bracelet steadied her, each pulse a whisper of comfort.

On the other end of this distant entanglement was Merrick.

She and her mother had once been connected this way. Across space. Across time. But this connection *felt different.*

This wasn't longing.

This was the beginning of something *new.*

When she thought of Merrick, she thought of that night in the wrecked drone, their skin soaked by rain, their bodies trembling from more than just the cold. She thought of their first kiss, her feet on tiptoes, his breath warm against hers.

This climb felt just like that moment.

Climbing higher and higher, the ground slipping further away, her heart racing, knowing that one wrong step meant falling, *but never once looking down.*

She thought back to that moment in the cave, when the Construct's hand had closed around her throat. She should have died. But then… a presence surged through her.

A force she couldn't explain.

It had surged through her like a tidal wave, filling her with strength beyond reason. For an instant, she had become something more than human. Something untouchable. It felt supernatural. Otherworldly.

Dangerous.

Merrick was the only one who spoke of it afterward, insisting once again that some divine "force" had chosen her, and this proved they were on the righteous path.

Jayde wasn't so sure.

All she knew was that, in her darkest moment, she had felt something consume her. A presence. Vast. Godly. It had steadied her. Saved her. And the longer she remained on Eurus IV, the stronger the presence became. A shadow in the back of her mind. It called to her, and one day, when she could no longer stand its beckoning, she and Merrick flew across the sea and set foot on the shores of the nearest continent. There, rising from the mountains, stood the ruins of an ancient civilization, stone monuments weathered by time, whispering to her of a forgotten power.

The sight of it turned her blood cold. But it wasn't just fear. It was recognition. Whatever had called to her in the cave, whatever power she had summoned, was there, buried within the ruins. The answers she sought were waiting.

And she would go.

Soon.

Jayde paused her climb and looked down at the colony below. The buildings remained as they always had. Blocky. White. Sterile. Their sharp edges and corners were softened only by the artificial glow of the dome lights.

Eurus IV had shattered her perception of the world. Life on Hypnos had been a canvas of white and gray. Clean and orderly. Like a means to an end. Control, she realized, could be woven into the soul in the most subtle of ways.

Now, she lived in a world of greens and blues, of golds and oranges. Life itself was a painting. Colors danced on the ocean. They drifted across the sky. They gleamed on the scales of reptilian birds, shimmered on the backs of aquatic creatures, and stretched across the horns of the herds that wandered the amber fields.

It was a world where she sat beside Thaddeus Lumen, painting the creatures they encountered onto a canvas of pressed grass. Their brushstrokes followed the ancient traditions he had taught her. White lines, bold blocky shapes. Faces. Figures wielding arrows. Their paintings echoed their story, but also the stories of those who came before.

She cherished that time. The quiet rhythm of creation. The way Lumen would stroke his beard in that thoughtful, fatherly way before saying, *"Very good. Now, what shall we paint next?"*

Jayde reached the top of the tower, gasping for breath.

Her legs ached, but there was no time to rest. She had to move quickly.

She swung her carry pack off her shoulders and pulled out her brush and paints, made from the pigments of berries she and Merrick had gathered along the ocean.

It was perfect for this moment. The berries possessed a vivid red color. Almost luminescent. Enough to stand out in the darkness as the lights of Hypnos dimmed for the night.

Before she began, Jayde took one last look through the glass of the geodesic dome, casting her gaze down at the barren expanse of the New Eden moon outside the colony walls. The glow of Hypnos spilled across the craters and jagged rocks, casting stark, angular shadows that only emphasized the lifelessness beyond the colony's fragile bubble of existence.

She exhaled, suddenly feeling the gravity of her mission.

Taking out her paints, Jayde set to work, her eyes darting up now and then, watching for any of the Construct's drones that might be patrolling the colony. She painted quickly, her hands steady despite the urgency.

It was a simple image. One she had painted many times before.

As the satellite dish slowly rotated, Jayde matched its pace, stepping carefully while her brush swept across its surface. Her imagination took hold, carrying her far from Hypnos, back to Eurus IV, where a flock of reptilian birds soared over an endless ocean. Their emerald wings shimmered in the sunlight, catching the wind as they rode the currents with effortless grace.

Unbound. Free.

The image stirred something deep within her, the same thrill she had felt the first time she saw them.

Now, it was her turn to share that feeling.

She stepped back to study her work, keeping a cautious distance from the platform's edge. Her painting was simple, yet it carried with it everything she had come to understand. A few swift strokes had brought it to life. A replication of the first sketch she had ever made on Eurus IV, scrawled on the side of their drone shelter with a burnt stick what seemed like ages ago. Now, refined with time and practice, the image was sharper, more deliberate. A reptilian bird, its wings stretched wide, poised for flight.

A symbol of what was possible. Of what was free.

She crossed her arms, taking in her work with a quiet satisfaction. Then, under her breath, she murmured, *"For you, Mother."*

With that, she turned and began her climb down the maintenance ladder, leaving her paints behind. It was a long, treacherous descent, and she placed each step with care.

When she was nearly to the bottom, she tightened her grip on the ladder, drew a breath, and let her feet lift free. She slid the rest of the way down, faster and faster, the wind rushing past her. For a moment, she felt weightless, like she was flying.

She would return again in time, to meet with the growing resistance spreading within the colony. Perhaps the scarred miner that had spotted her in the crowd would be among them now. She wanted to hear how she could help, how their movement was growing.

But most of all, she wanted to hear the whispers. The quiet stirrings of the people as they looked up and saw the painting of the reptilian bird, wings stretched wide in flight, emblazoned on the giant satellite dish.

And beneath it, that prayer that Merrick had once told her: WINDS BE WITH US.

THE END

Parker Lyons is a science fiction and horror writer who crafts unsettling, thought-provoking stories about the dark side of technology and the complexities of human nature. *REBEL PLANET* is his debut novel.

His influences are many, drawing inspiration from the likes of Stephen King, Stephen Spielberg, Guillermo del Toro and Tim O'Brien. When he isn't writing, he is either on the golf course, watching a movie, or relaxing on his back porch in Westfield, Indiana.

Follow Parker on Social Media:

For a FREE anthology of stories from **Midnight Carnival** visit:

www.TheMidnightCarnival.com